Praise for Torn

C000140275

"Brian McHugh's first nov
bringing a Scottish dimen:
recent Irish History. It sets us out on ̶ ̶̶
sea still in the eddies of what for many is a little known ̶̶̶̶̶ ̶
that of the Irish civil war of the 1920s. Wonderfully told, redolent
with traces of Conrad, and too, of Rider Haggard in this tale.
Action, history and a strain of the enigmatic, deftly drawn, courses
throughout. This first book is unmissable and we much look
forward to McHugh's next account of an enthralling journey."

Jack McLean, Literary Critic and Commentator

"Torn Edges is a gripping story that alternates between modern-
day Glasgow and 1922 Ireland of the Irish Civil War. This was a
nasty conflict that split friends, families and former colleagues.
Because of that it is often overlooked by Irish and Scots-Irish in
their celebration of their proud heritage. Author Brian McHugh
draws heavily on his own experience in the Gorbals, Govanhill,
Mount Florida and Cathcart as he takes us along familiar streets
and into well know pubs, restaurants and churches. All the while
intrigue builds up as we try to find out why a Glasgow murder
victim had a gold sovereign from the 1920s in his hand when he
died. Can librarian Liam Casey unravel the connection between an
old photograph of an Irish Free State soldier, a notorious massacre
and a stabbing in a dingy city lane? A superb first novel from
Brian McHugh. A great read, it seems certain it won't be his last."

Southside Press

"A great story. I was unable to put Torn Edges down. I found it to
be absolutely riveting and utterly absorbing. I thoroughly enjoyed
its pace and close understanding of the times and their
ambivalence and tragedy."

Jim Dickie

About the Author
Brian McHugh

Born of Irish parents, and brought up in the Gorbals, Glasgow.
Attended a Glasgow secondary school and studied engineering at
Strathclyde University.
Set up a small building company and returned to college to
complete engineering course.
Decided to become a teacher in the eighties and attended
Jordanhill teacher training college.
Teacher of design, technology and graphics. An active trade
unionist.
Main interests are current affairs, reading and the occasional game
of golf.
Currently live in the South Side of Glasgow.
Torn Edges is his first published book but he has written several
short stories including 'The day after the music died' published
Scottish Book Trust.
http://www.youtube.com/watch?v=O66jaAYDejA

Is currently working on the sequel to Torn Edges, due to be
published soon by Ringwood Publishing

Torn Edges

Brian McHugh

Ringwood Publishing
Glasgow

First published in Great Britain in 2012 by
Ringwood Publishing
7 Kirklee Quadrant, Glasgow G12 0TS
www.ringwoodpublishing.com
e-mail mail@ringwoodpublishing.com

2nd Edition April 2013

ISBN 978-1-901514-05-6

British Library Cataloguing-in Publication Data
A catalogue record for this book is available from
the British Library

Typeset, printed and bound in Great Britain by;

www.direct-pod.com

Acknowledgements

I'd like to thank the staff at Ringwood for their help in this publication. Sandy Jamieson was particularly helpful and supportive, and Lynsey Smith, the editor, gave me invaluable advice during the difficult editing process.

I would like to thank Ann Jarvis for her endurance and her hawkeyed proof reading skills in the initial stages and finally thanks, not least to my wife, Fran, for her patience and encouragement.

I particularly would like to thank Frank McGuiness for his contribution to the Second Edition.

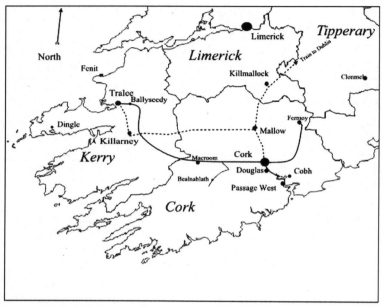

Part of the 'Munster Republic'. area around Kerry and Cork 1922

CHAPTER ONE

The Lane

Mick Hastings was almost impressed when he looked at the body. It nearly made up for his irritation at being called out for a serious assault fifteen minutes before he went off duty. The unfortunate victim looked as if he was simply lying at rest, yet he was almost certainly dead. The constable had told him as much when he arrived. This victim looked a bit different, a bit better dressed, better fed than the usual battered, ventilated, blood soaked stiffs that were Glasgow's stock in trade stabbing victim. The narrow lane, where the body lay, was unexceptional, one of the many dozens of lanes and streets that criss-crossed the grid pattern of the city centre. The area was well organised by the time Hastings had turned up. Blue police tape marked off the area and a couple of officers made sure that any curious members of the public were quickly moved on. He went in search of the reporting officer, found him, and introduced himself.

"Hi. I'm Detective Mick Hastings, I was told it was a serious assault but it looks a bit worse than that."

"I phoned an ambulance right away and tried to give First Aid but I'm pretty sure he's a goner, sir."

"I think you're right there. Did you get here first?"

"Better than that. I was just passing the lane when this lad came dashing out, seen me, and ran like hell up Bath Street. I looked into the lane and saw the body and the blood lying everywhere. My first instinct was to look after the victim, but I think it was too late even then. Still, it might be a good idea to have a look at the next lane up the street, if you don't mind me giving advice, sir. I'm not sure but I think he dived into the first lane on the right. Haven't had time to look myself. Might have dropped the weapon or something." Hastings looked carefully from the body to the lane entrance, nothing obvious lying around.

"No, no I don't mind you giving me advice," he said almost absent mindedly, "and you could be right. I'll take a walk up there now, back in a few minutes."

He knew from experience that the chance of finding a clue or a murder weapon diminished rapidly almost from the moment of the crime. He moved quickly up the busy sun-lit street, there was another slightly wider lane twenty yards further up. There was a bit more clutter here, boxes, dust bins, some rubbish bags. The lane, made dim by the surrounding buildings, was straight and downwards for about 15 or 20 paces, then turned sharp left for a slightly longer distance before exiting through a narrow close into Renfield Street. This, considered Hastings after walking the length of the lane, might be promising. He returned back to the opening and paused trying to put his mind into the head of the murderer, if indeed the runner was the perpetrator. Could be that it was an ordinary Joe who discovered the body and took flight - not always an unusual occurrence. Anyway, he thought, let's assume this guy was the assailant. He would have been anxious to get rid of the weapon; even seasoned professionals get spooked when they see the law so soon after a crime, they rarely believe in the miracle of coincidence. He started to walk back up the lane. He got lucky and spotted the handle within minutes; it was jammed between the bin and the wall just where the lane turned to the left. As he pulled back the bin the weapon clattered onto the ground. Hastings gave an impressed silent whistle. He looked at what he knew must have been the murder weapon; this was no kitchen knife, the handle was a beautifully turned piece of mahogany finished in polished brass. The blade, if it could be called a blade, was a four inch long silver metallic rod turned and shaped to a deadly point. He walked quickly back to the entrance and signalled to one of the beat constables standing on the main street. The policeman hurried over.

"Do me a favour. Guard this entrance for a few minutes I think I've found the murder weapon. I'll send someone down in a few minutes to bag it."

Things had moved on apace, in even the short time he was gone. A forensic tent was already being set up as he approached the scene. He spoke to the lead officer and informed him of the weapon. A member of the team was dispatched right away.

"By the way, Detective Inspector McKinney of Central Division is on his way over, I think he'll probably be the investigating officer."

"That's okay. I'll hang about till he turns up."

Hastings now turned his attention to the victim. A slightly portly man in his mid forties lay face up on the cobbled lane. Mick was struck by the neat and expensive clothes on the body. A cashmere Crombie overcoat covered a light weight grey Canali suit - both were lying open, exposing a white shirt with a faint pink pinstripe, below the shirt pocket was a neat hole oozing blood. For a brief moment he thought it must surely have been a small calibre bullet that killed him, but using a pencil he exposed the shirt further and looking closer he could see that the hole was neat and without a burn mark, the wound tied in with the weapon he had found. He also pondered the fact that the man had died surprisingly quickly, but then again, given the victim's age and the position of the wound, perhaps not. He felt the victim's face was vaguely familiar, not in some sort of famous way, but almost casual, like someone you know quite well but you come across in unusual surroundings like, say, a barman you unexpectedly met in a bank or someone you know vaguely from work suddenly appearing in a different town. He was about to turn round when he heard a soft tinkle, like a piece of metal, a coin falling perhaps. Bending forward he noticed a glint between the cobbles. Hastings lifted it, turning it in his hand. It looked like an old sovereign of some sort. He idly pondered the significance of the coin for a few moments. He looked around, the officers in the lane were busy putting up tape and still trying to shoo away the inquisitive pedestrians - no one was taking a blind bit of notice of him as he tried to catch someone's eye for an evidence bag. Hastings was as straight as they come and was a stickler for procedure, but something about this victim made him curious. He made his decision without too much thought and popped the coin into his jacket pocket; he would hand it over to McKinney later.

Des Capaldi often wondered why he bothered analysing his route to town –over the Glasgow Bridge or over the suspension bridge? The suspension bridge was slightly nearer and quicker. It was nicknamed the Toll Bridge by the locals as one was inevitably pestered by the homeless jakies that mooched around its northern end. They were mostly harmless and they were remarkably and entertainingly innovative, keenly attuned to any new development in the art of begging. The latest scam had included the acquisition of a skinny, mangy, Jack Russell type mongrel with a string lead that sprawled sad-faced next to the lucky recipient of the day. For sometime the dog had prowled the south bank of the river in the morning where he found an endless supply of half eaten hamburgers and sausage suppers. For sport he raced after seagulls and snapped playfully at the tail feathers of the fat pigeon that roosted in the low branches of the horse chestnut tree and then, when bored with that, he would take to crouching like a tiger in the long grass to await any squirrel that wandered within pouncing distance - but the squirrels were always too smart and too fast. Recently the dog's afternoons were spent loafing around the bridge with the down and outs that hung about the archway on the North side. Des had observed this phenomenon with half an eye and he occasionally turned it over in his mind. God only knows what possessed the dog to throw his lot in with a bunch of beggars and shiftless drifters. Perhaps, Des had concluded, the dog was happy and content there - felt part of the gang - loved and wanted, a place where he was fussed over and patted and spoiled: maybe to be tied up occasionally with a mangy piece of string and lie around looking forlorn was a small price to pay.

In any event, he made no conscious decision and found his feet carrying him over the Glasgow Bridge and into Union Street. It had been a long, busy day, for a Friday. He had worked that morning and most of the afternoon for a popular free sheet as a freelance sub editor. He had many contacts in the Press and was often called in at short notice for absences. It paid well. When not employed by the mainstream press he spent the rest of the time writing up commissioned articles for a variety of Sunday and weekly magazines. Music gigs, museum exhibits, trial reports, general bits and pieces usually anonymously, although he did get the occasional by-line. He also had a talent for decent photography, mainly sporting events but not averse to the odd spot of paparazzi work if anyone of any note happened to be in town. He ambled along Union Street in the bright evening sunshine; it was just after five thirty. He liked the City at this time of evening, in fact, he reckoned, Glasgow was a 'tea time' kind of place, a time where the bars and restaurants were busy but not overwhelmed and the crowds were good natured and happy, particularly on a Friday night. Later towards ten or eleven the atmosphere became at bit more downbeat with aggressive acne faced youngsters beginning to prowl and crowd the streets looking for nightclubs and other haunts of the demimonde. He walked passed Central Station and popped into the nearby dispensing chemist to say hello to Julie. They usually met at the end of her shift at six. She was there, very busy, but still managed a quick, cheery wave.

"See you later," she mouthed, and pointed to the clock and held up seven fingers. Finished at seven. It happened occasionally. Des gave her a sympathetic shoulder shrug and thumbs up. He would come back later to meet her and walk her home. In the mean time he was quite comfortable with having a bit of time to spare. He could visit a few bars, have couple of drinks, read the paper and chat to whatever mates he may bump into. He was on his way up Union Street to The Scriveners, a well know haunt of press staff and printers when his mobile phone rang. He stopped and stood in a doorway - he hated walking around with a phone at his ear.

His phone screen showed Mick Hastings.

"Hi Mick, what's up?

"Hi ... Just got called out to a stabbing…"

"Ach…."

"No, No wait a minute. This could be interesting. Where are you now? You're usually knocking around town at this time of day."

"Union Street, just before the Central station."

"Jeez, man you're practically there, couldn't be better. Walk up to the corner of Drury Street and I'll catch you there in about two or three minutes, cheers."

Des carried on walking, street murders didn't interest him that much, they were depressingly similar with both perpetrator and victim being virtually interchangeable. However he and Hastings went back a while and he had always been a good reliable source and knew Mick only phoned when he had something that might be a bit unusual. They met in the sixth year class in Holyrood, the largest and most popular secondary school in the south side of Glasgow. Des attended a private school for the five years, where he did rather well but didn't fancy going to college so young so, he like many before him, completed his education, at no cost, in a well established local school.

"School," said his father, "is not about education son, it's about making contacts, networking as you guys call it nowadays."

Des always nodded his head sagely, he never took a blind bit of notice of his dad's cracker barrel philosophical bon mots. As long as he was having a good time, made friends and could keep up with the work - who cared? Des and Mick weren't that close at school but they played football, played golf, drank and socialised with the same crowd over the past fifteen years. Their relationship was straightforward, they rarely made arrangements to meet but if they met in the pub they were glad to see each other: both used each other without guilt, there was none of the 'I owe you one' mentality involved that poisoned other professional relationships.

Des reached the murder scene in a couple of minutes and was showing his press card to one of the officers when Mick called over.

"He's OK, I know him."

"So Mick, another senseless frenzied stabbing in the mean street of ….."

"Quiet a minute Des, over here."

Des ambled over to the body.

"Ho man! - Cool threads, as they say in Miami."

"Take a closer look, does he look familiar?"

Des was about to shake his head when he hesitated, the face did look familiar. "Maybe he does... listen can I take a photo. I've got a compact digital here- no flash. We can look at it later."

Mick looked around ... "Okay Des, but hurry up, I'll stand in front."

Mick was getting slightly worried. He was beginning to break a couple of his own basic ground rules here. Des leaned over and took three photos in almost as many seconds and, as he said, no flash.

"Right Des. Look I'll need to see who's on the murder squad, probably McKinney, and hand the case over to him. Anyway my shift's about finished. I can meet you in, say, ten minutes."

"Okay doaky, where?"

"See you in the Black Dog," he said over his shoulder as walked to the knot of police officers at the lane entrance.

Des groaned inwardly as he turned and walked across Renfield Street and into Drury Street towards the Black Dog. The Black Dog, he knew, was a pub with pretensions. It had a baby grand in the corner with a typical lounge lizard singer who thought he was part of the Rat Pack. Fortunately for the customers the arrangement was badly amplified - no one complained. The singer had just finished 'Fly me to the Moon' and was about to segue into 'Mona Lisa'. Or was it the other way round, thought Des ten seconds later. He looked briefly and cynically at the overpriced 'cocktail' board, ordered a couple of beers and took a seat furthest away from the piano. He amused himself by reading the dinner menu and looking at the camera screen until Mick showed up a few minutes later.

"How are the photos?" Mick asked as he sat down.

"Not bad at all, all things considered."

Mick flicked through the three photos in the memory.

"I'm impressed, crystal clear, any ideas yet?"

"Like you said, remarkably familiar."

"I think he looks about forty odd so he's older than us," said Mick.

"Yet I get the feeling I've met him somewhere, you know, at a party or something. There is something else... this was in his hand."

Mick showed him the sovereign. Des turned it over in his hand, showing exaggerated shock.

"Hope you're not thinking of keeping this."

"No chance!" he laughed "I'll hand it in to McKinney tomorrow. I forgot I had it. I don't know why I kept it. It just seemed odd at the time."

Des turned the coin over in his hand.

"Gold sovereign, George the fifth – and in really good nick too."

"Worth much?"

"Hard to say how much it's worth. Mint condition, new ones are usually in more demand. These kind are usually jazzed up into sovereign rings much beloved of the local neds and medallion man brigade, I've seen loads of them. About two hundred quid for your average sovereign. People think they're worth much more, but these coins were produced by the million at the time.

"I think he must have had it in his hand when he was knifed."

"So, a straight forward robbery then?"

"Probably. Anyway, you've got some copy for the morning papers, let's leave it at that, and don't mention the coin in the story."

"As if," snorted Des. "Anyway, so how's it going? Haven't seen you for a few months."

They fell into a casual good-natured conversion, talking about their latest golf exploits and generally gossiping of this and that. Des was just thinking of heading off to pick up Julie when the singer in the corner had just begun to snap his fingers to the opening bars of 'High Hopes'.

"That's it. I'm out of here," said Des rising from his seat.

"If I can think of anything, I'll give you a ring later on, if you're still about," he said as they parted on the street.

"Sure," said Mick "I might go for a beer about ten but I'll be at home till then."

They relaxed in the flat; Julie had a hot shower while Des tidied up and began fixing dinner. While eating they talked idly of their day and looked forward to their day off tomorrow.

"By the way," said Des just as they were about to clear away the table. "I met Mick Hastings after I left your work, gave me a ring about a local murder. I took some photographs of the murder victim."

"Very nice, I'm sure."

Des took the camera out of the case.

"Yes, yes I know. But Mick and I thought he looked familiar and I thought it might be someone we both know. It might ring a bell with you - you're pretty good at putting names to faces and I know you'll be discreet."

"Mm - don't know, I'm not good at dead bodies."

"Don't worry, they're not gruesome, have a seat for a minute and see what you think."

Des opened up the viewer, selected the best angle and handed it to Julie.

She looked at the first photo and sat up sharp.

"My God! That's my cousin – Hughie Toner," she said.

oooOooo

CHAPTER TWO

Ireland - South Cork 8th. August 1922

Only one of the men paddling in the shallow waters of the River Lee recognized the buzzing sound in the distance.

"That sounds like an old Bristol fighter to me." said Charlie McKenna, shading and screwing his eyes as he looked into the bright early morning sunlight.

"That's a British aeroplane isn't it? What would a British aeroplane be doing flying around Cork?" shouted his brother Pat from the shore.

The three men in the water started to move ashore, gazing to the east as the low flying plane approached Hop Island.

"Get back to the car and get the guns, Pat," said Charlie.

The elder McKenna was a fairly large man in his mid twenties, broad shouldered with slim hips and with an open and pleasant face. A demeanour that tricked many into thinking that he was not only easy going, but easily fooled.

"Go on, get moving!" he shouted sharply.

They left the water and scrambled up the slight embankment. Pat quickly distributed the rifles with four rounds each.

"Think we should fire at it?" said Pat, putting the rifle to his shoulder.

"Lie down all of you," ordered McKenna.

The aircraft tilted slightly on its axis as it turned with the estuary curve, obviously making its way up river to the city of Cork. Charlie lifted his head to see more clearly.

"Well, well I've seen it all now," he said quietly.

"What's up, Charlie?"

"Did you see the roundels on that plane any of you?"

"Roundels?"

"Yes the roundels - the round identifying marks on the wings of a plane."

"Yes they were green and white weren't they?" said Pat.

"The British Army planes have blue and red on their wings. Looks like the Free State have bought themselves an aeroplane. Never thought I'd see the day when an Irishman..." He stopped as the plane turned slightly, straightened up almost at right angle to their position.

"And look," cried Pat excitedly "It has an Irish flag on its tail wing."

"Should we fire at it on the way back?" said one of the Martin brothers, unsure about what Pat and Charlie were talking about.

"Doubt if it would come back this way," said Charlie.

Charlie turned away, the chances of hitting a moving target were hard enough without amateurs like Pat and the two Martin boys firing away using their usual haphazard technique. At a funeral two weeks ago, Declan, the younger of the Martins, took part in a four gun salute where he managed to hit a telephone junction box, knocking out local communications for days. But it wasn't the chances of hitting a moving target that was concerning Charlie, it was the fact that the Provisional Government had a plane at all. The thought gave him mixed feelings, for in a way he was an unenthusiastic and unconvinced rebel against this newly formed government. It was a state of affairs that came about by a geographical accident, and more to do with personal loyalty than any hard held conviction. The sight had also, although he would have been reluctant to admit it, given him an uneasy sense of pride.

"Get your boots on," he said "we've still got a few miles to Passage West to cover."

They had stopped to give Kevin Martin a bit of a rest from driving. He had driven the Lancia car, accompanied by his younger brother, down from the town of Macroom during the night. The journey was long and arduous, and it was made doubly difficult by the bad state of the road and the feeble light from the headlamps. However he was given no respite and was immediately ordered to take Charlie and Pat on a recce to Passage West. There was a rumour that some Free State forces had landed there earlier that morning.

Charlie walked passed the Lancia, still looking at the gradually disappearing outline of the Bristol fighter. He was confident it wouldn't come back by the same route, the pilot, whatever his nationality, would know the dangers of returning over the same ground. Anyone who had flown a plane in the last war knew that any hostile forces about would be ready for the plane's return and would start firing almost regardless of their chances of a hit, a lesson not lost on pilots during that bloody and desperate encounter. He knew this simply because he had been there and had seen planes been brought down by the sheer barrage of lead that came up to meet them.

Although everyone knew Charlie was an ex-British Army sergeant and a veteran of the Great War, few ever asked, or dared to ask, about his time there or why he had joined the British army in the first place. Not that he could tell them much. Charlie had just turned eighteen when he left home to stay with a cousin and aunt in Glasgow. With the war now entering its second year there was plenty of work. Yet he had only been working in Glasgow for a few months before joining the British army, something that still baffled him to this day. He had recently convinced himself that he had somehow been tricked by his foreman in the Maryhill gas works to join up, but in reality it was the thought of going to France that excited him most, that and the fact that he could join up with the Dublin Fusiliers. The British Army had been recruiting heavily in Glasgow at this time, those men who were Irish or had an Irish background were free to join an Irish regiment, and the Royal Dublin Fusiliers "the Dubs" were popular among the Irish immigrant community in Glasgow.

He joined up and completed his basic training in a converted public park near Carlisle, and shipped over to France in time for the Battle of Hulluch, where he was lucky to survive a murderous artillery bombardment and even luckier to escape being gassed by the Germans – all on the same week as the Easter rising in Dublin. It was a baptism of fire. He learned the futility of the creeping barrage tactic and the crippling effect of the German machine guns in a month of sporadic attacks along a long line from Lens to Neuve Chapelle. During a respite in the reserve trenches, his company was assembled and asked if anyone had experience in the coal industry. Charlie stuck up his hand with about half a dozen others. They were marched along to the main depot and transported down the line by train to Amiens where he discovered he was to join a tunnelling company. His protest that he had merely worked with coal in a gas works and that he wasn't a miner were dismissed by the sergeant major as 'Neither here nor there, mate'. A young lieutenant joined in and said that if he didn't want to mine then he could 'Jolly well join up with engineers' explosive platoon'. One was as potentially fatal as the other but he decided working with explosives was probably less hellish than a life down a mine shaft. Charlie managed to survive and he was a quick learner. He handled explosives with the same degree of confidence as he could load and fire a rifle, but his most impressive virtue was his patience. He stayed calm and showed leadership when others around him panicked. The men admired him, looked up to him and it was no surprise that he rose up the ranks to sergeant.

They toiled for weeks under the clay at Hawthorn Ridge, hauling ton after ton of ammonal to the forward position under the German lines. Its detonation marked the first day of the Battle of the Somme. The carnage of the next couple of weeks led to continual mayhem behind the lines. Charlie was ordered back to his battalion which itself was continually being moved around to back up other army divisions and battle groups. After a year in France it all ended in utter confusion when he finally took a bullet in the leg after carrying a wounded officer back to the medical centre from the second battle of the Scarpe. Charlie was taken to the casualty clearing station at Arras and then for some inexplicable reason loaded on to a French hospital train that was about to leave for Paris - where he found himself idly lounging around the Paris Plage hospital for the next two months. Charlie was awarded the Military Medal for reasons that were never made clear, and finally posted to a small army administration base near the Gare de Nord in the 10th District as a wages clerk, none of which made any sense to him. Charlie was not inclined to argue; he had somehow managed to acquire a position where the duties were easy and the hours short. He made use of his time by travelling around Paris trying to master the French language, and, more importantly, trying to find a way of getting out of the army. Paris, at that time, was far enough from the front line to still attract the usual crowd of rentier artists and writers of limited talent and seemingly limitless cash who regarded Charlie as a working class hero. He acquired a taste for wine and even managed to acquire a passport during one boozy afternoon. Eventually he was surprised to be finally discharged on medical grounds even though he never felt fitter in his life. He simply showed his hospital record to a drunken medical officer who assumed that a two month stay in a hospital by someone with the Military Medal must indicate a serious injury. They posted him to Kent to await his final papers, when they came he was delighted to find that the Army Board had kindly issued him with a free rail pass to a destination of his choice anywhere in Britain, including Ireland.

He had thought of returning home to Donegal but he decided to return to Glasgow, mainly because he had a network of friends and relatives. In any event, getting to the town of Letterkenny was comparatively easy as there was a daily boat from Glasgow to Derry. An added attraction was a stop off in London, a city he was desperate to see after spending so much time in Paris: it would be interesting to compare both of these great cities of the world. He still had a lot to learn and he'd learn on the way or, as he told his bewildered soldier colleagues, "il apprendrait sur la voie" He had surprised himself by discovering he had a good ear for languages. He was not a native Gaelic speaker and took lessons at school but speaking Gaelic was considered a bit uncouth in many ways and in the main town of Letterkenny almost all business was conducted in English. In some ways Letterkenny, he had reflected recently, had more in common with Maidstone in Kent than it had with Cork. The reason he spoke better French than Gaelic, a language he found difficult, he had rationalised, was that English seemed to him to translate easier into French than into Gaelic.

His stay in London was enjoyable, if somewhat short and frustrating. He only had two days there, as each journey was specified on the ticket - not the 'open ticket' he expected. However he still managed to rush through the major museums and galleries. Back in Glasgow he even managed to get his old job as a stoker in the Maryhill gas works back again, but within a month he had the stirrings of tedium. He became restless and bored. He spent the time reading the papers for news of the war and then throwing them into a corner in frustration. He took to generally roaming around the streets for, although he was far from teetotal, he was never a great one for sitting around the dismal war time pubs. He read constantly, preferring to use the local library or, even better, walking down through St. Georges Cross and on to the enormous and well stocked reading rooms of the Mitchell Library near Glasgow town centre.

The invitation to America came right of the blue. Charlie had already thought briefly about going there, had made some inquires and knew that the easiest way to get there was by being sponsored by someone who was already well established there. Otherwise, because of the war, you had to have a trade or a special skill to even get past the first hurdle. He decided to bide his time and save up some money before thinking of what to do next. The McKennas were a large family and he was the third youngest of nine children, three girls and six boys. The oldest was Margaret who had left for America in 1896 on the promise of a job with her older cousin. She was fifteen and emigration to the US was a lot easier then. He was no more than two years old when she left; he had no recollection of her at all.

Now it seems Margaret was doing well and had written to her mother with the offer of guarantor for another family member to emigrate. His mother, as Charlie was later to find out, was a good judge of character and seldom let her heart rule her head. One of the other girls was already married with children of her own. Of the boys, three, including Charlie, had left home, the others she had come to regard as timid and unadventurous or simply not quick witted enough. Pat, the youngest boy, was smart, but still a child. She also had a fondness for Charlie; she had been good at school herself and recognised and knew that Charlie was clever and resourceful. She held him in high regard and realised that his talents would be probably wasted competing with others in the low grade work around Donegal and Derry. Charlie's mother had no great desire to see him come home– well, not yet anyway, and she told no one, including her husband, about Margaret's offer.

She wrote quickly to Charlie advising him to write directly to Margaret in Philadelphia, explaining her thinking to him and telling him not to worry about the rest of the family's reaction to her decision.

"I'll deal with anyone that complains," she wrote. Unfortunately, she hardly needed to add, he was on his own as far as money was concerned.

Charlie could hardly contain himself. He immediately wrote to Margaret regaling her with fond and entirely fictional memories of her. The paperwork came through a few weeks later, including a Paid-For Ticket as demanded by the regulations at the time. He would arrange to repay Margaret later. Although a passport wasn't necessary for an immigrant, his possession of one seemed to impress the authorities. He thought himself fortunate to have applied for one in Paris, considering it was done on a drunken whim. Within two months he was on his way to Belfast to pick up the Trans Atlantic steamer Adriatic, which had left Southampton three days before.

He wrote to an old army colleague, Sam Gorman, to tell him he was coming to Belfast. Sam wrote back by return post insisting that Charlie had to stay with him at his mother's house in East

Belfast. It was Charlie's first time in Belfast and it was an unusual experience. Sam was a Protestant who had joined 'the Dubs' as he put it 'out of sheer badness'. He also had been wounded in the Arras campaign and was discharged, or 'invalided out' as some put it. Before joining up, Sam was a skilled riveter and plater at Harland and Wolff's and, having a reserved occupation, had a bit of difficulty signing on for the army. He solved this by taking a short trip to Glasgow and telling a few lies.

Despite being quite obviously lame, his skills were in such demand that he was immediately taken back into the shipyard. He was a good, conscientious worker. Sam was also a middle ranking trade union official with hard socialist views who despaired of the wilder excesses of the rampant triumphalism of his Protestant neighbours. He had the typical city dwelling working class physique, having a thin and wiry shape combined with pale sombre features which belied a great sense of humour and natural charm. Charlie also knew him to be almost insanely brave. He was a strong character with firm views and used his wit to great effect in the arguing and bickering that passed for debate in the trenches.

The city centre of Belfast reminded him of Glasgow, in appearance and character and the people were oddly similar to Glaswegians in their use of communal words and language. He had noticed how Sam was often mistaken for a Glaswegian by their English, and more surprisingly, their southern Irish colleagues. While he was in Belfast, Sam introduced him to his great passion, football. He followed the fate of several football teams in Belfast, his favourite being the local team Glentoran and took Charlie to see them play one of their rivals, Cliftonville. Being wartime it was billed as a 'friendly' match. Charlie enjoyed the game and the general spectacle, but it was hard not to notice the simmering, underlying sectarian hostility in the crowd. After the game they walked into the city centre looking for what Sam called a 'neutral' pub.

"Things are looking bad here, Charlie," said Sam after buying a couple of pints. "We've had bad riots recently since some of them southern MPs have started to boycott the London Parliament. Carson is back ranting about Home Rule and Rome rule. It's calm at the moment but things can get really ugly around here – and it doesn't take that much to start it off."

Charlie had very few political thoughts about Ireland before the war but the debates in the trenches, particularly Sam's, had made a deep impression on him. Sam was often the lone voice against what he called 'daft romantic nationalism', not that he had any love of the empire or capitalism he would be quick to point out, but that the real battle was against big business and their exploitation of the working class.

"So what are you going to do, Sam?" asked Charlie.

"Not sure if there's much I can do about it," replied Sam. "There's talk of partition as being the best answer, even among the boys in the union - not convinced that I agree, but most of the Protestants up here are all for it. As far as I'm concerned, sure it doesn't make any difference to me if we're exploited by some bowler hatted bigwig singing 'The Sash' or some bead rattler dancing around with a shillelagh, they'll still demand sweat and blood off all us eventually. But we live in dark times and if anyone starts to argue with some of the more bitter Unionists or defend Catholics in any way, they're just as likely to be murdered as well as anyone else, believe me..."

They continued their chat over another two or three beers, talked of the war, books, politics, roaming from one topic to another. Finally they left in good humour.

"Now don't you be singing them silly rebel songs, or you'll get us both killed!" said Sam laughing and putting a finger to his mouth with exaggerated caution as they both held on to each other and tottered up the road.

The next morning Sam walked Charlie through the thin black drizzle that seemed to be Belfast's permanent weather feature, to the quay side of York Dock.

"Here, I didn't realize your ship was going to be the Adriatic! Look, see that row of rivets along the top gunwale – I did them," he announced proudly. "Ah yes, Belfast built! You can't beat it!"

Two cranes were loading a large cargo of textiles into the hold as they walked to the solitary gangplank. One or two figures appeared on deck and, even though it was clear that very few passengers were embarking from Belfast, a few lonely streamers were beginning to be thrown from the rails.

Charlie turned.

"Goodbye, Sam. It was great to see you, I hope everything goes well. I'll write to you first thing, and let you know how I'm getting on."

Sam shook his hand warmly and slapped him on the back.

"Sure. You do that, old boy," said Sam imitating the upper class accent of the officer rank. "Good luck, chin, chin and all that!"

Sam stood back on the quay side, holding a streamer and waving until the boat disappeared into the mist of Belfast Lough. Charlie never saw him alive again.

oooOooo

CHAPTER THREE

Unadventurous

"Don't you remember a couple of New Years ago we went to a party at my Uncle Hughie's after the bells?" said Julie. "He has a house in Govanhill not that far from my mum and dad's place."

"Mm..., come to think of it I do, but that can't be him, your uncle must be seventy if he's a day."

"Nearly eighty, if not more, I'd say. No, not him, it's his son, young Hughie."

"Young Hughie! Look, this dead man is in his forties..."

"Yes, yes, I know that but they just called him that to distinguish him from his father." Julie replied patiently.

Des looked at the image again and thought for a minute.

"Ah yes!" he said, slapping his head lightly "I do remember him. It's coming back to me now. I only spoke to him for a few minutes. Irish guy, big tip for himself, likes to talk like a gangster. I know he's a relative of yours but not quite my cup of tea - if my memory serves me right."

"Wrong on the Irish bit, he's one of these 'plastic paddies' as my dad used to call them. Start talking about the old country, give them a few drinks and the 'Oirish' accent becomes more pronounced and more bizarre. Almost right about the gangster bit, though more what you would call a fly man rather than muscle. Building trade, supplying labour, a bit of stolen goods, fencing gear in the black-market, general fraud - usual stuff. He had a few contacts over in Belfast that he liked to boast about. Tried to make out he was well in with the Provos and the like."

"For a pharmacist you seem well up in the world of petty criminals!"

Julie shrugged.

"Kind of grew up with it I suppose, not directly. But when I was younger we went to Ireland every year and met a lot of relatives, usually stayed with them. If you're brought up in a city you tend to romanticise the countryside a bit. But believe me there is lots of tacky behaviour in the rural areas as well. One of my granddad's brothers-in-law sold dodgy poteen and was a general drunken no-user. Uncle Hughie's lot always seemed to me to be crafty, sly, always trying to get one over you. My sister absolutely loved it, still does. Loved to wander around, talking to the old ones, drinking tea and having the crack as they say, but I was a bit less enthusiastic. I always thought they considered us as outsiders - they often called us 'the wee Scotties'. Eventually, as I got older, I started to go to Spain and Italy with the school and began to find Ireland a bit of a bore. I've only been back about two or three times this past ten years, mainly for weddings and funerals. I also felt that the Toners and the others seemed to get more troublesome and more course and uncouth the older they got."

"Ah yes, a refined young lady like yourself ..."

Julie picked up a cushion and threw it.

"Be quiet, I'm enjoying reminiscing here."

"Sorry, carry on, so you knew young Hughie then."

"Well, he was a bit older than me but I knew the rest of them, his younger brother and his sister Eileen who was much more my age."

She paused for a minute reflecting.

"Yes, Eileen was nice but the rest of them were, in my mother's immortal words, 'stamped with the same brush'."

Des laughed out loud.

"Great one for the mixed metaphors, my mother," sighed Julie.

"In case you're wondering," she continued. "Uncle Hughie – Old Hughie Toner - was my father's brother in law. He was from Donegal, around from where my father's lot came, and a bit of a waster as well. He ended up married to Noreen, my father's younger sister, so fair game for criticism from my mother. My mother thought that some of her husband's family were nothing but a bunch of low lifers. Her own family were in her eyes, of course, perfect."

Des poured another glass of wine for each of them.

"You Irish guys seem to revel in your family history, something I lack an interest in. Other than my immediate family, back to grandparents is enough for me. In fact, one of my grannies was Irish. The family name, Capaldi, originated in a place called Picinisco in Italy, or so my dad says. He knows that his great granddad was Italian and that's going back well over a hundred years, that's as far back as I want to know. What's the point?"

"I couldn't agree more. I'm quite happy about the Irish background bit, but some of my relatives like to wrap themselves in a tricolour and relive the Irish wars as if they were yesterday."

She stood up.

"There's an old school friend of mine who called her daughter 'Bealtaine' I mean, for God's sake, no one seems to know how to even pronounce it! It apparently means 'May' in Irish Gaelic, and from what you just told me, she's probably less Irish than you are."

Julie paused, and then added.

"You know, sometimes it makes you wonder if some people will ever want to be become part of the indigenous population."

"Never mind - carry on," said Des.

"Yes. There was always a bit of an atmosphere about. My grandfather, Charlie McKenna, spent most of his life here, in Glasgow, although he often talked of his time in America and occasionally about his time in the army during the First World War. Come to think of it, I'm sure I seen a photograph of him in a uniform somewhere. Spoke decent French, believe or not."

"Not many of you paddies speak French."

"Oh aye! And you speak fluent Italian of course..."

"Morte fascista!" shouted Des flattening up his palm and giving the socialist salute.

Julie closed her eyes.

"I learned that from old Aldo who ran the fish and chip shop in Allison Street."

He went silent.

"It means death to the fascists, by the way," he added lamely.

"Can you be quiet for ten minutes?"

"Apparently," she continued "Charlie, my granddad, learned the language in France while he was there during the War. I always got the vague impression that he was involved in the troubles after the War, somewhere down south, around Cork. I remember him going down there a couple of times to look up some old friends, usually went by himself. Maybe my dad could tell us more. Strange, even although he never talked that much, he seemed a lot smarter, more... how would you put it? ...more worldly wise than the rest of his family. He seemed to have a fair bit of money as well, he left my father a real tidy sum, round about £200,000, and that was fifteen years ago."

Des gave a silent whistle.

"That's a lot of cash!"

"Yes I know. Caused a real family argument too. My mother was embarrassed. We were reasonably well off, had a big house, well educated, went good holidays and always had a car and the rest. My dad, as you know, was a faculty head in a college and was well paid. My grandfather's remaining relatives over in Ireland were really shocked to find out that old Charlie was pretty well loaded."

"I've never thought about asking, but what exactly did your grandfather do for a living?" said Des.

"He had retired for years even before I was born, but I think he worked on building sites for most of his life but seemed to have a decent job on the management side of things, mostly working for the old Glasgow Corporation."

"Seems a fair bit of savings even with a good job," said Des. "I wonder how he managed it?"

"I suppose you're right. I never gave it much thought, couldn't imagine him doing anything untoward though. He was a steady sort, unadventurous. Seemed quite happy to potter around the garden. My mother's family didn't want for much either, come to

think of it, pretty middle class by the standards of the day."
She glanced up at the clock.

"Look, Des, I must call my mother. Young Hughie was a bit of a toe rag, but he was family after all."

"Wait a sec Julie. Let's get a few facts confirmed. Do you think that Toner was killed for his Irish connections?"

"I don't know one way or the other. He never struck me as having any interest in politics, but stranger things have happened, I suppose. Anyway he ran about with a bunch of low life hoodlums so I expect anything could have happened."

"True," said Des. "The biggest fallacy of all time is honour among thieves. Most of these guys would maim and murder their best pal if it suited their purpose."

"Anyway," he continued, "if you've got to phone your mother tell her you've heard a rumour and for goodness sake, tell her not to contact his family - that would be a disaster for everyone, particularly Hastings. In fact, let's leave it until I contact him - he should still be at home."

"Right then," said Julie. "I'll clear away these dishes while you do that."

He picked up the phone - he was lucky. Hastings had just finished showering and was about to head out shortly. Des told him that Julie was almost sure that it was her dad's cousin Hughie and was about to launch into all he knew about young Hughie.

"Its okay, Des. He has already been identified as Hugh Toner. I think who ever done him in was disturbed before he could rob him. He had his wallet and stacks of I.D. on him. His family have been informed."

"I think I know why you thought he was familiar. Julie says you might have met him with us. He was at a New Year party a few years back. Do you remember that house in Mount Florida? We all arrived after the bells."

There was a short silence.

"Let me think. Was that the night we had to walk from Central Station because we missed the last train?"

"That's right!' said Des. "I'd almost forgot about that."

"Yes, I remember that night well, we all had great time. Ah! Just a minute, of course, I remember now. I didn't speak to him much. Bit of a loud mouth if I remember."

"Got it in one old chap - the very man!" said Des "Julie's going to phone her mother for a natter, any problems with her mentioning this?"

"Don't suppose so, just tell her not to mention my name or I'm in big trouble."

"She won't. She is quite discreet."

After Julie left to make the call home, Des pulled out his laptop. He knew from long experience that for Julie this would be a half hour phone job. While waiting for the computer to boot up, he poured himself a glass of light beer. The hard part, as Des knew, was making up the heading, so settling down, he gave the story his usual working title "Glasgow Man Murdered in Frenzied Knife Attack!" The writing flowed easy; there were two approaches - Red Top Tabloid and Broadsheet. For a run of the mill story at this stage he knew exactly what the sub editors were looking for. He ran off a first draft and sat back:

"Last night Strathclyde Police launched a murder hunt when the body of a forty year old man was discovered in Renfield Lane in Glasgow city centre. Detectives were called in after police discovered the body early yesterday evening. Officers and forensic specialists were yesterday scouring the surrounding area for clues as to how the man met his death. It is believed that the murder weapon may already have been found in a nearby dustbin. Detective Chief Inspector Peter McKinney, who is leading the investigation, said: "Our inquiries are still at an early stage and we are examining CCTV in the area."

100 words

End

Satisfied, he e-mailed this off to his tabloid contacts. A bit of rearranging and a few more erudite additions like:

"Police said because of the nature of his injuries, the death was being treated as murder."

"Police were awaiting formal identification before naming the victim."

The quotes were entirely fictional of course, but few detectives or senior policemen objected, particularly if the quotes were suitably bland and, more importantly, their name and rank were mentioned.

Again he emailed this off to his contacts. An easy £200 at least, he thought. He could hear Julie starting off the usual long goodbye to her mother. He drummed his fingers along the side of the keyboard and decided to have a look at some examples of sovereigns on the net. Incredibly, well, for him at least, he found an illustration of the exact coin he was looking at that very afternoon - George V 1916 gold sovereign. A rough guide to price showed them to be worth, just as he thought, around £200 a pop, not a great amount but he had seen men murdered for less.

As Julie entered he turned the screen around.

"I forgot to mention this," he said, "but your cousin Hughie had one of these in his hand when he died."

Julie moved closer and closer to the screen.

"Well now," she murmured, "isn't that interesting!"

oooOooo

CHAPTER FOUR

The Ambush

"Let's get going," shouted Charlie.

The two Martin boys pulled on their shirts, dried their feet as best they could and put their socks and boots on as they hurried back to the van. They had enjoyed the paddle and the brief body wash in the cold seawater. All four looked and felt dirty and scruffy, none worse than Charlie. He hadn't had a bath in ages and his hair was becoming long and greasy and was flopping over his forehead. He hadn't shaved for at least a week. An old greasy British ex-army greatcoat came down past his knees and covered his outer clothes which were now becoming matted and stiff. Occasionally the greatcoat would fall open to reveal a leather holster with a Colt revolver strapped around his waist. Recently he was beginning to take on the appearance of a Mexican bandit rather than a disciplined soldier.

"Put the rifles back and remember to put the safety catch back on."

They started chattering excitedly about the appearance of the airplane as they packed away the guns.

"Let's go," snapped Charlie. It was hard not to like the boys but they had never seen serious action and they were already treating the patrol like a school day outing.

His official instructions were vague. Charlie was told by his commanding officer to take a couple of men and head down to Passage West 'to see if anyone had landed anything'. Charlie, like many others, was surprised by the incredible mobility of the newly formed Free State Army who seemed, if anything, to be more enthusiastic and more professional than even the British had been. They had already captured Waterford and Limerick. The battalion Charlie had been attached to was scattered, with dead and wounded everywhere, in a pitched battle just outside Kilmallock in County Cork. Even although the raw recruits of the Free State foot soldiers took a bit of a mauling, the officers were well trained and knew how to run a field battle. He could hear distinct Belfast and Dublin accents shouting for field fire to be brought up and signalling for flanking movements.

Serious doubts were entering the thoughts of Charlie. In a way, he had little time to think things through the way he liked, weigh up the rights and wrongs, balancing the safest and fairest way forward not just for himself but for the men under his control and command. Things were becoming confused. Uncharacteristically he was becoming perplexed: he wasn't even clear what to do if he did find Free Staters at Passage West.

"Right Kevin, get this machine moving and head down the coast here."

Kevin, at twenty, was the older of the Martin brothers and could handle the captured Lancia with surprising skill. His brother Declan, on the other hand, was a large heavy built teenager with a slower wit and who rarely spoke.

"According to this map it should be another four miles or so," Charlie continued. "You boys have been round here a while and should know the place, keep your eyes open for anything unusual." It was an exceptionally glorious morning, just past seven o'clock. On their left hand side the early morning sun dazzled across the bay, slowly burning away the dawn mist on the water. On their right lay the deep lush green fields of South Cork. There was no traffic and the only noise was the squawks and cawing of curlews and herring gulls. After a few minutes Kevin started to slow down the heavy Lancia as they approached a sweeping right hand turn which was gradually taking them from the bay and into the countryside. As the Lancia ground to a halt Charlie asked him why he was stopping here.

"Look further down the bay there. It looks like a ship at anchor," he answered.

Charlie decided that Kevin must have the eyes of a hawk, he could see nothing.

He pulled out a small six inch telescope from his field coat, and to the amazement of the Martin brothers, extended the four draws which tripled its length.

"What am I looking for, Kevin?"

"Straight ahead, to the left of that bit of land there."

"Ah yes! Looks like a small passenger boat, a ferry or something. What's odd about that?"

"Never seen a boat of any kind anchored down there. They usually ship up all the way to one of the quays in Cork or pull in at Queenstown."

As Kevin was answering, the soft early morning mist cleared for a few moments and Charlie saw a light tender pulling away from the ship. Charlie immediately recognised its cargo – a British Army eighteen pounder standard field gun.

He kept the telescope focussed on the tender for a few more moments even as the mist swirled round again, he was trying to compose his thoughts. This looked bad. He recalled the engagement at Kilmallock where he had seen a house and outbuildings well defended for several days only to be abandoned after a few minutes of shrapnel bombardment by one of the very same field guns.

He snapped the telescope shut and slipped it into his inside pocket and looked around.

"We need to go back."

He looked around him.

"We can't turn here, the road's too narrow. Move on down the road and find a place to turn," he said sharply.

Seeing the look on his face the rest of the men wisely said nothing.

The Lancia moved smoothly for a hundred yards and stopped again. Kevin switched off the engine and stood up putting his finger to his lips and pointing with his other hand to a spot further down the road. Again Charlie could see nothing but this time pulled out the telescope without prompting. He scanned the area that Kevin indicated until he glimpsed a slight movement about two hundred yards away, just off the roadside. This man's eyesight is beyond the humble hawk and verging towards the truly supernatural, thought Charlie. A small cloud of smoke or steam came from the area. Charlie indicated for silence and left his car seat and moved down the road keeping to the tree lined right hand side. He covered twenty yards and slipped behind a large ash tree. Again he used the telescope, this time he could make out some uniformed figures around an armoured car that had pulled off the road. It was probably an armoured version of the Lancia they themselves were driving; steam was billowing from the engine. This was even more bad news, for the car must have been unloaded from the ship, no mean task in itself, and travelled this distance from the beachhead. In that case the ship, by Charlie's estimation, must have anchored some hours ago and must have been able to land men and equipment without any opposition.

There was noise coming from area, men talking and the quiet hiss of the escaping steam. The men, obviously from the National Army, looked confident in their new uniforms but they were twisting and turning a map and pointing up and down the road. They looked lost.

Charlie removed the 'scope and stared at the scene for a few moments. He wondered if these guys were the vanguard of a larger force or did they simply race ahead and take a wrong turning in their haste. From the look of them he suspected the latter. He returned to the car.

"Kevin, if you came from Passage West and were heading to Cork would you come this road?" he asked quietly.

"Aye you could, but there's a better road going through Upper Rochester."

Charlie thought for a few minutes then decided to take a real chance.

"Start driving down the road slowly, me and Pat will follow

behind. We'll be armed. Drive past their car and stop. Shout out and ask if they need help, me and Pat will take them by surprise."

Charlie took out his American colt revolver and gave one of the better rifles to Pat.

He patted the Lancia.

"Let's go," he said.

Before Kevin started the engine there came the sudden crack of distant gunfire, Charlie indicated for silence again and hurried back to his original vantage point. On viewing the group this time, he noticed no sign of concern about the gunfire, no rush to arms or running for cover, but there was an obvious look of increasing concern on the faces of what Charlie took to be the two commanding officers. By this time Charlie had already made up his mind to ambush the patrol, in a way he had no choice, the Lancia simply could not turn on this road - it was ahead or nothing. He had also made up his mind that this whole Civil War, as he was now coming to see it, was doomed to failure. A sea landing, he knew from experience, is one of the most difficult and dangerous manoeuvres an army unit can plan and the easiest for a well organised defence to repulse. For Charlie, an army unit to land virtually unopposed was amateurish and reckless in the extreme.

An alternative, which he was beginning to turn over in his mind, was to simply surrender. He was convinced that he could persuade the others to follow suit without too much opposition. The Martin brothers, wily as they were, had little perception about the actions they were now engaged in: fighting the British army and the RIC for Irish freedom was an easy concept for them to comprehend - fighting for a clash of egos and ideology was another. His brother, he reasoned, would simply do as asked out of loyalty.

However to surrender, he reckoned, could be a bit of a step into the unknown, Charlie was a reasonably well known figure. In theory his rank was Captain in the engineering company of the Irish Republic Army. Such commissions were voted for by the men of the battalion and Charlie was voted in after the battle of

Crossbarry. Part of the problem was that he personally knew, or at least had heard of, many of the officers in the present Free State army. He also knew Liam Lynch, the chief of staff of the anti-treaty forces, quite well. It was Lynch who persuaded Charlie, with a mixture of charm and flattery, to stay on in Cork despite his misgivings about Lynch's 'Munster Republic'. However Charlie had almost an inbuilt loyalty to anyone, or indeed anything that commanded his respect, a characteristic which is at once admirable, but potentially fatal.

However the die was cast and the crucial point was simply their present position. Charlie took stock. He took into account his men's enthusiasm and youth, they were easy to command. They had the additional upper hand of surprise; the Free Staters looked too confident and therefore liable to be lazy about security and simple field craft. Even as he observed, two other soldiers - privates he guessed - emerged from the armoured car and started sauntering around the vehicle smoking cigarettes. He went back to his men.

"A slight change of plan."

He talked quietly and confidently. He had learned during the war that whispering orders to men seemed to panic some of them.

"Myself and Pat will move down the right hand side of the road where there is more cover, when the time is right we move over to the left."

He pointed down the road.

"Can you see that clump of high bushes about 10 yards from their van?"

Kevin and Declan nodded eagerly.

"When we cross over to the bushes, you start moving. As you pass their vehicle shout out and ask if they're looking for help, just as we agreed before."

He paused.

"Before we go, keep your eyes on the road. Do not, for God sake - under any circumstances - look in our direction."

An anxious and excited look passed between the brothers.

"Come on," he said to Pat.

It took less than three or four minutes to get to the point opposite the bushes. Charlie could now hear the officers talking, not distinct enough to understand their conversation, but clear enough to recognise the sing song, almost anglified, accent of educated Dubliners. He was almost embarrassed by their slovenly discipline. The two officers turned and looked down the road, jabbing at the map. There was no sign of the other two soldiers, the privates. Bending low they crossed to the other side of the road. Another few distant rifle cracks almost covered the sound of the Lancia starting up, not that it mattered - the officers looked otherwise engaged. The Lancia seemed to take an age to pass them, the two Martin boys looking almost comically serious as they stared stubbornly ahead. The officers looked startled as the Lancia drew level.

"Conas ata tu," shouted Declan.

Seeing the officers baffled look, he added "Do you need any help?" in English.

One of the officers started to fold up the map.

"Er, yes my good man we were er... wondering ...."

"Put your hands up and don't turn round," Charlie said in a clear voice, loud enough to be heard, but without shouting. Pat had his gun trained on the other two soldiers who, needing no instructions, dropped their cigarettes immediately and put their hands in the air.

"I'm an officer of the Irish Volunteers, and I give you my word that you will come to no harm if you follow my instructions," he said in the same clear voice. "Now, all of you kneel down."

When the officers were kneeling Charlie walked behind.

"Unbutton your holster with your left hand. Keep your other hand in the air."

Charlie knew this was a deliberately awkward instruction, almost humiliating, but it keep the prisoner's mind and body off balance during a critical time. Charlie had briefly considered the problem of being identified, whether they should adopt false names or not, but decided it would complicate a simple plan.

After all, he thought, it's not as if this was a bank hold up.

"Kevin, move forward and remove these gentlemen's side arms, one at a time and bring them over here. Declan, you stay in the car."

Kevin moved forward carefully, pulling the gun from each holster as instructed. Charlie picked one up, a brand new British made Webley, still with some of the manufacturer's grease on it. Charlie was now in a slight dilemma, this part had gone so smoothly he had little time to think about the next step. Again the crack of gunfire. Was it getting nearer or was he beginning to imagine things? First things first.

"Kevin, get back into our car and use this space to turn her round. Declan, over here, take Pat's gun and position and you, Pat, guard these two."

"Use this if you have to," he said, handing over one of the officers' guns to Pat. Charlie picked up the other gun and, putting his Colt on the ground, placed the new Webley in his own holster. He walked over to inspect the armoured car. It wasn't, as he first thought, an armoured version of the Lancia, in fact it wasn't really an armoured vehicle at all: it was more of a large delivery van reinforced with metal panels. He opened the side door. The back had room for two seats and the front was crammed with what looked like full boxes of ammunition, British Standard issue, packed around them were empty sandbags to keep them from moving around. A closer look revealed that a row of boxes in the centre, of roughly the same shape but of smaller size and dimensions, were in fact wooden and blue in colour. The ends had a hastily applied stencil in white stating 'Soarstat Eireann' - Irish Free State and below that 'An Roinn Airgeadas' in smaller letters. Charlie frowned, Free State and what?

He tried to think clearly again. His knack for language meant that he could usually translate a phrase by working or guessing a few words and then putting them in context. *Airgead* he remembered could mean money and *roinn* could mean divide up as in dividing a room or a department, possibly it could mean something like the department of finance or simply 'The Treasury' in Gaelic. Charlie was intrigued. In any event, he decided, the ammunition would come in handy and in the meantime with much twisting and turning Kevin managed to turn the Lancia round and was now facing Cork.

His men turned expectantly when he removed himself from the van. He called Kevin over.

"We don't have any rope or chord to tie these men with, do we?" asked Charlie.

"I don't know, but I doubt it," replied Kevin.

"That makes things awkward."

He was silent for a few moments then he gestured Kevin to follow him. He took a few paces back towards the Lancia and turned. The noise of the engine partly drowned his voice.

"Listen carefully, Kevin. Take the two privates about ten yards down to the end of this widening and get them to lie face down on the ground. Tell them, in English, that we're moving off in a couple of minutes but that there are another two of our men at the end of road that will be keeping an eye on them. They've to lie there for an hour then they can move off," he paused. "Have you got that, Kevin?"

"Yes, sir," he replied.

Charlie was taken aback, not only by Kevin's immediate understanding of his instructions, but by the fact that he called him sir - praise indeed from a Kerry man. He thought for a second then called over Declan, instructing him to remove the blue boxes from the back of the van and to place them into the boot of the Lancia. He returned to the officers kneeling on the ground again approaching them from behind, he tapped what he deduced was the more senior on the shoulder.

"Stand up slowly."

The officer leaned forward pressing his hands on the ground to give his arms leverage and then pushed himself up. Standing behind him Charlie realised that the man was tall and well built, possibly an athlete of some kind. He was also looking more relaxed.

"Lift your arms high and don't turn round."

Charlie started to pat the officer's body starting under the arms and then moving to the front, when he reached the jacket pockets he heard a jingle of keys in the right hand one and felt a bulky package in the left. Both pockets had been left unbuttoned. As he removed these items the officer turned slightly.

"Don't turn round and don't worry, I'll return your stuff in a minute"

Charlie slipped the keys into his own pocket and started to quickly scan through the documents, they were all in English. He was right in his guess of the Gaelic translation, some of the documents were headed 'Department of Finance - Provisional Government of the Irish Free State' and referred to or were addressed to Lieutenant Colonel Simon Barrett and his adjutant Captain John Kelly.

"I take it you are Officer Barrett?"

Other than a slight glance to the left, the officer remained silent. Charlie walked back to the Lancia where Declan was about to heave in the last case.

"Put that one on the back seat, Declan."

He shouted over Kevin.

"Think you could drive their van back to Cork?"

Kevin laughed.

"Sure sir, I used to drive an old Austin van like that every day back in Tralee."

"Good. Load up the van with whatever guns you can find around here, take those rifles and ammo over there. Take the other officer in the back and get Declan to guard him and here take this," he reached down and handed over his old Colt.

"Keep it," he added.

"We'll move out first in a few minutes. You follow behind. I'll stop after a few miles, I want to drop our prisoner off first, it'll be somewhere along that road we used when we came in, you know, the long straight part with the stone wall on the river side of the road. After another few miles we'll drop your man off as well."

Charlie went back to the Lancia and opened the boot. There were only three keys, one of which was obviously a spare for the van; the blue box was hinged on the short side the other side was padlocked, it opened with the first key he tried. He lifted the lid.

At first Charlie thought that the small cylindrical tubes, packed sideways, were some kind of explosive, perhaps some new kind of dynamite. The tubes were about an inch in diameter and packed sideways the length of the box, about twelve inches They were covered in tightly wrapped wax paper. He pulled one out, dammed heavy, he thought, good job Declan was a big strong lad. These boxes, small as they were, must have weighed a fair amount. Charlie, given the evidence of the boxes' origins, reflected again and began to assume that they were some sort of coinage. He was about to open the cylinder by cracking it against the side of box, but thought better of it, if he was wrong he would blow himself to kingdom come. He started to unwrap the wax paper from the top of the tube.

oooOooo

CHAPTER FIVE

Liam in the library

Des and Julie went grocery shopping on Saturday, crossing the 'Toll bridge' early in the morning. It was always free of the usual penitents, with or without dogs, at this time of day.

"I suppose even jakies need a day off," remarked Des when he first noticed this trivial occurrence. He later realized that they simply moved to much more fertile ground on a Saturday. They took to standing casually beside the ticket vending machines at the city car parks, where they chatted affably about the weather and tut-tutted about the pot holes in the tarmac to the harassed car parkers who, having raked through their pockets or purses for change and having shoved in several quid into the machine, felt an embarrassed obligation to turn over what was left in their hand when pleasantly asked to 'spare a bit of change for the homeless'. When they returned to the flat loaded down with shopping, they divvied up the household chores and set to work. When it approached 12 o'clock they called a halt. Julie said she fancied a jog around Glasgow Green followed by a work out and swim at the local gym. Des decided to take a visit to the Mitchell Library to do some research on one or two of his current projects. His idea of exercise was a round of golf and the occasional five a side game of football.

"You're not taking the car are you," said Julie as she locked up flat.

"No. I'll just hop over on the underground," Des replied. "See you about three or four this afternoon, I'll phone you before I head home."

He walked round to Bridge Street station. If Rome has the most pointless underground system in Europe, then Glasgow must be a close second, thought Des as he boarded one of the two tiny carriages that barrelled their way endlessly around the 'Outer Circle' of the system, passing through miniscule stations in the dead areas of Glasgow. Desolate areas from where the early twentieth century travelling public had long since departed. Des disembarked at St. Georges Cross and walked out with the only other passenger, a bemused Japanese tourist clutching and staring at an opened map, obviously baffled why anyone in their right mind would build an underground station in the middle of a motorway intersection. Des walked down to the library and entered by the main doors dawdling at the notice boards looking at current and up and coming events. As he started cutting through the main reading room on his way upstairs he heard a loud shout.

"Des! How are you, me old fruit?"

It came from behind the librarians counter and it came from Liam Tracey, an old Irish, South Tyrone diehard and legendary drinking phenomenon from Des's folk music period.

"Liam! Good God! How's things?" replied Des, genuinely delighted to see him again. "I forgot you worked here."

"Ach it's a living," said Liam lowering his voice in response to the raised eyebrows of the regulars.

"Come round here," he said walking towards a back office. "Come on in, it's okay, I can seen the counter from here."

He swept a pile of magazines from a sagging chair.

"Here, take a seat."

Des sat down. "Great to see you Liam, you haven't been seen around town for a few months, where have you been?"

"Went back home. My mother was ill for a wee while, she's brand new now. Seventy five odd years old and can still drink me under the table. How's yourself, still flogging stories to the press? How's Julie these days?"

"I'm still working away and Julie's doing fine."

Des talked away about Julie and other recent events and they carried on gabbing for five minutes catching up on gossip and tales of mutual friends.

"By the way Liam did you ever know a relative of Julie's, a cousin of some sort, called Hughie Toner?"

"Jesus, is he Julie's cousin? Ah well can't choose your relatives I suppose..."

Des cut in before he made any more comments.

"He died last night, possibly murdered."

"By God, did he? What happened?"

"Don't really know, but Julie reckons there might be some vague Irish Para-military connection. He had a gold sovereign on him that Julie says came from Ireland. I know that doesn't make a lot of sense, but ..."

"If you will excuse my slightly immoderate language in this place of enlightenment and illumination," Liam replied, spreading his arms to include the entire library, "but Hughie Toner was an absolute and insufferable arse. Irish paramilitary connection? Are you stone mad? In fact, I bumped into him and a few of his cronies a few months ago in Sharkeys Bar," Liam continued, "Their accents got bloody worse as the night wore on, a mixture of Brad Pitt and Sean Connery. My God! It was like a surreal outtake scene from 'Derby O'Gill and the Little People'. Not only that but..."

"Now then, Liam, no speaking ill of the dead and all that," said Des, quickly stopping him in his tracks. From past experience he knew that Liam's ramblings could quickly get out of control if left unguided and quite often ended with Liam, drunk or sober, bursting into song for no apparent reason.

"Anyway I'll probably get a couple of reports printed up in some of the papers and on the odd occasion you can get follow up commissions, so some background info is always a good filler. I just thought I'd spend a bit of time looking up some books on the Irish troubles after the First World War."

"Can't see the connection between Toner and the Troubles," said Liam, scratching his head. "Anyway! Look up nothing! Go no further, old fruit, I'm your man," roared Liam slapping his desk. "What I don't know about the Troubles is not worth knowing about!"

He stood up.

"I usually finish about one o'clock on Saturdays," lowering his voice as he looked up at the clock. "Met me in twenty minutes in the Avalon Bar, it's across the road from the side entrance."

"Have a pint of stout waiting. Now I've a few bits and pieces to finish here, so get going," he said shooing Des out of the office.

Des stood at the busy bar flicking through the selection of daily newspapers left in the rack of the Avalon. He found his piece was picked up by a couple of Redtop dailies and 'The Scotsman'. He would get in touch with them later for any follow up commissions. As he finished reading the front page he heard the commotion as Liam Tracey arrived. Physically, he was a large, hirsute, barrel-chested man, one of these people who knows everyone and, it appeared, that everyone knows, which accounted for all the ballyhoo and shouting as he wandered and weaved his way through the bar. Before becoming a librarian Liam had lectured in the Arts; politics and modern studies but mainly in history. He was also the lecturers' trade union rep. A position, which combined with his impressive and erratic drinking habits, proved to be a deadly combination. He was not sacked, but left the college under a bit of a cloud. A 'mutual arrangement' was the term used at the time.

"Good man, Des!" he said as he swallowed about half the pint in one go.

"Another two pints mine host," he added seamlessly as he rubbed the froth from his greying beard. He nodded to a table under the television. "Let's take a table over there."

"Now then what's all this about research into Irish history? Why bother when you can make it up as you go along."

"That's nonsense, you're an historian yourself and you don't make it up," said Des

"No I don't, but everyone else in Glasgow does," replied Liam with a straight face. "You should hear some of the guff I have to listen to in some of these South Side pubs. Make you laugh out loud so it would. Anyway I've learned to say nothing and just nod my head wisely from time to time. Now then what's all this about Toner and the Troubles?"

"Well nothing really. It was just that me and Julie were chatting about Toner when she started to talk about her grandfather, Charlie, who she reckons fought in the British army in the First World War and might have had something to do with the republican side during the troubles. It kind of caught my interest more than anything else."

"Nothing unusual in her grandfather being in the British Army, loads of Irish fought in the British Army and tens of thousands of them died during the Great War and scores of them took part in the war of independence thereafter, in fact a lot of them became highly regarded because of their expertise, including the great Tom Barry himself."

Liam paused and looked into the middle distance.

"A toast to a great general - General Tom Barry." He took a gulp of stout.

"Indeed," said Des, still sipping from his first pint.

"I'd hazard a guess and take it Julie's granddad was a Donegal man, like most of the Irish in Glasgow. What was his name again?"

"Charles or Charlie I think his name was. Yes, he was from Donegal."

"If he was, then old Charlie wouldn't see much action up there. Most of the fighting during the War of Independence took place either in or about Dublin or down south around the Province of Munster - Cork, Kerry, Tipperary that neck of the woods. The War of Independence lasted around two and a half years and was followed by a bloody awful civil war lasting, in military terms, for a couple of months but managed to get dragged out for nearly a year. The Irish never admit it, but there were more army casualties and atrocities in the Civil War than the previous three years against the British and the RIC. A civil war and tragedy that was effectively airbrushed out of history - in my humble opinion."

42

"Is that it?" said Des.

"In a nutshell - yes. Oh yes, I know by the number of songs and ballads that have been written that it appears to rival in scope the Hundred Years war. But believe me, the war of independence lasted from the first action by Dan Breen in January 1919 until the truce and cease fire of July 1921 just over two years. You could say that it had a long historical beginning, stretching way back, and some would debate and say the violence never did quite end with the truce, particularly in the North, but most agree that by then the campaign for independence was won."

"That all sounds about right, I'm sure Julie said something about her grandfather going off to Cork on the odd occasion, when she was very young. Apparently to look up old friends. She said he usually went alone."

"Probably a wise man. Memories ran deep for a while down there, but most of the people involved have died off by now. Nowadays the young ones couldn't care less. I was there a couple of years ago, great place, brilliant bars, loads of places with bands singing crazy Irish songs. He burst into song.

"They shot them in pairs as they came up the stairs,
Sean Tracey and Dan Breen"

"Jesus, you couldn't make those songs up, could you," he said shaking his head.

Liam looked serous for a moment, Des knew what was coming.

"To my namesake, the great Sean Tracey…" he intoned, taking a large gulp from his glass. He paused, looked at the rest of his pint and continued, "…and not forgetting the mad Dan Breen." - finishing off the pint with a flourish

"Indeed," Des sighed again taking a sip from his own glass. "That'll be another pint then, Liam."

As he stood at the bar he could see Liam reflected in the mirror stroking his beard and looking quite pensive.

"This could all be very interesting," said Liam as Des returned. "There's not that many people have got a close connection to the early troubles. Most of the bam pots I meet would have you believe the grandfathers died in Dublin on the steps of the GPO building clutching a blood-soaked tricolour."

"Details," he added as he lifted the next pint to his lips, "that's what we need, man, more details."

"We're going over to Julie's place tomorrow. I'll see what I can find out. Her mother is always on about Ireland"

"Ah the lovely Grace McKenna! Don't you depend too much on her. Believe me, the older they get the more they exaggerate and romanticise. Best bet is to get solid evidence. Records, passports, photos that sort of thing."

"Funny you should say that about photos," said Des sitting up. "Julie mentioned photos last night and I've just remembered that last year, Julie's Auntie Rosie - that's one of her dad's sisters - was looking at a box of photos. She showed me one of old Charlie and another one of his brother in army uniforms."

"That's the very kind of thing we need! British army uniforms were they?"

"I assumed so."

"Ach! Assume nothing, they could be Free State uniforms, they were very similar. See if you can get a hold of them or even better scan them into a computer and then e-mail to me, I'll write down my e-mail address for you."

Liam rummaged through his pockets and found an unused bookie's betting slip and a matching pencil.

"If you get it to me for Monday morning I can meet you on Monday after work," he said as he wrote down the information. "We have some brilliant software for picture enhancement and some excellent printers that I can use in the library. Monday's an early finish for me so I could meet you about four. Let's make it half four in The Scotia Bar. Now then, another pint, Des. My shout."

"Make it a half pint - one for the road," said Des.

"You know, the Irish Civil War is very interesting, very difficult to get an angle on sometimes," Liam said seriously, as he put down the fresh drinks. He was slowly drifting in to his lecturing mode.

"How bad was it?" asked Des

"Well at least three thousand dead. But it's not just about the 'butcher's bill', as they say. Let's put it like this. After the Civil War politics in Ireland have been skewed and twisted almost to this day."

He leaned back against the wall.

"The two main political parties of Ireland were forged in the crucible of the civil war!" he cried dramatically, forming his hand into an upturned claw.

Several people from the bar looked over

"Forgive my flowery language, Des," he said taking another draught of stout. "It's the Irish in me."

Nothing to do with the drink then, thought Des dryly.

"Anyway, for decades, and unusually for a western European country, there was no real what you might call class politics in Ireland, no real Right versus Left, none of your Conservative versus Socialist Progressive. At best you could say Fine Gael took the pro-treaty position, vaguely right of centre and Fianna Fail the anti-treaty position and vaguely left of centre," he closed his eyes for a second. "Come to think of it, saying Fianna Fail is even remotely left of centre is perhaps stretching a point."

"But you could also say," he continued, "that the Civil War was, in its own awful way, inevitable."

"How is that?"

"It's quite unnerving to see how similar historical events nearly always follow the same tragic path. There is the great revolt against the colonial tyrant, the victory, the colonial oppressor power pulls out, then the struggle for power between the leaders of the revolution begins. Having had a common enemy for so long, they had remained allies - as soon as the common cause goes..." Liam stopped, spread his hands and shrugged his shoulders.

"...Revolution followed by civil war and conflict. Not always the case but it's almost a disturbing universal formula."

"In the period of the Irish troubles, just after the Great War and into the early twenties, there were several countries in the same position," he continued. "The Russian revolution was followed by a terrible civil war, the same happened in Hungary after the fall of the Austro-Hungarian Empire. Even Finland, a country now reckoned to be one of the world's remarkably civilised countries, had a revolutionary uprising against Russian domination that left a staggering fifty thousand dead in the civil war that followed - all this in a country with the same population as Ireland. In most of these wars it was a straight forward conflict between left wing socialist and right wing monarchists and reactionaries. The Civil War in Ireland was different; although some still say it was a struggle between left wing republicans and reactionary traditionalists, but I tell you, it would take a bit of doing to convince me that Michael Collins, De Valera, Liam Lynch and their ilk were either red blooded socialist revolutionaries or even conventional conservatives."

Des cringed and waited for a song.

"Don't worry, Des. No songs about these guys."

"You know, is it not the oddest thing?" he said rubbing his beard. "Every toe rag who threw as much as a stone during the troubles managed to get a lengthy song penned about themselves. In fact, there seemed to be more balladeers than protagonists. Yet the two main leaders? Not as much as a bloody catchy tune."

"Anyway," he announced, "there's no need for us to be philosophising at this time of the day. If you want a blow by blow account of Irish history and a re-run of the Civil War go to Heraghty's Bar any Friday night. You might not learn much but it'll give you a bloody good laugh if nothing else."

After gulping down the rest of his pint Liam announced that he was heading for his usual Saturday rampage through the South Side.

As they rose from their seats Des asked.

"Whatever happened to that best selling book you were going to write? You remember - the one you told me you were doing some researching for that last time we met."

"Ah yes, the book," he sighed.

"Yes indeed, I did some research and found that that the best sellers have three distinct themes, one is obviously plenty of sex, another one is hospital stories, you know, nurses and doctors that kind of thing and of course a good cowboy book always sells well. So I thought if I could combine all three I would be on to a winner."

"Well, how is it going then?" Des asked as they stepped on to the pavement.

"Not great, but I do have a title, it's called…"

He hesitated.

"… 'The Nurse wore Spurs' "

"See you on Monday," he shouted as he rushed across the busy street.

CHAPTER SIX

The Douglas Barricade

Charlie stood behind Officer Barrett.

"My driver will lead with the first vehicle," he explained. "As you can see the front is open, but the driver will not hear any of our conversation. I intend to release you about two miles up this road and your fellow officer will be dropped off about a mile further on, you will not be harmed in any way. However don't try anything that you may regret."

Throughout the entire engagement Charlie consciously kept his face, if not quite hidden, at least out of direct view, particularly from Barrett and the other officer.

"Now go and sit in the front seat directly behind the driver and face forward, your colleague can go in the other car."

When the convoy was ready he told a slightly nervous Pat to drive at a steady pace up the road for a couple of miles and stop at the large abandoned warehouse where they had stopped earlier that morning. Pat did not have the swaggering confidence of young Kevin Martin but, nevertheless, he was a competent driver. Charlie banged the side of the van and shouted "Let's go!" as he swung into the jump seat directly behind Barrett.

They travelled silently for a few minutes getting used to the swaying of the heavy Lancia on the uneven road. Charlie leaned forward. He swung his arm out, then slowly brought his closed right fist in front of the officer's eyes, he opened his hand. Lying in the palm of his hand was a bright, brand new English sovereign.

"Interesting shipment you were carrying there, Mr. Barrett."

Barrett looked at the coin and turned away. He seemed to hesitate, thinking about what he was about to say.

"You could be making a big mistake here," he said calmly.

He shifted in his seat.

"Can I turn round a bit," he added. " I realise you don't want to be recognised, but it's a bit odd talking to the back of someone's head and trying to listen to the person behind at the same time."

"Turn a bit if you find it more comfortable," replied Charlie

Simon Barrett put his long arm along the back seat and turned to the side, exposing his clean cut and boyish profile to Charlie.

"From what I can see you seem to be an experienced and intelligent military man. I hope I can speak frankly to you."

He stopped, waiting for an answer.

"Carry on," said Charlie cautiously. "I have an open mind."

"This....This uprising, this civil war cannot be allowed to continue. You and your comrades are fighting a lost cause - that's if it can be called a cause at all."

Barrett began to look flushed and angry.

"The political situation in the North is being compromised by this... ridiculous sideshow. It's being orchestrated by a few hotheads who can't put their guns down and a few politicians who lost power and refuse to accept a democratic vote."

"That's enough," snapped Charlie "I don't need a god-damn lecture in Irish politics at this time of the morning!"

Charlie settled back in his seat, rattled, he took a few seconds to compose himself.

"Now lets get back to the case in hand," he continued, "namely the reason you're transporting several thousands of pounds in treasury money into a battle zone."

"Twelve thousand actually," replied Barrett regaining some of his original composure. "Two thousand in each box, and that's taking the sovereigns at face value. As you have probably guessed, I'm not a military man, I'm a senior civil servant and a lawyer, so is my colleague Kelly. We've been seconded by the new government

49

into the national army for the next few months. There were several, well, let's just call them tasks, that it was felt would be better carried out by those who were less tarnished by the politics of the past year. Lawyers, diplomats, skilled negotiators and that kind of thing. Unfortunately this morning the military commanders at Passage West were more concerned about their fighting troops than us. We were almost the first to disembark, which wasn't planned. The original idea was to land a small reconnoitring force followed by a larger fighting company but after firing off a few shots the irregulars had simply abandoned their posts. Just before dawn we were unloaded with the first disembarkation. It was still not quite light when we made the mistake of having a drive around. When you found us we were totally lost."

"As for our shipments, as you called them, these are destined for certain …shall we say …payments. These have been authorised by General Collins himself. After we capture Cork… and that is planned to take place by tomorrow night… negotiations will begin and this war will end."

"Take my word for it," he added as he turned his head to the front again.

Charlie leaned back in his seat. He knew exactly what Barrett was talking about; this money was for bribes and 'wanted men' rewards, possibly more bribes than rewards he suspected.

The car was silent for a few minutes when Barrett turned his head again.

"Look, I know you don't want to talk about the politics of it all, but think of the reasons why we've reached this insane war. We all know that most of the real fighting during the struggle took place down here or in Dublin. The southern divisions based down here had more than a third of the entire armed men in Ireland fighting the English - mostly successfully. The place was ungovernable. The problem is that Cork and Kerry do not comprise the whole of Ireland. In the rest of Ireland, even in Dublin, we were struggling badly and in deep trouble. As General Mulcahy said to the Dail, before the treaty, 'far from driving the British out of Ireland we would be lucky to drive them out of a fairly good sized police barracks'…"

Charlie heard Pat applying the brakes.

"Time to leave, Mr Barrett."

Charlie sat back in the shadow as Barrett stepped out of the Lancia and started to walk back down the road. After a few steps he stopped and turned round.

"Before I go, let me tell you this. This war could be over in a week with that bullion and if it continues it could turn very nasty. Think carefully before you make any decisions."

Charlie stayed silent for a moment then banged the side of the door.

"Get going!" he shouted.

Charlie waited for a few minutes until the Lancia started to turn slightly to the left before he signalled Pat to stop again. This time he jumped out and looked down the road, he could just about make out Barrett standing in the middle with his hand over his eyes gazing up at the little convoy. He walked back to the other vehicle.

"Right Kevin, let your man out here and tell him to start back down the way we came, then come up here and see me."

He carried out his instruction to the letter and came bustling back up to the Lancia. Charlie held up his hand and told him to stop where he was, and pointed to the gun in Kevin's belt

"A bit of advice, Kevin. Never a good idea to keep a Colt revolver tucked into your trousers," he said drolly. "Put it in a holster, there's one in the Lancia that I took from the other officer. Make use of it."

"Now," he continued. "We are going to head back into Cork, keep your distance behind me and keep your eyes open in case I have to stop. For Gods sake don't run into the back of me, with the amount of ammo we're carrying we will be flying through the air to Cork."

"We're not that far away from Rochestown. It's just up the road a bit," said Kevin.

"Okay I might stop there, but only if we have to, I'll sit upsides Pat from now on. I'll move my hand up and down if we're about to stop"

"Grand," said Kevin, as he removed the Colt gingerly. "I think I'll just go and get that holster you were talking about."

There were off in a few minutes and as they turned more fully to the left and further inland, Charlie could see the first few houses of Rochestown. In the meantime a stiff wind started to blow up Lough Mahon and the sky was now slowly clouding over. As they approached the town Charlie could see a couple of armed men had stopped a bus which seemed to be heading in their direction, presumably the local bus to Passage West. He could see the driver was already clambering out of his seat and one of the gunmen was now taking a keener interest in the two vehicles heading towards them. Charlie signalled to stop about thirty yards from the bus and jumped out and held up one hand, he left his great coat open so the men could clearly see his side arm.

"Morning fellas. My name is Captain McKenna of the Engineering Company," he said clearly and loudly about ten yards from the men. They looked at one another, slightly relieved.

"Morning to you, sir," the taller of them replied, as they shook hands. "Joe Sullivan, Cork City Brigade."

"Seems we have a problem, Joe. I'm just back from Passage West or as damn near it as you'd want to be."

Charlie turned away for a second to give himself time to think, for all he knew these guys could be Free State sympathisers, highly unlikely, but better try to keep things general rather than specific.

"It appears that..." he paused again, "That the enemy have arrived by sea and in some force."

"Well now, that's what we'd heard. The rest of the brigade is setting up in Douglas. We were told to come here and stop traffic, anything the Free Staters could commandeer and use as transport," said Joe enthusiastically. "That's why we stopped the bus."

The passengers were now off the bus and seemed to show less enthusiasm for the enterprise than Joe, in fact one or two were beginning to grumble loudly.

"We're waiting for some sappers to come down and blow up the bridge then we can set up some positions to attack the buggers as they come up the road."

"Good man and good thinking. I've managed to relieve the 'Staters' of a van full of ammo here," he said waving to the other vehicle. "It might be an idea for us to head over to Douglas, they might be in need of some of it there."

"You're right. We just walked from there, it only took half an hour or so. Keep on this road for about a mile till you reach a crossroad. You'll see the sign for Douglas, the town is only half a mile from there."

Charlie thanked them and turned back to the Lancia. The eager Martin brothers started shouting "Adh mór ort" to everyone as they headed off on the road to Douglas.

Traffic started to appear very shortly after they set off for Douglas, not much, mainly delivery vans and the occasional private car. People seemed to be going about their business in a fairly calm manner. Charlie was still unsettled, uneasy. What Barrett had said had unnerved him; it was too close to the way he was beginning to think himself these past few weeks. They turned right at the crossroad and soon found Douglas in a state of ferment, with armed men pulling over wagons and carts in an effort to create street barriers. Sand bags were being used to fill in the gaps. Incredibly they were not even challenged as they manoeuvred around the barricades. Charlie stopped both vehicles on the main road and stood on the seat to get a better view of the frantic activity around him. He immediately spotted a tall white haired man who seemed to have some authority, giving orders and trying to organise some of the men into work groups. Charlie left the Lancia, instructing Pat not to move under any circumstances.

"Conas ata tu," shouted Charlie as he approached what he now took to be the leading figure.

The tall man kept on waving and giving instructions quickly. Finally he turned around.

"Thanks for asking, I'm fine," he replied in English, sounding both harassed and suspicious.

He stopped and stood still looking closely at Charlie, trying not to be impressed by the Webley revolver hanging by Charlie's side. He cocked his head to one side.

"I know you from somewhere, don't I? You don't sound as if you come from round here," he continued, still suspicious.

"I was up at Kilmallock just a few days ago. It's probably up there you seen me. I'm Captain Charlie McKenna, I'm from up North – Donegal."

"Yes, of course, sure I remember you now," he said relieved. "How the devil are you? Have you been sent by Lynch to give us a hand?"

"Not exactly, what makes you think that?"

"Sure I've just been talking to him on the phone, I'm Joe Riley by the way," shaking Charlie's hand heartily. "He said he'll try to send some more men up here."

"General Lynch is here - in Douglas?" said Charlie quickly.

"No, but we have a good phone link up to Fermoy. He set up new headquarters there. He wants to keep up with things happening in Cork."

"A phone link you say! That's excellent news. Listen, I have a whole load of ammo in the back of that second van over there. We managed to capture it from the 'Staters' down near Passage West this morning. I'm wondering what the General would regard as the best place for it. Do you think I could get in touch?"

"Should be no problem, the phone is in that hardware shop over there. It's the local Post Office as well," he replied pointing down the street to the large building on the left. "You can head on down there now but it'll be another ten or fifteen minutes before I can finish this off."

"Okay," replied Charlie. "See you down there."

They parked outside the makeshift HQ and wandered around stretching their legs. The Martin brothers managed to scrounge some tea and sat inside talking in half Gaelic and half English to the young girl operating the small telephone exchange. Another couple of young lads, ostensibly guarding the place, with old Mausers hanging round their shoulders, joined in the general banter. As Charlie walked impatiently up and down then going in and then out of the shop, he noticed some old paint and some brushes lying in the corner.

Some interesting ideas, almost the makings of a plan, were beginning to form in his mind.

"Fellas, would you mind if we used some of this old paint to hide the markings on this van?"

"Not at all. Carry on there," shouted one of the youngsters.

He took a tin of blue coloured paint and one of the better brushes outside and called Pat over.

"See the blue boxes we have in the Lancia, go over now and use this paint to cover the writing on them. I know it's not an exact match but it'll be near enough, Think you could manage?"

"Just the writing?" said Pat.

"That'll do fine, if anyone questions you, tell them to come and see me."

The job only took Pat ten minutes and he had just stored away the brush and paint and joined the rest of the lads when Joe Riley came hurrying up the road.

"Sorry about that Captain, we seem to have a lot of rookie volunteers here today. I'll get in touch with Fermoy now."

"Mary," he shouted to the young girl. "Would you get that number we used this morning."

The next ten minutes involved a great deal of dialling and redialling by Mary and a great load of cursing and swearing in both Gaelic and English by Joe. Finally he made the connection.

"General Lynch, it's Joe Riley here down in Douglas," roared Joe down the phone. "There a Captain McKenna of the engineers who wants a word with you, sir."

Charlie couldn't make out the reply but Joe handed over the phone.

"Here you are, Captain," he said handing over the receiver.

"Hello Liam, Charlie McKenna here."

"Hello Charlie." The line was a bit crackly, but fairly clear. "Good to hear from you, haven't seen you for a week or two. How did you manage to fetch up in Douglas?"

"Long story, but I'm here now," said Charlie. "Liam, I was looking for some instruction from you. I managed to capture a load of ammunition - around 20,000 rounds I'd guess. I'm wondering what would be the best place for it. I'm inclined to leave it here but if you have more need of it elsewhere…" He went quiet, letting the query linger.

There was a moment's hesitation.

"Yes, that's probably the best idea, get hold of the brigade quarter master and let him handle it." Lynch sounded uncertain and preoccupied to Charlie. He turned away from the phone.

"Who's the brigade quarter master?" Charlie asked Joe.

He thought for a moment.

"Well suppose in a way, I am," said Joe. "Dermot still hasn't returned to Cork yet and I'm the senior company quarter master, so I suppose it falls to me."

"Joe Riley, the man you were talking to, is the acting brigade QM down here, sir"

"Oh," said the General slightly surprised, "that'll be okay. Let Joe handle it then. Charlie could you try to make your way up here. I could be doing with your good council. Now, I'll have to go. There's a hundred and one things to do here and there's someone on the other phone. Can I wish you health and luck and hope to see you in the next few days. Put Joe back on again."

"See you soon Liam," replied Charlie handing back the phone.

A brief one sided conversation consisting of many nods, looks and glances over to Charlie followed. Riley ended with a cheery "And good luck to you sir!" and put the phone back carefully on the cradle.

"Right captain, follow me," he said as he made his way smartly through the corridor and into a back room.

He took a bunch of keys from a drawer and opened the top door of a tall safe that stood on the corner. Charlie couldn't quite see inside the safe but it seemed to be full of papers and files. Joe withdrew a metal box about the size of a large brick which he opened with a smaller key on the same ring.

"Now then," he said as he pulled open the lid. "Two hundred

pounds I've to give you."

He pulled out two banded bundles from many others and tossed them on to the table.

"You can count it if you like, but it's all there."

"What's this for?"

"The ammo of course, General says you're to leave the lot with us."

Riley flicked through the rest of the money mentally counting the bundles.

"You can't say the Cork brigades don't pay their way," he added proudly.

Charlie knew the QM's carried funds, usually from central HQ, a process often augmented by the occasional bank robbery. They used such funds to pay for additional equipment, firearms and ammunition regardless of where they came. It was one way to encourage the volunteers to commandeer enemy arms and equipment after an engagement. He knew to refuse such a generous offer would be regarded as an insult. He tucked the money into his inside pocket.

"I'll give some of this to the men."

Joe busied himself putting things away and locking up the safe.

"I'll leave you to do the right thing, Captain," he replied, slightly disinterested.

"Now then, Mr McKenna," he continued, walking down the corridor. "Let's see what we can do with this load of ammo we've acquired."

Joe stepped out to the street and started to move towards the Lancia.

"The ammo cases are in the van behind," Charlie said quickly.

Joe hardly broke his stride and simply veered towards the van, throwing open the door when he reached the back. Charlie caught up a few moments later.

Riley was talking to himself.

"Good selection, Lee Enfield .303 and Mauser 7.92, I see."

A slight pause

"Any side-arm bullets? Ah yes, over here."

He continued moving the cases around, muttering to himself. Charlie leaned against the door.

"Ex-Army man I take it?" said Charlie.

Joe stopped and looked at Charlie keenly.

He turned away.

"I suppose it takes one to know one."

He hesitated, and continued.

"Long time ago, served in South Africa for two year, joined as a boy, Royal Munsters, finished in '04."

He looked around confidently.

"I wouldn't broadcast it though," he added under his breath.

Charlie slapped him on the back, smiling.

"You're right, it does take one to know one."

As they walked back to the shop front Charlie gave Joe a brief explanation of his own army background and what had happened that morning.

"I don't want to tell you what to do, but you might think of sending some men with some of this ordinance back down to Rochestown. I'm pretty sure our Free State prisoners will have made it back by now and will have told their commanding officers that the road to Rochestown is clear, well, at least for the few miles that they had to walk back. I've got to head back into town but I think it would be better if I left the van and leave the Martin boys here as well, they're only young lads but have done well this morning. I know there was no fighting or shooting involved but they carried out their orders quickly and without fuss. I have known plenty others that would have panicked in the same circumstances. I'll have a word with them in a minute."

"That seems like good sense. As for your boys, well, I can only ask them if they want to stay. A lot of the lads are going home when they hear that their home town is in trouble. Where are they from anyway?"

"They're from Kerry, somewhere up near Tralee I think."

"I doubt if they'll do much good up there. The Free Staters took Tralee a week ago. I was there, the whole thing was a farce, over in a few hours. We were outnumbered and outgunned although I think we did a bit of damage. I managed to get myself bloody captured. They kept us locked up in the barracks overnight and the daft buggers let us go in the morning after a bit of interrogation. They were too busy trying to get as many troops as quick as they could to Kilmallock. I just walked down the road to the station calm as you like and managed to get the train back to Mallow. Funny enough, the fella that questioned me - he didn't talk like you, sounded like a Yank or something, but he said that he came from Donegal like yourself, name of Peebles."

This gave Charlie a bit of a start. Peebles, surely not George Peebles of all people he thought.

He tried to be relaxed and offhand.

"Peebles you say! Come to think of it there were a few people of that name around Letterkenny, didn't get his first name did you."

Joe gave him a withering look.

"It wasn't exactly a conversation in a bar over a few pints," he said tetchily

"Sorry Joe, no offence. Look, I really need to get moving," he added. "I'll be back in a minute."

He left Joe and walked back towards the shop, as he did so he discreetly pulled out four fivers from one of bundles in his inside pocket and transferred them to his greatcoat pocket. When he reached the doorway he shouted out to Pat and the Martin boys to come outside for a few minutes, which they did reluctantly. Charlie could see why, Mary had been joined by another couple of giggling girls behind the counter.

"Pat, get the Lancia ready, we're moving out."

He pulled the other two aside.

"Well lads," he said addressing the two young men. "There's a couple of things you'll need to think over, but first I want you to take this money."

The twins looked astounded as Charlie handed over two five pound notes to each one of them. The Martin brothers came from a culture that had existed almost money free, most food and goods were essentially bartered. The only time money changed hands was at the monthly market where a five pound note could buy you anything from two heifers to ten loads of turf.

"Don't worry. It's from the quarter master. It's for capturing the ammunition. Make sure to keep those bills safe and change them for coins and ten shilling notes in the bank here or in Cork when you get there, okay?"

"Now, Joe says you can stay with him and the rest of his men," continued Charlie. "He says that's up to you, he can't force you. If you want to leave, you can if you want to, but I'm afraid the van stays here."

The way they glanced at each other and back to the shop made Charlie think that their decision was being made there and then.

"Anyway, good luck boys. I hope I'll see you again some time," he said as he walked away. The two boys mumbled their goodbyes as they hastily returned to the shop and the girls.

As Charlie walked towards the Lancia, Pat was already seated and had the engine running. He stood beside the door and waved to Joe, who was still staring into the ammo van, pensively stroking his chin.

"Well good luck. Might see you sooner than you think," he shouted over the noise of the engine

"Thanks," replied Joe distractedly. "Er…and good luck to yourselves."

"Adh mór ort," he added, waving his hand in dismissal.

Charlie jumped in to the passenger seat besides Pat.

"Back to Cork, is it?"

"For the time being," he answered, and paused. "But I think you and I will be taking a trip up to Tralee tomorrow."

oooOooo

CHAPTER SEVEN

Cork City

They met a bit more light traffic as they approached the centre of Cork. Charlie told Pat to slow down and pull over to the side of the street.

"It would be better if we changed over. I'll drive from here on in. There's a small hotel on Georges Street that I want to book us into, it's called Conway's. I've stayed there before and I'll find it easier than you."

"...and don't look so worried," seeing the look of alarm on Pat's face. "It's not that grand! I'll do the talking, just do as I say and you'll be fine."

They crossed over the Parnell Bridge then left up Georges Street for a couple of hundred yards. They turned in behind the hotel where there were some old stables that were now used as parking bays by the hotel customers. Charlie parked the Lancia there and left Pat in the car. He removed his holster and gun and shoved them under the driver's seat then made his way round to the front entrance.

There was a familiar figure in the foyer.

"Good morning, Mrs O'Sullivan."

The house keeper took a moment to recognise him.

"Mr. McKenna what on earth have you been up to? You look like an escaped convict!"

"Yes I've been up the hills. I had to avoid some trouble near Kilmallock. I've just arrived back."

"Here, let me help you off with that filthy coat."

Charlie started to tug off his great coat with her help.

"Could you arrange some rooms for me and my brother for a day or two?"

"I could indeed…." she hesitated, "…and a bath?"

"That would be grand."

"You'll be having lunch as well?" she added.

"Wouldn't miss it, Mrs. O'Sullivan. I'm going out for an hour, for some tailoring. If you can have the baths ready for then I would be very grateful. By the way I wondered if you had a key for the stable. We have a car and I'd like to lock it up."

"Sure none of that will be a problem, I have the key here and don't you be worried about the time, to be honest what with all that's going on, we're not all that busy this week."

Between them they managed to manoeuvre the car into the garage. Charlie told Pat not to bother spending too much time straightening things up as they would need to bring the car out again after lunch. Before they locked up the garage Charlie removed his side arm and holster from under the seat and locked them in the boot. They walked back through the hotel and turned right, heading back down Georges Street where there were several gents' outfitters and tailors.

Again Charlie told Pat not to get alarmed and to keep calm and quiet while they were in the shop. Charlie stepped confidently into the shop looking around for someone in charge.

"My driver and I have been out and about, as you clearly can see," Charlie announced to the thin faced, rather anxious looking floor manager who approached them. He spoke clearly and distinctly, not quite aping an English accent, but with hardly a trace of any kind of accent. "I'm afraid we got caught up in a bit of a melee just outside the city, my clothes are practically ruined. My usual tailors are in Limerick but, unfortunately, I have some business in Tralee tomorrow and I really couldn't go like this, could you fit us out? I don't have an account here, I take it cash will be okay? Only large English notes I'm afraid."

"That will be no problem, sir," replied the now reassured floor manager.

"I'll select a few things then and pay for them now. I take it you can deliver them to us after lunch? We're lodging at Conway's just up the road."

"Oh, I think we can do better than that, sir."

The floor manager fussed around, shouting over assistants, and insisting that anything and everything would be no problem at all. He eyed Charlie up and down.

"I think there are a couple of ready made suits that will fit with a few alterations," he said, pulling forth a grey worsted and a hound's-tooth from the rack.

"Mr. Goldstein will take them to your hotel before lunch and have them back with the alterations in an hour or so. A few shirts perhaps?"

Charlie ordered an entire wardrobe from shirts to shoes.

"I know my sizes for the shirts and things so I'll leave the suit fitting till later, I'm sure Mr. Goldstein can replace them for another size if need be when he returns with the alterations. Now then Mr ..."

"Mr Flood, sir."

"Mr Flood, good! Now what about my driver?"

"This way, sir."

The floor manager, leading the way, directed them both downstairs to the outfitting department where a more modest suit and other items were selected and purchased for Pat.

"I think that's everything, where do I settle the account?" said Charlie when everything but the two suits was packed, bundled and wrapped in sheets of brown paper.

"Just follow me, sir," replied the floor manager with a slight nod. He led the way upstairs to the accounts department.

"Buckley!" he said loudly, snapping his fingers for attention. "Make up this gentleman's account."

"If there is anything else you require, let me know immediately. If you'll excuse me, I'll attend to this customer," he said smoothly, and with a barely perceptibly oily bow, he glided over to a large ruddy- faced farmer.

Charlie and Pat casually looked around at some hats and caps as they waited for the bill to be made up. Buckley hailed Charlie over and passed over the bill without comment. The bill was nearly fifteen pounds, about as much as Charlie had already roughly calculated. He had already separated some notes from the main bundle before he arrived at the shop, he handed over three of them to Buckley.

Buckley retired to the back office for a few minutes

"Your change, sir," he said as he passed over a ten shilling note and some coins.

"Thank you. We'll be on our way."

"I'll get someone to follow you with your purchases."

"That'll be fine."

They turned left on leaving the tailors and walked back towards the Hotel. They had only travelled twenty yards when they heard the rattle of a cart behind them. Turning round they saw a small boy pushing a two-wheeled barrow loaded with their parcels and what they took to be Mr Goldstein, wearing a derby hat, trotting behind.

"By God! Now that's what I call service!" said Pat.

"Come on Pat, let's hurry on or they'll be trying to fit my suit on me in the street," said Charlie laughing.

Charlie took his bath while the parcels were being lugged upstairs and laid out on the bed. He dressed in his new linen and pulled the long cotton shirt over his head before calling for Goldstein.

"Not too bad a fit," said Goldstein tugging and pulling at the jacket, slashing the material with chalk. "The trousers are perfect. Let's try the hound's-tooth."

The other suit required almost the same alterations.

"Back in half an hour," said Goldstein almost rushing to the door.

"They don't hang about these fellas, do they," said Pat

"Here," said Charlie throwing over a newspaper. "Have a read while we're waiting."

Goldstein was back even sooner than he said with both suit jackets altered. Charlie tried them on, they were perfect.

"Well done, Mr. Goldstein," he said standing in front of the full length mirror.

"A small gratuity for your trouble," he added, slipping him half a crown. Goldstein tipped his hat, said his thanks and promptly vanished.

Charlie looked at his pocket watch "Ten to one, let's go down for lunch."

Mrs O'Sullivan fussed over both of them and seated them at a window overlooking a back entrance to the old English Market on Georges Street.

"We'll both have soup followed by a corned beef dinner and a bottle of beer each, Mrs O'Sullivan."

He noticed a look of concern from Pat.

"You're okay, it's not that blasted bully beef that you're used to back home. Its salt cured Cork brisket beef, you'll like it."

The meal did not disappoint Pat. A serving of mutton and barley soup was followed by a plate of boiled potatoes, a mash of buttered carrots and swede and two large slices of Cork corned beef. They talked mainly of home. Their brothers, sisters, cousins, and gossiped about neighbours who lived in the same town land or parish as themselves or 'townies as they called them back in Donegal. When tea was served, Pat lit a cigarette, sat back and relaxed.

"I've made a decision," said Charlie. "I've decided to go back to America. This war is finished."

Pat was less shocked than Charlie expected and gave him a reply which was equally surprising.

"I think you're right, Charlie."

Pat leaned forward tapping his cigarette into the ash tray.

"Oh, I know I'm not as well read as you or as well travelled, but I do understand things. I came down here because there was little action up North and anyway most of them up there have accepted the Free State - maybe it's because they are in the firing line, I don't know. But something is not right with all of this down here."

"I'm sorry Pat. I'm an idiot. I didn't release you had that many thoughts on it."

"That's okay, this is probably the first time we've actually

65

discussed it."

"I assumed you had taken the road of the anti-treaty wing - thirty two county republic, no oath, no partition." said Charlie.

"I did at first, but I'm beginning to have doubts."

"I think I know how you feel," said Charlie leaning forward. "I'll tell you this, I got to know Mick Collins quite well. Always liked the Big Fella, as they call him, but like a lot of people down here, I felt we could have got a lot more out of the English in the treaty. But in the past few months I'm beginning to get the feeling that he was set up."

"By De Valera?"

"No, not just him. De Valera's a cunning politician - not a soldier, but a fool who thinks the world revolves around him. But people that think like him, like to think themselves purists and idealists. I've always noticed that fellas who claim to be idealist never like to be seen to compromise. I learned a lot in America. There's an old Jewish saying that says an idealist is someone who thinks because a rose looks beautiful and smells great it will make a better pot of soup than a cabbage. Negotiation can be a dangerous business and to get a deal you're likely to get your hands dirty. Idealists always like to appear saintly and untainted. Believe me, dirty hands spoil the image."

"Why did you keep on fighting then?" said Pat.

"Some principles perhaps, but mostly loyalty to the rest of the men in the brigade I suppose."

"What changed your mind?"

"About six weeks ago I managed to get a letter from a friend of mine who had returned to Belfast from New York. He told me a good pal of mine, an old army colleague had been killed - assassinated, murdered, call it what you like, during the riots of July 1920, two years ago. In fact it must have happened shortly after the first time I came back. His name was Sam Gorman, he was a socialist and a trade union man. Worked all his days in Harland and Wolff - except for the time he joined up, of course. He was always arguing that the real enemy were the capitalist ruling class and it didn't matter if they were wearing an Orange

Sash or dancing a jig and singing in Gaelic. Oh sure, he would take the republican side, but he was always warning us about the short sightedness and the danger of what he called 'daft romantic nationalism' which he reckoned would drive away any support from socialist and trade union Protestants in the North. A man of courage and faith. A great lad..." Charlie paused for a second, "...he was killed trying to defend Catholics in the Short Strand."
Pat thought about this for a minute.
"I can understand all that, but why would it change your mind?"
"Because now I'm not too sure what it is I'm fighting for, and if you're not too sure – why bother?" he sighed. "Anyway, I'm fed up with it all. I left a girl in America and I'm beginning to miss her more and more."
"So what's your plan?"
Charlie looked over at the clock on the market tower and then back to Pat.
"Follow me," he said quietly.

oooOooo

CHAPTER EIGHT

The Postcard

Des was by nature an early riser. He usually got up early on Sunday, particularly if playing golf. He irritated the hell out of Julie as he padded about taking imaginary shots and whispering even more imaginative commentary asides like -
"Yes ...and this it for Capaldi ...the putt to seal the Open."
 She was always relieved when he finally opened the door on his way out.
"Don't forget we're going to Mum's this afternoon," she shouted lazily
"Don't worry, I won't," he replied as he closed the door behind him.
The previous evening had been quiet. Julie had expressed mock horror at Des still being sober after bumping into Liam Tracey in the afternoon. "He must be losing his touch," she said "you're usually birling after a session with Liam." That evening they passed a couple of hours in the local Greek diner named, with little thought of originality, Zorbas. A so-called Greek 'taverna' where they were on good terms with the manager - a man of mysterious origins, few of which were Greek. They chatted quietly about their plans to get married next spring when, after ordering coffee around nine, the place suddenly started to fill up with a party of women primary school teachers out on the razzle. Within half an hour the women were all up dancing like dervishes and forming finger snapping, swirling, screeching circles. When the

Greek dance music stopped they all flopped back into their seats and the waiters rushed around like mad refilling their glasses with wine. Within a few minutes the music started up again and they all raced on to the floor, whooping and yelling, waving their arms in the air - fingers snapping like castanets.

Des and Julie returned home to a decent movie on the telly and an early night.

Des and three of his mates hacked their way across Cowglen golf course from 9 o'clock till lunch time when they retired for a couple of bacon rolls and a welcome beer in the club house. He was back in the flat for 2.30, plenty of time to get changed for the visit to his prospective in-laws. They left in the late afternoon, deciding to take the bus rather than drive. Grace, Julie's mother, usually had dinner ready around 6 o'clock on a Sunday. A bit early for dinner, but, as far as Des was concerned, for Grace's steak pie, any time was good enough.

The early evening was still warm enough for Julie, Des, Grace and Julie's father Eddie to sit out in the garden for an hour or so before dinner. The conversation rambled around the events of Friday and the fate of young Hughie Toner.

"Never really took to him even though he was my sister's boy," said Eddie. "He was a lad who was always in and out of the shadows, as my father used to say. Still you wouldn't wish it on anybody, would you?"

"A burden and a cross to bear for his poor mother, that's what I think," said Grace shaking her head grimly.

"Some of that family were out and out crooks," she added rather pointedly as she made her way indoors.

"I'll go and get the dinner out."

"Don't mind Grace, she never got on with my sister Noreen," explained Eddie as they passed through the French widow. "Some perceived slight many years ago. In fact I've forgot what the whole damn thing was about in the first place. Don't tell that to Grace though, or there'll be hell to pay."

Dinner was as good as Des anticipated and they talked mainly about upcoming holidays, Eddie and Grace were planning a trip to the USA.

"We're staying in New York but I quite fancy a trip to Ardmore, just outside Philadelphia. My father lived there in the nineteen twenties," said Eddie.

Julie turned round to Des

"That's my Grandfather, Charlie McKenna," she said, "the one I mentioned the other night."

"Oh, I didn't realise that you knew where your grandfather lived in America," said Des to Julie.

"Neither did I - until now," she replied. "Although I don't suppose I ever thought about it that much."

"He met my mother out there as well. They got married in Atlantic City."

"Crikey, married in Atlantic City!" said Julie suddenly sitting up. "Now that's what I call a good idea!"

"I don't think the wedding budget will quite run to that, my dear," added Eddie quickly.

"Only kidding, dad!"

"It was really odd," continued Eddie. "According to the shipping records he seems to have gone to America for the first time in 1917 on board a ship called the 'Adriatic'. Yet he was in Cork about four years later. I've never bothered looking at the records again but he seems to have reappeared in Philadelphia in this place called Ardmore in early 1923. Anyway, I'm not hoping to find that much. My father didn't talk a lot about his early life. Had to drag everything out of him."

"Was your mother an American then?" asked Des.

"Not at all! She came from the same town as my father did in Donegal. In fact if you went down to the bottom field in my dad's old house you could just about make out the chimney stack of my mother's house."

"That's amazing!" said Julie. "They went all the way to America when they could have met each other at home at the local shindig."

"Not as amazing as it seems. I suspect that Donegal immigrants, like all immigrants, stuck close to one another and used each other as contacts for jobs, digs and other arrangements. It probably wasn't that unusual to meet people you knew at locally arranged social events, in fact, probably quite common."

"Julie reckons your father took some sort of part in the Irish Troubles just after the First World War."

"Hard to say, I suspected something of the sort but I never really knew. His appearance in Cork would suggest something like that, the War of Independence, or 'The Troubles' as they used to call them, were strange times. I remember my father saying, rather sarcastically, that when he came back from America in the thirties that it was amazing that every Paddy in the Gorbals seemed to have been a member of the IRA during the troubles. I remember the Gorbals quite well. I was about ten or eleven years old when we moved up to this house. Odd to think of you two living down there now, the place was a bit of a rundown slum in the forties and fifties."

"Now, don't you listen to him," said Grace. "You didn't live in a slum. The McKenna's were always well off. Your family had that big flat in Carlton Place, toilet, bathroom, separate kitchen. For god's sake your living room overlooked the River Clyde! You'd be paying a fortune for a house like that now."

"Okay, we didn't exactly live in poverty but we weren't rich," Eddie replied. "Anyway, give me a bit of space. I was a social work lecturer for thirty years, being brought up in the Gorbals gave me a wee bit of street cred," he added good humouredly.

"Right then, time for coffee and a spot of brandy," said Grace. "Let's have it outside while it's still light."

Des gave Grace a hand with the coffee while Eddie and Julie busied themselves with the brandy and the glasses. They sat out in the garden drinking and chatting. A pair of finches chirped noisily in the box hedge and the late evening sky to the west, directly in front of them, slowly changed from mid blue to fiery red. High dark purple clouds with orange streaks began to appear and Venus glowed like a mini sun above it all. It was a spectacular sunset, yet so commonly seen at that time of year that it barely merited a mention from the four people sitting around the garden table. They moved indoors as the sun went down and the air started to chill.

"Mum, do you remember those old photos you had of granddad and dad's Uncle Pat? You know, the ones where they're wearing uniforms, let's dig them out and have a look. Des was telling Liam Tracey about them and Liam said he wouldn't mind having a look at them."

"Yes," said Des, "Liam said it's a bit unusual for anyone to have any first hand knowledge of the troubles. Reckons there were all sorts of things that were covered up or never mentioned. Maybe I could scan them into the computer and take a copy or e-mail them to him."

"Liam Tracey," said Grace. "It's a while since I've seen him about. No young woman got her claws into him - made a decent man of him yet, I take it."

Like most women of her age, Grace had a soft spot for Liam. He was a large bear of a man and had a mature and roguish handsomeness about him; he was also, of course, an outrageous flatterer of women and a shameless flirt. Qualities that only the most committed of bachelors can get away with in the company of older married women.

"I'll get the photos down. I know exactly where they are."

While Grace was upstairs, the others cleared the dining room table, clearing away the glasses and condiments, putting dishes into the dishwasher and tidying up the other clutter from the room. Grace pulled over the large coffee table to the sofa seats.

"Now then," said Grace. "It's ages since I've had a look at these." She scattered some of the photos on the table.

"This will make you laugh," she said picking one up. "Here's one of your grandmother in a bathing suit, she's the one in the middle by the way. I remember her telling me it was taken in Atlantic City around 1930 or so."

Julie looked at the underexposed photo of a pretty young woman with her two friends cavorting about a beach.

"It's funny how the whole thing looks much older. It looks almost Victorian rather than nineteen twenties flapper. I suppose swim suits hadn't changed much in all those years."

She looked at the picture again and, although she would have been reluctant to admit it, she realised that she looked unnervingly like her grandmother. Des flipped through some of the photographs.

"When did you say your Charlie returned to Glasgow?" he asked casually.

"I remember he kept what he called 'his papers' in an old biscuit tin," said Eddie, "there was an old passport; it had some visas, old postcards, birth certificates and that kind of thing. We used to look at them out of curiosity when we were young. There was a card that had a picture of the steamship 'Cameronia' on the front and a date on the back, I can't remember exactly but I'm sure it was sometime in 1934."

He reflected for a moment.

"Yes, I suppose it all kind of ties in"

"What do you mean?" said Julie

"Well there was a wedding certificate in the tin dated 1933 from Atlantic City and my older brother was born in Glasgow in 1934 so it makes sense to assume that Charlie returned to Glasgow around 1933 or 34."

Grace pulled out another couple of photographs and spread them on the table.

"Here's one of your granddad, a portrait. I'm pretty sure this is one of him in a British army uniform and look, this one here is his brother Pat, also in a uniform."

Des had a closer look.

"The uniforms look similar but the jackets look different, maybe they were in different regiments or something."

"No that's my father in the British Army during the Great War, definitely," said Eddie. "And I'm sure he left the army at least a year before the war ended in November 1918. I'm also pretty sure that Uncle Pat joined the Free State Army around 1922. When I was young I remember Pat talking about being shot at when he was patrolling the lanes of Cork and Kerry when he was in the army. I thought at the time he meant lanes like we have here, you know, the ones between streets, but I think he meant more like country lanes."

"They're both handsome young men," said Julie.

"Yes of course, runs in the family," said Eddie, sweeping his hair back with exaggerated movements.

Grace raised her eyes to heaven and sighed.

"Right Julie," she said. "Now let's look at some of these photos that Eileen brought over from Ireland last year. She said that a cousin of ours was cleaning out some ancient dresser in your grandfather's house when she found this envelope with some old photos in it. Apparently she didn't recognise anyone in them and was about to throw them in the bin when Eileen arrived. She thought your dad might know somebody in the photos, so she gave them to me. I forgot all about them until now."

There were five photographs in the envelope and one postcard. They looked at the photographs first. Eddie recognised and identified almost all of the people in them. They were group photos of aunties, uncles and cousins from way back.

"Look at this one," said Eddie pulling one over.

"This is a photo of my dad as a young man. The older man beside him is his father, my grandfather. My grandfather was born in May 1865, two days before the end of the American Civil War."

"That's incredible!" said Des. "Are you saying that Julie's great grandfather was born during the American Civil War? That doesn't seem to make sense! My grandfather is still alive and kicking and still in his seventies. His own father only died about ten years ago...

"Hold on Des, don't get excited. It's easily explained. My father was one of the youngest of his family and he was born when his father was in his thirties, he in turn married late and was in his forties when I was born. I was in my late thirties when Julie was born. See, it's all about timing as they say. Anyway let me see that postcard it seems to be blank."

Eddie picked up the card and turned it over.

"Oh," he said, "it's another photo of a soldier, looks like Uncle Pat again."

He placed it on the table, photo side up. Julie picked it up, turning it back and forth. It was the photograph of a young man in army uniform standing almost to attention in what looked like a farmyard.

"I wonder if that was common in those days?"

"What do you mean?" said Grace.

"You know - to make a postcard out of a photograph."

"I don't know, perhaps it was a fashionable thing to do. Look you can see where he tore a piece off the side of the photo to make it fit the postcard frame."

"Oh yes," said Eddie, picking it up. "That's interesting, I never noticed that."

"Talking about interesting, what about that gold sovereign I showed you last night?" said Des.

"Oh that's right!" replied Julie.

"Mum," she continued, "do you remember granddad gave me a gold sovereign when I was five and just started school? You kept it in a little velvet bag for me, I used to take it out and play with it now and again."

"Yes I've still got it. I kept it with the others."

"The others?"

"Oh yes! Your Granddad gave out sovereigns on many occasions. Your dad was given at least three and I was given two, one for my wedding day and one for my fifth anniversary. There's about eight of them upstairs. They all have the same date."

"That's a pretty valuable collection," said Des. "They must be worth a couple of hundred pounds each."

"Don't you worry Des. I keep them in a safe place."

"Along with the Van Goghs," said Eddie.

Grace gave him a glare and continued.

"For years I used to think he bought them individually, you know, as each occasion arose he would buy one as a keepsake."

"Didn't he?" asked Julie.

"No, he must have bought a job lot of them or something. Your dad found three left in what remained of a roll of them, they were in your granddad's old trunk, the one we cleaned out after he passed on."

"You never told me that," said Julie.

75

Grace shrugged "What is there to tell? It's not as if there's a secret hoard or anything. I'll go upstairs and bring them down and let you see them. They look really nice when they're all together."

The rest of them continued to look over the photographs until Grace returned. She came into the room with a satin bound jewellery box which she placed in the middle of the table. She opened the lid to display the coins. They were, as she had hinted, quite spectacular.

"How do I know which one's mine?"

"That one there, third one in from the top row."

"Oh isn't that nice," cooed Julie, picking it up. "Its ages since I've seen this."

Des was about to say "How do you know..." when Grace coughed. He caught her eye: she gave him a quick wink.

"Not that it matters, of course, they are all identical," she continued quickly.

She lifted the top tray of coins off, underneath was another shallow space.

"The ones we found in the trunk are under here," said Grace, lifting out some paper wrapping. "The top tray was designed to hold eight, but I never bothered to get a new one made. So I just left them as I found them."

Des picked up the coins and the wrapping; it looked like the waxed paper surrounding a roll of cash, something of value - like pound coins. There were still three sovereigns at the bottom of the roll.

"There's some writing on the side..." said Des folding it up to see it better.

"What does it say?" asked Julie

"Well it doesn't seem to be in English; it looks foreign or something. Hand me a pen and a bit of paper. I'll write it down."

Des laboriously wrote down what was on the paper, continually turning the wrapping this way and that.

"There we are," he said, placing the paper where all could see.

'Soarstat Eireann' it said.

"Is that it?" said Grace with a tut and a flick of her head. "I thought it might be something romantic or dangerous like 'Casino de Monte Carlo' or 'Property of the Third Reich.'

"What does it means?" said Des.

"Soarstat Eireann?" she said. "Oh that's just Gaelic for the Irish Free State."

"I wonder where Hughie got hold of one of these coins?" said Julie.

"Maybe from his mother or perhaps from his uncle Pat. His mother and Pat were quite close. Pat never married."

"Yes, Pat was quite the quiet one," remarked Eddie.

"Quiet one! Off his bloody head more like!" said Grace. "Hanging about that old house day and night, muttering and moaning. Frightened the life out of me half the time."

"Yes I suppose he was a bit …disturbed," said Eddie

"A bit disturbed? Oh yes, I suppose that's one way of putting it," said Grace grimly, "…and, as I was about to say before I was interrupted…he was another one for dishing out the odd sovereign. God knows where they got the habit from, must have been an old family custom or something."

They had another coffee with cinnamon biscuits and brandy and made arrangements to phone each other whenever the funeral arrangements were announced. Grace chattered and talked for a while about the photographs, Ireland and the McKenna family's odd obsession with handing out sovereigns before Des and Julie rose to go home.

"Listen, Des," said Grace. "Why don't you take the wrapped up sovereigns with you and you can show them to Liam when you meet him? I know Liam would be interested. You can put them back the next time you come round."

"Don't you think they might be a bit too valuable to be carrying around?" said Des.

"True, they're worth about a couple of hundred pounds each," said Eddie, "but if you think about it, your laptop is probably worth more."

"I suppose you're right. I'll show them to Liam and then bring them back. In fact, if the funeral is later this week I can get them back to you then."

"Don't worry about it, Des," said Grace with a wave of her hand. "They've been lying around here for long enough. I'm sure they'll come to no harm."

They walked out to the hall.

"By the way Eddie, do you think I could use your computer for few minutes, while these two say their long goodbyes," said Des nodding over to Julie and Grace. They were still chattering away about the funeral plans and who they thought would turn up. "I could scan these in and e-mail them to Liam. It'll save me setting up the laptop when I get home."

"Of course Des, feel free. The computer is already on, I was using it earlier."

Des turned on the scanner in the next room and prepared the two photos for scanning. He used the scanner software to set up the photos as Jpegs and labelled one of them charliephoto.jpg and the other one as patphoto.jpg. He composed a quick e-mail to Liam and was attaching the two files as Julie came in with the rest of the photos.

"Aren't you sending this one as well?" she said holding out the postcard.

Des looked at the postcard again and shrugged his shoulders.

"Yeah okay, why not, I'll need to come out of this e-mail to scan it in."

He placed the postcard face down on the scanning surface and switched on. As he returned to the e-mail, Julie leaned over his shoulder, her hand affectionately tickling his neck.

"I see you gave the attachment titles a lot of original thought, charliephoto and patphoto," she said as she looked at the screen. "What are you going to call this one? No, don't tell me, let me guess 'postcardphoto'"

He turned round to face her, putting his arms around her waist and gave her a kiss in one elegant, flowing movement.

"Don't be sarcastic," he said, letting her go. "It's so unbecoming!" He smiled and wagged his finger.

"Now then, in the pursuit of originality…" he typed in a name

78

rapidly. "I now name this file..." he paused for dramatic effect ...
'torn_edgephoto'."
He pressed the send button.

oooOooo

CHAPTER NINE

The Bonded Warehouse

Charlie unlocked the stable and followed by Pat, he walked to the back of the Lancia and pulled opened the car boot.

"You made a decent job of painting over the writing. Do you know what it said?"

"My Irish isn't that great but I took it to be government property, something to do with a bank, I thought."

"Not bad. Not bad at all. Department of Finance of the Irish Free State. Headed up in the Provisional Government by the great Mick Collins himself no less."

Charlie took the small key from his wallet and opened one of the cases. He withdrew the tube he had already opened and shook a few of the coins into his hand.

"I doubt if you have ever seen one of these before so I'll tell you what it is."

He turned one of the sovereigns between his fingers

"This," he said, "is a British gold sovereign, worth a pound sterling at face value. These cases here are full of them."

Pat gazed at the wooden boxes, looking slightly bewildered.

"Don't bother trying to work out how much is there. I can tell you. Twelve thousand pounds worth, according to Colonel Simon Barrett and I'm happy to take his word for it."

"Twelve thousand pounds! But how... what?" said Pat.

"Payoffs, bribes, maybe some reward money, probably a mixture of all three. It's fallen into our hands now and I think I've found a way of keeping it, or least some of it anyway."

"Phew! Twelve thousand pounds, Jesus, that's a King's ransom. I can hardly think straight."

"Yes, it's a lot of money," said Charlie.

He drummed his fingers on the box, thinking.

"Anyway, first of all I want you to take these four rolls and put them in your inside pockets, that's a hundred pounds."

Pat hesitated.

"I don't know Charlie, it seems a bit like stealing to me," he said.

"We'll discuss the rights and wrongs later, in the mean time take these," said Charlie, placing two rolls neatly in Pat's palm. Pat weighed them in his hand.

"They're very heavy - for the size of them."

"Just put them away. Here's the other two."

Charlie filled his own inside pockets with four of the rolls.

"Now let's head for a bank."

"There plenty of banks at the bottom of St. Patrick's Street," said Pat.

"Sorry Pat, I should have said - my bank."

With Pat leading the way, they walked through the hotel lobby, again turning left after leaving the building. They cut through Princes Street into Patrick Street, as the locals called it, and then walked down towards the river until they reached the Provincial Bank building.

Charlie stepped self-assuredly up the stairs and into the banking hall: by now Pat was learning to simply follow on and say nothing. Charlie noted that the bank was surprisingly busy; perhaps word had got out about the landings at Passage West, which in turn was leading to a minor panic. If it was, then it suited his purpose just fine. He looked around as if trying to recognise someone and then, making up his mind, he walked over to one of the few unoccupied teller desks.

"Good afternoon, I wish to make a small deposit to my account. Here's my bank book and account number," he said producing a wallet size notebook from his back pocket. The teller opened the book, looked at the name and then looked up at Charlie.

"Ah, yes, Mr. McKenna. I think I've had the good fortune to have dealt with you in the past."

The teller flicked through the pass book for a few seconds.

"I see you still have an American address on your book, do you wish to change it Mr. McKenna?"

"Not at the moment. I intend to return to America fairly soon and I will still, of course, be using your New York branch."

"Very well, Mr McKenna. Now, how can I help?"

"I have a hundred pounds in notes and a hundred pounds in sovereigns. I was obliged to take the sovereigns in a business deal up in Limerick, seems that some people up there are getting a bit nervous about the turn of events in the past few weeks and beginning to get wary of paper money. Damned nuisance if you ask me."

"That will be fine Mr. McKenna. I'll get it marked up by the cashier."

The teller counted the notes carefully and unravelled the rolls of sovereigns. He wrote out an internal account note and took it to the cashier's gate.

"You will be called to collect your book shortly Mr. McKenna."

"That's fine," said Charlie, turning to Pat. "I was just wondering, while we're here do you think my brother could open an account? He's in the same business as me. He already has an account in the Ulster Bank, up north, but it would be more convenient to open an account here as he is always up and down to Cork these days."

"Yes I can do that, although he'll have to leave a decent deposit to open an account at such short notice"

"Hundred pounds enough? Damn sovereigns again, I'm afraid!"

"One hundred is more than enough. Now perhaps I can get some details?"

The account was opened quickly and smoothly. Pat answered each question quietly and calmly, with the occasional prompting from Charlie, slowly growing more confident as the procedure moved on. He was handed over a new account book which he handled with a barely disguised pride. At the same time Charlie was called over to collect his own book. By the time they left, there was a queue beginning to form outside the bank door.

"Well Pat, that's at least a hundred quid each so far. Let's see what we can do about the rest. We'll go back and get the car."

They retraced their route back to the hotel and managed to manoeuvre the car out of the stable. This time they avoided the shortcut and drove down to the river and crossed the St. Patrick's bridge. Pat had to change gear abruptly by double declutching to get motoring up the steep hill and was relieved when Charlie told him to turn a sharp right into King Street. Charlie pointed out the houses and shops burned down in the Black and Tan reprisal raid in 1920. There was still a distinctive acrid, smoky smell, even after all this time.

"Where now?" asked Pat.

"Carry on down to the railway station. There's a bonded warehouse between the station and Penrose's Quay, you'll see it in a minute," said Charlie.

"You seemed to know this place well."

"I've had some dealings with the warehouse in the past," said Charlie.

They drove in silence for a couple of minutes. Pat was deep in thought.

"What exactly is a bonded warehouse?" he finally asked.

"Well it's a kind of a warehouse that is carefully guarded or 'sealed' as they say, a bit like a large bank for expensive goods and imports like machinery or bulk imports like wine, tea and coffee. Sometimes for expensive material like silk and precious metals.

"Metals like gold you mean?" said Pat.

"Not necessarily," said Charlie turning to Pat. "I mean fairly large quantities of copper, brass, bronze and the like or, even more valuable - machined parts made of these materials."

"How did you get to know...?"

"I'll tell you later, turn right here."

Pat turned right and through a large opening in a warehouse building with the name 'Cohen Brothers. Import and Export' painted elegantly above an arched doorway. Heavy hinged doors lay to the right and left, rather like a large factory.

"Park up beside that office sign there," said Charlie. "You stay in the car for now. This might be a bit tricky and take a wee bit of time and it's better that I talk to someone without any distractions. I can think straighter. If all goes well, I'll come back out. And don't show any surprise if I introduce you as my managing director or something along those lines."

"Don't worry about me, after today's events I'm just about ready for anything. I brought that newspaper with me, so take your time."

The first hurdle was a rather frosty middle aged receptionist in the front office who informed him that Mr. Isaac Cohen was not available. This hardly surprised him. He was lucky to be recognised by the bank teller. To meet two business contacts within a day, under the circumstances, would have been fortuitous indeed.

"That's fine. Your company has handled business for myself and my associates on several occasions. I'm sure you'll have a record somewhere. To be honest, as it happens, I don't need to speak to Mr. Isaac directly. What I need is some storage room for material that I intend to ship up to Belfast in the course of the next few months. I'm sure there is someone else who can handle this small bit of business."

"It'll be Mr. O'Donnell you need then," she said coldly. "I'll ring through for him."

Mr. O'Donnell proved to be remarkably compliant.

"So," he said after some discussion, "essentially you would like to store some boxes containing rod lengths of phosphorous bronze in one of our storage rooms."

"Yes indeed," said Charlie, "I must admit I'm getting rather worried about the situation - well, let's call it the 'civil situation', down here. We drove down as far as Limerick yesterday from Belfast. We spent the night there and picked up the boxes early on this morning from Queenstown. The material was originally manufactured in France to strict specifications from one of our main customers, a large subcontractor who supplies shaft

84

bearings to the ship building industry. It was my original intention to collect the bronze and take it back to Belfast. The thing is, Mr. O'Donnell, we were stopped several times on the way down by armed men, and of course we had nothing of value in the car so we passed through without incident. I think if we were to journey north with anything of worth we may get our goods requisitioned. Not that any of these brigands would know the true value of machined bronze. They would probably sell it off as scrap, which would be even more infuriating. I've phoned our office and our customer is not too desperate for supplies yet, and under the circumstances would be willing to pay for storage for some months."

"Yes that seems reasonable enough," said O'Donnell. "What sort of volume are we talking about and I also assume that you want it bonded."

"No it doesn't need to be bonded, the import tax was paid on delivery, but unfortunately I have to take the paperwork back up to Belfast for payment."

O'Donnell tapped his teeth with his pencil.

"You'll have to produce it when you return to collect your goods, you know that of course."

"Yes, I realise that, but in the meantime our first concern is the safety of our goods. The official paperwork can be organised later."

"Okay. So what volume are we looking at here?"

"Not that much."

He stopped for a second to think. He had originally thought of putting the entire consignment in but decided it might be wiser to keep the opened crate with its eight missing rolls just in case anyone noticed the difference in weight, there was also the chance of banking some more of the sovereigns in the course of the next few days or weeks.

"Four cases about this size," said Charlie using his hands to demonstrate the dimensions of the wooden cases.

"Oh, that's easily arranged. You're talking about four foot square. I thought it would be much larger. Still, it'll cost about a fiver a month for a secure cage, mind you, that's including insurance. Quite a lot for such a small consignment of bronze," replied O'Donnell still scribbling notes onto a pad.

He looked at Charlie.

"Cost almost as much as it would if it were gold!" he added with a short laugh.

"Indeed," said Charlie with a thin smile. He turned away slightly unnerved, he knew that what O'Donnell said was light hearted and was purely coincidental. Nevertheless he walked a few paces tapping his lips lightly as if in deep thought; he gave a short cough and turned around to face O'Donnell.

"What if we sign up for a year?" he continued, still pacing. "What I'm thinking is that we move quite a few specialist machine parts through Cork and it might be worth our while having some good, secure storage space for future use."

O'Donnell scribbled a few calculations in his notepad.

"I could give you a small secured area for fifty pounds a year. That includes up to £2000 insurance for your goods. You'd have to pay the full fee in advance, I'm afraid."

Charlie placed his finger on his pursed lips for a few moments.

"Mm... that seems reasonable, Mr O'Donnell. It's a deal, as the Americans say."

"Let's go and get the documentation started. I'll take you up to my office. Just follow me." O'Donnell was pleased, even with the insurance premium, this was not a bad bit of business for his employer. Charlie was even more pleased.

Charlie returned to the van after completing the paperwork and instructed Pat to remove the top case, the one they had already opened, and place it in the storage area behind the spare wheel. This done he told Pat to drive further into the building and locate Block 3 where he had arranged to meet O'Donnell and one of his burly warehousemen. Block 3 was well signposted and they reached it in minutes. The warehouseman loaded the four cases onto a small hand trolley and wheeled it into the building on the ground floor.

"Stop at room sixteen," said O'Donnell, removing a bunch of keys from his pocket. The heavy door was opened to reveal a fairly small room lined with steel mesh cages. Each cage was about five foot square with the steel mesh extending to, and cemented into, the ceiling.

"I've signed over cage five to you," said O'Donnell talking a smaller bunch of keys from his other pocket which were clearly marked for room sixteen. Each individual key was also clearly marked. He opened the deadlock allowing access to the enclosure. Pat gave the warehouseman a hand this time knowing that the cases were quite hefty for one man to manoeuvre. When the cases were stacked away the warehouseman pulled the door closed with a loud clang that echoed through the building. Far too much like the sound of a prison door for Pat's liking.

O'Donnell took out a square 4x4 card and wrote the time and date at the top.

"Will I title it in your name? Your company's name? Or ..."

"Title it in the subcontractor's name," Charlie hesitated for a moment. "Sam Gorman, of Belfast."

Charlie and O'Donnell stood at the door, said their goodbyes and shook hands as Pat reversed the car to face back out to the street. O'Donnell walked round to the driver's door.

"Good luck," he said to Pat, "Hope to see you again."

They would meet again - but under very different circumstances. Pat gave him a cheery wave as he pulled away.

***

"Turn right and carry on down to Glenmire Road railway station. I want to check out the times of the trains to Tralee," said Charlie as they approached the main doors. Pat followed his instructions and as they travelled the short distance to the station they could hear in the far distance the light but distinct sound of artillery and rifle fire coming from the south west.

"I thought we would be taking the car to Tralee," said Pat as he parked the car outside the main entrance.

"No, I think we need to leave the car here - in Cork, I mean. It's bound to be recognised eventually and I suspect Mr. Barrett will be hot on our trail as it is. Let's go in and find a timetable."

The trains to Mallow were regular, at least one an hour locally and another five going to Dublin daily but stopping at Mallow. The problem was to get the right connection to Tralee. Between them, by trailing between three timetable boards, they managed to organise their final itinerary. Ten fifteen to Dublin, get off and change at Mallow for the half past eleven to Tralee South. Charlie was about to purchase the tickets there and then when he looked up at the station clock, it was now almost four o'clock.

"It's getting late. We'll get the tickets in the morning, let's go back to Patrick Street, I think we need to buy a few more things," he announced. "Drive up as far as you can go, near a place called Robert Day's, saddlers."

Pat was able to park the car near the Methodist church; the saddle shop was almost opposite.

"What are we getting this time?" asked Pat.

"Just a few things. Some luggage. Suit cases or kit bags or ideally something that the Americans call a carpet bag, maybe. You stay here, I'll be back as quick as I can."

Charlie came back twenty minutes later carrying one new, standard canvas Navy type kit bag and a sturdy leather suitcase. He shoved them both into the back seat.

"Sorry, I took longer than I thought. I decided to get some shaving kit for us as well."

"Jesus, Charlie, you think of everything!"

"No I don't. I'm making most of this up as I'm going along here. I'm just trying to keep us out of danger if everything goes wrong. Now let's head back to Conway's and put this stuff away. We need to think about getting rid of the car."

The hotel was quite near at hand. Pat drove to the top of Patrick Street and was turning left when he said, "I've got an idea about the car."

"Oh yes! Let's hear it then," said Charlie.

"Why don't we drive it closer to Douglas, we can abandon it there. It should be easy enough to get a taxi back to the hotel from there"

"You might have a good idea there, Pat."

"I might as well park in front of the hotel then."

They carried the luggage into the hotel, only to be stopped by Mrs O'Sullivan who seemed to appear out of nowhere.

"Not thinking of leaving us already?" she said, glancing at the bags.

"Oh no, just some new luggage I had to get for a ... a trip tomorrow."

"I see, what happened to ..."

"Er, what time's dinner tonight?" said Charlie trying to change the subject. "I have to go out for a while and I wouldn't want to be late."

"Seven o'clock suit you?"

"Seven's just fine," he replied, edging up the stair case. "Just fine."

Pat opened the door of his room and threw the kit bag on the bed; Charlie followed taking a seat and placing the suitcase between his knees.

"Hope we haven't left ourselves short of time now, Charlie."

"Don't worry. We'll be okay. I was thinking of your idea, only thing is it might be difficult to get a taxi back from Douglas after all they're not that thick on the ground even in town."

"Why don't we hire a taxi from here? You could follow me out and then give me a lift back," said Pat.

Charlie laughed.

"You're beginning to worry me Pat! You seem to be getting the hang of this caper."

He lifted up the kit bag.

"But first let's get some of these sovereigns up here. We'll both go back down to the car and take as many as one of us can comfortably lift in one go."

"How many rolls do you think there are in a box," asked Pat.

"Well let me see. Barrett reckoned there was £12,000 altogether in five boxes which is £2,400 in a case." Charlie put one hand on his brow to do the mental arithmetic and started to think aloud. "25 coins in a roll means 4 rolls for a hundred pounds or if you like 40 rolls for a thousand pounds. So, 80 rolls would give you two thousand pounds. The other £400 would be 4 rolls times 4 which is 16. So there we are, 80 plus 16 would give you 96 rolls in a box."

"That's a bit of an odd number."

"It might be something to do with the weight. I didn't lift one, are they that heavy?"

"Not really. I think it's just the surprise of something that small weighing so much. I would say a box would weigh less than a two stone bag of spuds."

"That's about 25lbs in America, the weight of a 2 or 3 year old child. I'm pretty sure either one of us could manage to lift that kind of weight easy enough."

Charlie unlocked the boot, placed the kit bag inside and looked around discreetly. Although the street was busy no one took any interest in two well dressed men huddled over a car boot. He quickly checked that the safety was on the Webley and stowed it and the holster in the bottom of the bag first. By grabbing and shoving five or six rolls at a time, shifting the sovereigns took less than a minute. Pat humped the bag on his shoulder, taking a few seconds to judge the balance and his movement.

Charlie slammed down the boot lid and both then walked back into the hotel. This time Charlie led the way to head off the indomitable Mrs O'Sullivan should she suddenly decide to appear again. They managed to make it back to their rooms undetected where Pat was relieved to drop the kit bag on the bed.

"Now for the taxi," said Charlie pulling back one of the curtains. "I noticed a garage down the road when we were down at the car. Look," he said pointing out the window, "you can just about see it from here. I'll take a walk down there and see what I come up with. Leave the kit bag here and we'll go back down stairs to the Lancia."

"I'm sure a couple of pounds will encourage them to come up with something. You wait in the car until I get back," said Charlie, as they found themselves back on the pavement.

Five minutes later Charlie came rolling up the street in the back of a Crossley Landaulette.

"The driver knows a good way to get to Douglas from here - so you follow us."

The small convoy drove back down Georges Street and made their way to Douglas in less than fifteen minutes. The further they travelled from the city the more ominously quiet the streets became.

Charlie halted the taxi at the start of the main street in Douglas and told the driver they would return in less than ten minutes. When Pat pulled up behind them, he pulled open the passenger door and jumped into the Lancia.

"Where is everyone?" said Pat anxiously.

"They've probably been warned to stay off the streets," replied Charlie. "Don't worry about it."

He glanced up and down the road.

"Drive up here until we can just see the Post Office where we were this morning and we'll leave the car there. Leave that empty crate in the boot and the keys on the seat, I'll be surprised if it's still here in an hour. Let's go."

They closed the Lancia's doors. Before they left Charlie bent forward, making sure that the keys were easily seen, as he did so there was a sudden crackle of gunfire, it didn't seem that far away. They hurried back to the taxi.

On the journey back to the city centre they listened and nodded as the driver prattled away about the rumours spreading through the city. Finally they returned to the garage where Charlie parted with a pound to the garage owner. They walked slowly back to the Hotel. It was just gone six and the sky was just beginning to darken.

"I don't know about you, but I could go a nice pint of stout now," said Pat.

Charlie stopped and looked at him.

"Well now, Pat! That's the second good idea you've had today!"

oooOooo

CHAPTER TEN

America

For the most part, Charlie's first trip to America was a tortuous mixture of long, terrible tedium with the occasional excitement. The time on board was filled with endless rounds of cards, followed by poor and predictable meals. After dinner there were long listless walks around the deck, restless nights and the occasional bout of sea sickness. The passenger list consisted mainly of middle class American and English technicians and engineers: there were only a few fellow Irish immigrants on board. On the first few days there was, of course, the initial excited conversations and speculation of fortunes to be made and people to be met. Few of the young men, Charlie observed, had any idea of the distances involved in travelling from one place to another in America; one minute they were going to Chicago, the next they were heading for the gold mines of California or the cattle trails of Kansas. Most of them had hardly left their home county in Ireland, let alone travelled the vast distances they talked about so glibly. After the first couple of days Charlie started to keep pretty much to himself, reading some books he brought and talking to the sailors, some of whom, he had found out, had served in the war. To his surprise one of the sailors, Jack Peebles, was a townie of his from the nearby village of Dromore who told him to be sure to look up an elder brother of his in Philadelphia who was supposed to be a big shot in construction and could probably get him a job easy enough. The sailor's brother went by the name of

George Peebles, had been in America since he was about ten years old and, according to Jack, had 'a funny American accent'.

Towards the end of the seventh day Jack informed him that landfall was due the next morning and that the ship was dead on course to reach New York Harbour for 9 a.m. In Paris, idle curiosity and boredom had made Charlie wander up to Rue de Chazelles to see the workshops of Bartholdi, the creator of La Liberté. He had since looked at many photos and postcards and he was particularly keen to catch a glimpse of the statue coming from the sea at daybreak. He arranged for one of the middle watch sailors to rouse him after last bell at 4 a.m. Charlie was wide awake and already dressed when he heard the knock on the door. He got up quietly trying to avoid wakening his three third class companions, who were restless and complaining enough at the best of times. The sailor was waiting outside the door to take him up on deck; third class passengers had restricted times to use the deck, at this time of the morning he was assured, it should be no problem.

Once up on the chilly empty mid-deck he was left to his own devices. He huddled on an aft deckchair until the sun started to come up on the port side. To starboard he could just make out the lights of another ship passing, slightly silhouetted against a low lying coast. As the sun slowly rose a land mass on the port side started to appear. The ship was by now powering down at a fair lick between the narrows and the entrance to New York harbour and some of the First Class passengers were beginning to stroll and chatter along the decks above him. Staten Island to his left suddenly appeared so close that he felt he could easily jump off and swim ashore. The engine noise and vibration suddenly stopped and the ship slipped through the water quietly. Charlie realised that he had become so used to the noise that the ensuing silence was almost unsettling. In the middle distance he became aware of a small flotilla of tugs and ferries heading towards them including, he supposed, the Health Inspector who would clear the boat for the port of New York. The ship slowly came to a stop and started to drift slightly. Those few passengers that were potential immigrants were required to register in Ellis Island and were put aboard the small transfer ferry and immediately taken there. Things and events seemed to happen at breakneck speed: it was only when he had completed the paperwork below deck on the ferry and finally came above that he got his first sight of the Statue of Liberty. It seemed to fly past them. Combined with its enormous base it was huge and it loomed above them casting the little transfer boat into a brief shadow in the early morning sun. At Ellis Island the twenty odd passengers were registered in the enormous echoing reception hall in an orderly and efficient manner and returned to the main ship which, by this time, had docked in New Jersey. Charlie waited patiently on the pier side for his luggage while the younger of the New Americans dashed around, pointing excitedly across the Hudson at various land marks they thought they recognised. When his luggage arrived he made his way to the nearest ferry, crossed the Hudson and into West Manhattan not far from 34th Street where he walked the mile or so to Penn Station. He would have liked to stay longer in New York. In fact it had crossed his mind to stay there rather than face the journey to Philadelphia; however the next through train was in less than half an hour which more or less made his mind up for him. He bought a single ticket, and then spent the time eating his first hot dog and wandering around admiring the marble finish of the architecture and watching the busy concourse of the station.

The train was nothing like he had seen in Europe; it was larger and seemed much higher off the ground. As soon as they took off, some attendants scooted about selling coffee and hamburgers while others collected tickets and roared out the names of the stations as they passed by. When they did stop at a station, the carriage was invaded by urchins selling candy bars, cigarettes, sandwiches and anything else that was legal. The journey was exhilarating and wasn't that long as the train hurtled through the Pennsylvanian countryside at a tremendous speed; it was quicker than going from Derry to Letterkenny.

At the station his sister was delighted to see him and introduced her fiancé, Giuseppe Ulivi, an Italian who arrived in Philadelphia at the age of ten, yet still spoke with a remarkable Italian accent. "Just call him Joe," she said, giving Joe an admiring glance. "By the way, I've arranged a place for you with the Nolans, you won't remember them but they were friends of our father's back home. You can stay there till you settle."

The Nolans had a kind of boarding house in a place called Fulsom Street, an Irish neighbourhood surrounded by bars and diners. A lively area, crowded, but safe. Charlie was introduced into the local Irish social club that Friday night. The club was mainly run by Donegal immigrants. Since the war immigration had virtually ceased, particularly for the Irish, and he was treated as a little bit of a novelty. People gathered around to ask for news of this one and that one. He answered patiently and as honestly as he could, but the older women in particular drifted away realising that he was hopeless - too quiet for their liking and not as good a scandalmonger and gossip as they would have wanted. A few of the men hung around asking him if he had any contacts in the town and supplying him with a few work leads.

"You wouldn't know a George Peebles would you?" he asked, suddenly remembering Jack's brother.

"Oh sure! He's quite a big building contractor - and from your neck of the woods too. He'll give you a start, no bother," said someone. "George is an okay guy, but worth watching. Ned Ferry over there works for him. He's a ganger for Peebles."

He started to walk across the room.

"Come on over and I'll introduce you to Ned."

That Monday morning Charlie was taken to a building site downtown and was given a start right away. It seems that the young men of America were now joining the US Army in droves, leaving a bit of a shortage of labour. The first American troopship had left New York that month for Europe, adding to the sense of excitement. Old hands told him that cinemas seem to appear almost overnight, with entrepreneurs opening up old shops, warehouses, local halls, even garages to give movie shows. Movies of the smiling troops leaving for 'over there', sanitised shots of the Western Front and of course the latest Tom Mix cowboy pictures. For several weeks Charlie walked about almost in a trance. Everything seemed newer, fresher and somehow younger here. He had a job that seemed to pay about twice as much as back home and his money appeared to go twice as far. Within a couple of months he had even saved enough to buy Rosie and Joe a handsome dinner service for their wedding which was by far the most lavish social occasion he had ever attended.

The reception took place in the Irish club which was bedecked by Joe's apparently endless supply of older sisters in banners, bunting, flags and flowers all of which were in the green, white and red of Italy. Wine flowed freely. The married couple had hardly completed the marriage waltz round the hall before Joe's sisters took to the floor grabbing men from every corner. Charlie drank little and was surprised to see George Peebles turning up later on. George kissed the bride and shook hands with the groom and gave them twenty dollars in an envelope. He continued glad-handing round the room when he could find a way through the wild dancers that tore across the floor, punching arms, slapping shoulders and trying to shout loudly above the music. Charlie had just finished from getting whirled around the room by one of Joe's larger sisters and was standing on the side trying to get his breath back when George Peebles slapped him on the back.

"How are you, young man?" he roared.

Charlie turned around to face him.

"Ah! You're Charlie McKenna," he continued. "I know you. You're working for me on that new office building downtown."

As Peebles had scores of men working for him, Charlie was taken aback and flattered to realise he had been recognised. He was unaware that George had the charmer's gift of remembering names and faces without even trying.

"The foreman pointed you out that last time I was down there, said you were a smart worker and was thinking of putting you in the shuttering squad."

"Well, I wouldn't say no to that."

"Come over here and have a drink, there are plenty of tables now they've started the serious dancing," said Peebles.

"Sure Mr Peebles."

"Call me George, Charlie. Call me George."

They sat a table near the dance floor where Charlie called over the waiter.

"A beer for me and a …"

"A Whiskey Highball - Jameson's with some lemonade and ice for me," said George. "It's not often I go drinking," he added, "another couple will do me."

"Where are you from, Charlie?" he asked.

"Not far from yourself, near Dromore. I met your brother Jack on the way over."

"Did you now? He's the youngest of the family, I've offered him work here but he keeps putting me off."

"Sailors get fond of roaming around. Maybe when he's a bit older."

"Maybe he will. I came here when I was ten - accounts for my accent. I went to school here, and then worked for my uncle in a carpenter's shop. Hated it. Hated being inside - joined the army at fifteen. Sent out West to fight them Indians."

He talked with a kind of odd Irish-American accent with a fast staccato delivery and pronounced Indians as Injins. Charlie was about to mention his own army service but he was interrupted by the waiter bringing the drinks, in the meantime George rattled on.

"Yes sir. In the end I made it into the US marines at eighteen. Took part in the invasion of Cuba in 1898 during the Spanish American War. Made Captain by the age of twenty two and got an honourable discharge after getting shot in the belly in the Philippines."

It sounded like a well rehearsed litany to Charlie, who nodded impassively.

"Came back to start up this construction company. Never looked back since."

"You've done well for yourself," said Charlie, when he realised George had stopped talking. "I had a spell in the army myself, over in France most of the time."

"Ah! An Irishman who didn't take part in the Easter Rising then?"

He paused for a second and eyed Charlie closely.

"Must be one of the very few - according to the ones I've met recently," he added dryly.

"No, 'fraid not. Far too busy avoiding being shot at and gassed by the Krauts in that week," said Charlie with a quiet laugh.

"What kind of operations were you involved in? What rank were you?" said George suddenly taking an interest.

"Eventually made it to sergeant, people like us don't get to Captain's rank in the British army. Mostly infantry detail, as you would call it, but I got to use explosives during the Arras campaign."

"The Arras Campaign?"

"A big offensive during April and May in France earlier this year not far from the town of Arras, about 100 miles north of Paris. Used miners to dig under the trenches, loads of explosives used there. Finally took a bullet in the leg and was discharged."

George was silent for a moment.

"Interested in politics?" he said.

"I take an interest, sure."

"You seem a straight forward kind of guy. I know people who might want to meet someone with your experience."

Charlie shrugged non-committally.

George finished his drink and called over the waiter. He gave the waiter five dollars. "This should cover this table's drinks bill for an hour or so."

"Ah be quiet!" he said, as Charlie rose to protest. "And here ..." he continued to the waiter, pulling out another five dollar bill. "Get one for yourself and the rest of the waiters."

"I'll be in touch, Charlie. By the way, you'll be in the shuttering squad on Monday. I'll see to it. Good luck now and I'll see you later."

***

Shuttering involves making up the wooden forms for concrete. A kind of external moulding box that the liquid concrete can be placed in to set. The next day the wooden forms or shutters can then be removed leaving a solid concrete shape, like a column or a wall. It's essentially carpenter's work, but needs semi skilled workers and smart labourers to make a good squad or gang. It pays much better than general labouring and to be in a good shuttering squad is considered a bit of a prize job on a building site. Charlie found himself in such a squad on the Monday morning.

George Peebles rarely visited his sites or dirtied his boots by wandering around, but could often be spotted in some high vantage point observing the progress of the work. The speed of the work, meeting of deadlines, hiring and firing and general discipline was controlled by site foremen who were in turn, controlled by the personal site agents of Peebles.

It didn't take Charlie long to become well established and soon began to organise the labourers more effectively, getting them to strip and clean the shuttering with cheap whaling oil to make them easier to remove from the quick drying concrete.

After two months, in January of 1918, the agent came up to the top storey and called him over.

"Mr. Peebles is down in the office, he'd like a word."

Charlie walked down the four flights of stairs to the street level office wondering, in the back of his mind, if he had done something wrong.

"Ah! Charlie McKenna! How the devil are you?" shouted George, shaking his hand vigorously.

"Have a seat," indicating a dust covered armchair. "You're doing well I hear."

"So far so good."

"Indeed, indeed," said George lighting a cheroot.

"I wanted a quick chat, Charlie. I remember you mentioned you had a bit of experience with explosives in the army."

"Yes, that's right," said Charlie a bit cagily.

"I'm thinking about taking some work on in New York which might require skill of that type. They're building subway lines all over New York town, some of them are elevated, but a lot of them need tunnelling."

"I didn't know you had work in New York"

"Got some work up there, but those Italians are taking most of it," replied George slightly irked. "They can play a bit rough those Italians."

He pronounced Italians as Eye-talians.

"Anyway," George continued, "I wouldn't mind you going up there for a while, get a bit of experience. I've got a bit of work around 42nd and 43rd Street. Building the new underground station, it could be the start I need to get more work up there."

Charlie looked at the floor for a second.

"I hadn't thought of moving yet," he said slowly.

"Don't tell me. Some dame you've fallen for, right?"

Charlie reddened slightly. "Well I've been walking out with someone, a girl who lived besides us back home."

"Well tell me something new!" said George with a laugh. "Charlie, why worry? New York is only two hours away for God's sake, you can be back down every few weeks. It'll make her keener."

The reality was, of course, that he didn't have much of a choice. To finish up with Peebles would have been employment suicide in Philadelphia, not only did he pay the best rates but Charlie was now well in with what was becoming an elite shuttering squad. He found himself in New York the following week.

Charlie was given accommodation in a tenement just off 11th Avenue, a tough and rough area of mainly shanty town Irish which sported several vicious gangs. However he kept to himself and concentrated on his work on the subway. Essentially George's part in the arrangement was merely supplying a gang of eight skilled workers as subcontractors for the blowing of rock obstacles, and he was right, Italians dominated the workforce. It didn't take long for the first 'protection' approach to be made in the form of $50 a week 'union' fees. George came up to New York when told of this development and insisted that they pay nothing; he knew several of the local gang leaders who would jump at the chance at mixing it with the Italians. Charlie was more circumspect.

"You forget George; we're in the firing line here. Why don't I go and see who's behind this union business and have some discussions with him."

"Are you raving mad? Talk to them! These Eye-talians will have you killed if you question their methods, you either pay or don't pay, kill or be killed."

Charlie hesitated.

"Do me a favour George," he said calmly, "send my brother-in-law Joe up here for a few days, just in case I need someone who can speak the lingo. In the meantime I'll make arrangements with the Italian who approached us. I'll ask to meet his boss."

George paused for a minute and looked at him with a mixture of anxiety and admiration.

"I hope you know what you're doing, Charlie. Maybe you should take a few of O' Donnell's heavies with you in case things get rough."

Charlie grinned cheerfully.

"Don't worry about me, George. I'll be fine."

Next day Charlie sought out the 'Union Delegate' who had an office on 10th Avenue not far from 43rd Street. The office was a grubby shop front with a plate glass window and a hand written sign which stated 'The Union of Subway Workers and Labor'. No such union existed, according to George, or if did it was unknown to him and his Tammany Hall cronies. Charlie walked into the office and noticed someone leaning against the shadows of the left hand wall with his eyes closed. He asked about the local union delegate. The rough looking hoodlum opened his eyes slowly and looked Charlie up and down

"So, who wants to know?" he said a with a broad Brooklyn accent.

"It's no big deal, there's a team of us up from Philly who might be interesting in joining, that's all."

The thug slid off the wall and opened and entered a door at the back. Charlie could hear voices coming from the room in a mixture of Italian and Brooklyn English. Finally a smaller more rotund man, with a loud tie and chewing a cheroot appeared flanked by the cartoon hood.

"What's the problem?" said the smaller one opening out his arms.

"Well the problem is that one of your delegates asked my squad to join the union, your union," said Charlie pointing to the grimy sign. "Thing is me and my guys are already union members of the Western Federation of Mine Workers."

The smaller fat guy looked bit uneasy. He was smart enough to know that the Western Federation of Mine Workers, the WFM, was still a powerful organisation and if these were bone fide members that could be awkward.

"My name's Aldo di Dio the local chapter president. This is er... a local arrangement we have here."

"What, for fifty bucks a week? Between eight of us that's six dollars a week each, that's more than double what we pay a month in the WFM."

"Well like I said, it's a local arrangement," said di Dio, hitching up his trousers. "We'll pay your WFM union fees for you. The rest is for strike funds. We have some disputes in New York. We need to get the funds from the rest of the workers to cover their wages."

"I can see that you might need the money if that's the case," said Charlie appearing to be reasonable. "I'll get in touch with the New York branch to see if that is the union position…"

"Hold on, there's no need for that, or to go and complicate things. We've already made the arrangement," said the fat guy looking increasingly unsure.

"Ah it's no problem," said Charlie affably. He had now swung the situation to make it look as if he was going to do them a favour. "In fact my brother-in-law is coming up to New York. He's a full time WFM delegate and speaks Italian. I'm sure we can come to some arrangement."

Di Dio suspected he was being outmanoeuvred and stayed silent. Charlie continued confidently. "Look we're all trade union guys here. We don't mind helping out. But you're right, things might become complicated if the WFM become involved. Instead of you paying our dues we'll pay our own and then the squad can give you a voluntary contribution of, say, ten dollars a week to help your strike fund."

Again di Dio looked uneasy. He was a minor member of a local

'Mano Nera', a Black Hand gang and pretty well free to organise his own scams and extortion rackets as long as he paid the Capo. If the authorities and official unions became involved he could find himself in trouble, and in more ways than one. Di Dio looked at Charlie closely, he thought he was bluffing about his connections, but couldn't tell by his almost bland expression. What he did know was that this Irishman might prove unnecessarily troublesome, all for the sake of a few dollars.

Di Dio rubbed the back of his neck and made a great show of nodding his head wisely.

"Yes I can see what you mean. Perhaps our arrangements in New York may appear to be over elaborate to you. Maybe your idea might suit all parties better."

"Good. That will save my brother-in-law a trip. He hates leaving Philly. The new arrangement will start next Friday and your man can collect the money from me. By the way, I'm assuming our 'voluntary contribution' will give us certain local welfare rights and protection, after all working underground can be a dangerous profession," Charlie paused. "For everyone involved." Charlie tipped his hat, walked out of the office and took the first train to Philadelphia.

"Ten dollars a week! Are you out of your mind? I could get Manny O'Donnell's gang to kill the lot of them for that. Christ I must be paying you guys too much!" shouted George as he paced around the office.

"That true, you're paying us well enough. That why we're only asking you to pay half the money."

"Well that's big of you! Do you expect me to fork out five dollars a week to some jumped up dago for the privilege of working there?"

"Relax George it's all taken care of. These guys are small fry, a couple of Moustachioed Petes who watch the movies, but you can bet they're connected to the Black Hand somewhere along the line. For a couple of dollars it'll keep them off our backs while we're up there." George continued to groan and give out loud tuts. "It's the principle of the thing!"

"You want us killed for a principle? Oh come on, George! I've seen you give waiters a bigger tip. Only yesterday you were complaining that it was pay or don't pay, kill or be killed."

George began to calm down and threw himself angrily on the grubby armchair in a puff of dust. After a few minutes of silence Charlie noticed George's shoulders were beginning to heave and then he suddenly exploded with a roar of laughter.

"I did say that, didn't I? Now you get us off the hook with the price of a waiter's tip!" he chortled.

He stood up, still laughing and waved a finger at Charlie.

"You know something Charlie, you should go back to Ireland – you'd make a great politician!"

oooOooo

CHAPTER ELEVEN

Alice's Restaurant

Mondays were usually busy for Des. Most Scottish papers produce a football or sports special which pulled in a few of the writers and subs on a Sunday night leaving a few newspapers short handed on Monday mornings. Des started at seven am and finished around noon, after a quick workout and swim he was back in the flat for just after one o'clock. Hastings phoned just as he entered the hall and was closing the front door.

"I've got a bit of info on our man Hughie that you might want to hear. Nothing great, but you might want to talk to Detective Sergeant Munro, Alex Munro, from Southern Division. He's over here in Central on some other bits of business. I'm taking him for lunch if you want to join us."

"Sounds good," said Des, who rarely passed an opportunity to make a contact with the police hierarchy. "Where are you going?"

"I'm taking him to Alice's Restaurant, about 2 o'clock"

"Alice's Restaurant, are you nuts? That's a dive!"

"The man likes ribs and cabbage. Who I am to complain? By the way, I handed over that sovereign to McKinney on Saturday morning. Do me a favour and don't mention it to Munro."

"Sure. No problem on that one. But hey! Alice's Restaurant!" said Des with a chuckle. "You're a real cheapskate Hastings, no mistake. See you at two."

Des pottered around the flat, tidying up and getting into some casual clothes. He left at 1.45 making sure he had a handful of change for the usual moochers at the end of the bridge who always treated him like a long lost friend at this time of day. He walked along the Clydeside to Bridgegate cutting through the top end of an area known as 'Paddy's Market'.

If you were a romantic traveller you might call the place a flea market. In fact it was very much at the lower end of the flea market business, if such a concept exists outside the third world. A place where midden bins looked as if they had been looted and emptied on to the pavement and scattered in a semicircle around the dishevelled market hawkers. It attracted the usual collection of low lifers, drug dealers, thieves, shop lifters and assorted unsuccessful criminal riff-raff of the underworld. It was also held right underneath the back windows of one of Scotland's major courthouses, Glasgow High Court.

Des walked on for fifty yards to Alice's Restaurant. It was the only restaurant in Western Europe, as far as he knew, that had only two items on the menu, Ribs and Cabbage with potatoes or Ribs and Cabbage without potatoes. Hastings and Munro had just sat down as he arrived. A thin faced, shapeless waitress with washed out blonde hair approached, small notebook and a chewed bookies pencil at the ready.

After a quick agreement round the table, Hastings ordered.

"Two with potatoes and one without"

"Mulk?" snapped the waitress.

"Yes, milk all round will do fine"

She put her notebook on the table and ponderously wrote 2+ and then 1- and finally 3mks. Seconds later she was back with a mixed collection of cutlery which she tossed casually on the table. The restaurant was busy, mostly with genuine workers and some hawkers from the market. It had yet to attract the usual bunch of trendies and left wing politicos from the nearby gentrified Merchant City. The trouble was that Alice's wasn't quite 'ethnic' enough to attract the truly trendy and just a wee bit too working class to attract the left wing politicos. Another disadvantage to the above posers, who liked to linger and chatter over lunch, was the speed at which the food was delivered - hardly surprising considering the limitations of the menu. However, even more damning was the fact that they didn't do iced tea, green tea, minted tea, cappuccino, espresso neither singolo, doppio nor macchiato, café carajillo, café latte or anything else that encouraged the non-eater to linger about, cluttering up the place and taking up valuable seats.

Des was introduced to Detective Sergeant Munro and they had just sorted out the tangle of cutlery, when three large soup bowls arrived at the table, each filled with a rack of pork ribs and a heap of cabbage, all in a boiling pool of salty cabbage water. In an unaccustomed fit of restaurant etiquette, the two smaller bowls of steaming potatoes were served 'on the side'. A jug of ice cold milk was placed in the middle along with three glasses, none of which were of the same size, shape or design. Des had just lifted his fork to start eating when the bill arrived. It was the same sheet that the waitress wrote their order on, only now it had the amount owed printed in pen in large letters at the bottom of the page.

The waitress stood and silently glared at them, it was obviously the tradition to pay before you ate.

"My treat," said Hastings cheerfully, pulling out a ten pound note. He was about to hand this to the waitress when she stood back and nodded her head in the direction of an enormous old fashioned till where the owner sat picking his teeth. Hastings stood up and went to the counter with his tenner. Le patron took the tenner, gave it a sharp snap and held it up to the light to make sure it was genuine. Satisfied, he crashed open the till, threw Hastings a couple of coppers of change in a saucer and thumped the bill with a large PAID red ink stamp and casually continued with his teeth picking.

"What a performance! You'd think we were dining in the Paris Ritz the way these guys carry on," said Hastings as he finally sat down.

"So, Mr Munro, Mick tells me you know our late, mutual friend Hughie Toner," said Des, starting to eat.

"Kind of. He was a bit of a player in the early eighties, liked to let people think he was some sort of IRA man with contacts."

"And was he?" asked Mick.

"Are you kidding?" said Munro with a laugh. "Belfast people on either side of the sectarian divide never really trusted the Scots, particularly Glaswegians. Any organisations they had over here attracted all sorts of chancers and were totally riddled with informers who sang to anyone, from the local police to MI5. The IRA and UVF kind of played along with the idea and used the local wannabes for safe houses and the occasional piece of money laundering. In return they got a bit of protection for their own extortion and construction trade scams."

"Any arrests?"

"Very few. Suited us not to hassle these guys. Oddly enough, they kept the local bampots and neds in some kind of order. That is until the drugs boom started of course, and then it was every man for himself."

They carried on eating in silence for a few minutes. The pork ribs were excellent, if a bit messy. The cabbage was fresh, cooked to perfection and best tackled with a spoon. The Ayrshire potatoes were light and fluffy, and were wonderful when mashed into the cabbage juice.

"So, do you think he got done in for his Irish connections?"

"No, you can forget about that," said Mick. "The man who done him is sitting in a Central Division police cell right now. His name's Jack Brady, well known toe-rag. We caught him last night trying to flog some sovereigns in the Red Parrot Bar, about a hundred yards away from the murder scene. On Saturday morning I saw McKinney and gave him a gold sovereign that I found near Toner. He went round personally to every bar and restaurant in the neighbourhood and showed them the coin and told them that, because a suspected robbery had also taken place, that this was now an official murder inquiry. That made the owners nervous - murders are bad for business in their eyes. The next day the Red Parrot manager phoned. I was first on the scene, just in the door, when this loony dressed in a complete 'Junkies AR UZ' sports outfit tried to flog me a couple of those sovereigns. You would hardly believe it. Makes you wonder what goes through these guys' minds."

"Steal now - think later. That's their motto, as far as I can see," said Munro.

"So how did it all happen then?" asked Des.

"Post mortem suggests Toner was well tanked. He was last seen staggering about in Madsen's bar, a bar that's even dangerous when you're stone cold sober. Master criminal Brady spots Toner showing off some 'gold doubloons', as Brady insisted in calling them, and decides to rob him at the first opportunity. Uses a chib that he somehow acquired from some pal who worked in a supermarket. Nice piece by the way, a mahogany handle, a butcher's sharpening steel with the blade cut down and pointed."

Mick stopped for a moment.

"It never ceases to amaze me the time and effort these guys make to manufacture weapons," he reflected shaking his head.

"Anyway, Brady says he was too stoned to remember anything at first. Now says he didn't mean to kill him, he just waved the knife in front of Toner to 'give him a fright' and was only 'defending himself' when Toner had the temerity to take offence and to loudly object to being robbed in broad daylight."

"Case over then," said Des.

"Pretty much," added Munro, before Mick could answer.

"I wondered ..." he continued.

He hesitated briefly, glancing at Mick.

"...We think it might be helpful if you alluded to Toner's Irish connection if you're writing this up."

Des looked up, interested.

"I could do. Although, in the end, that kind of thing depends on the editors. There's also a bit of a family connection which might complicate things. Any particular reason?"

"Well," said Munro, choosing his words carefully. "There's a small unit based in Southern Division that takes an interest in, shall we say, Irish affairs. We try to maintain our contacts with the Garda and the PSNI. I know things seem to be quiet to most people over here, but, to be honest, there is always something bubbling under the surface over there. The professional criminal in Ulster always used paramilitaries as an excuse. These days the unionists are more into drugs and protection rackets and the nationalists are into cross border smuggling and, believe it or not, EU farming scams. However there are one or two still involved in radical groups like the Real IRA and Continuity IRA who still want to carry on the 'Struggle' as they put it. They're not all that well handed but it's been difficult to keep tabs on them. They've pulled off a few stunts recently, some with fatal results but God knows what they're up to."

Des wiped his lips with a napkin he pulled from the dispenser.

"I'm not too sure where this is going," said Des, suddenly startled to realise his napkin had a large Santa Claus in one corner with the legend 'Merry Xmas 1976' printed on the underside.

"Not really anywhere, I suppose. Toner's funeral is on Friday and one or two of us might decide to turn up. If you give him a bit of background then you never know who might turn up – it's just a long shot."

"No skin off my nose," replied Des with a shrug. "I'll see what I can do."

By now they'd finished sucking and gnawing at the rib bones and were busy wiping their hands with the 1976 Christmas napkins. They pulled back the chairs and left the restaurant. Mick left a fifty pence tip in the saucer beside the till that drew another malevolent glare from the waitress who sauntered over to clear away the debris.

"Thanks for the lunch, Mick. I enjoyed that," said Munro patting his stomach and giving a discreet rift. "And nice to meet you Des, give us a ring if you're looking for a bit of press copy. Here's my card."

Des gave his thanks and slipped the card into his top pocket.

"By the way," added Munro. "I've left my car over at the Sheriff Court so I'll just leave you here. Good luck."

They said their goodbyes and Des and Mick continued to walk back up the Saltmarket, eventually stopping at the corner of St. Andrews Street where Mick had to turn right to get to his police station. Des had already decided to walk up to Argyle Street and mosey around a couple of book shops.

"I'm meeting Liam in the Scotia Bar in about an hour or so if you want to join us," said Des

"I don't finish till after five, so I'll give it a miss. Thanks, just the same, and tell Liam I was asking for him."

"Sure thing, Mick. Catch you later."

***

The lower east end of the town centre is a peculiar area of strange cafés and odd shops like tattoo parlours and creepy places that specialise in military paraphernalia and fantasy board games. There are dance studios that share premises with weird religious cults: experimental theatre groups that rehearse loudly at the back of large shops fronted by Tarot card readers and palmists. He spent the next hour or so drifting in and out of the various interesting music and books shops that were dotted around this part of town before making his way to The Scotia Bar in Stockwell Street. Liam was standing at the bar flicking through one of several newspapers supplied by the establishment and drinking a black coffee when Des entered.

"Des, old man, what'll you have?"

"Off the drink, are we?" said Des eyeing the coffee.

"Don't drink on a Monday or Thursdays," replied Liam looking shocked, "Or Sunday after 6 o'clock for that matter."

He paused for a second.

"Although I have been known to relax the rules," he added, "…on the odd occasion."

"I didn't know you were so rigorously regular in your drinking, Liam. Please forgive me," Des said in mock humility. "I'll join you in a coffee, an Americano for me."

Des, like most of Liam's close friends, knew that Liam didn't drink any where near as much as he liked people to think he did. In fact, he often took a great delight in hamming up his Drunken Irishman act.

Liam ordered up, folded up the paper, put it back on the rack and they settled down in one of the booths.

"Got your e-mail and photos this morning. And here," he said, handing over a bag with two books, "you might want to read these for a bit of background if you're doing some research. They're library books, so bring them back when you're finished."

Des pulled out the first one; 'The Long Fellow', a biography of De Valera.

"Don't bother reading all of that, after the Civil War it becomes a total bore," said Liam, waving his hand in dismissal.

"What about this one, Michael Collins 'The Lost Leader'?"

"A load of old Romantic nonsense, just about readable, unfortunately you may need to read all of it."

"Why is that?"

"I don't want to spoil it for you Des, but you might find that he gets killed at the end of it."

Des looked at the books briefly and put them back in the plastic bag.

"What about the photos?"

Liam took out three 6x4 photos and laid them on the table.

"I put them through a photo software package, tidied them up and made them up to the same size," he said. "Very interesting. The first two are straightforward. This is one of Julie's granddad in a British army uniform of around the First World War, looks like he made sergeant, at least going by the shape of the cap. This other one, the one with his brother... What's his name by the way?"

"That's Julie's uncle Pat, although I suppose it's really her great uncle Pat."

"...It also looks like a British army uniform," he continued. "But it's more likely to be a Free State Army uniform, it's got the typical round collar but I couldn't see any other insignia."

He put the two portrait photos to one side.

"Now in this other photo, the third one, Pat is definitely in a Free State uniform," said Liam, pointing to the full length photo of a uniformed soldier. "I've seen dozen of photos like this, if you look in either of the books I gave you, you'll find similar uniforms."

He plucked at his beard.

"Thing is, what is he up to?" he said.

Des picked up the photo and looked closely. He shrugged his shoulders.

"What do you mean, what's he up to?"

"Do you know where this was taken?"

"Julie's mum thinks it was probably somewhere in Donegal."

"Hmm. Pretty lush vegetation for Donegal, I've been there - rocky and windswept for the most part - looks more likely to have been taken down south, somewhere like Cork or Kerry. As I said on Saturday, that's where most of the action took place during the civil war."

"The photo's been torn along one edge..." he continued, tapping the photo.

"Ah! But the original was a postcard. He could have torn it to fit the size of the card!" replied Des.

Liam looked up, frowning.

"Do you really think so? Let's think this one through then...

"A soldier walks into a photographer's and asks the assistant if they could make this photo into a nice postcard to send to the folks back home. 'Sure thing, sir,' replies the assistant. 'Oh dear! It's too wide, I won't bother using this handy paper guillotine or this pair of scissors that I normally use to trim photos, I'll just rip off this edge'."

Des held up his hand.

"No need for sarcasm, just a thought," said Des, slightly peeved. "Mind you he could have torn it before he took it to the photographers, or postcard maker, or whoever it is who makes these things."

"Now that's a more likely explanation. But why?"

"Obviously something he didn't want anybody to see or..." Des thought for a moment.

"... or there was something in it that he wanted to hide?" added Liam.

"Possibly," said Des picking up the photo again.

"And there are another couple of things."

He started to tick them off using his fingers

"One, what is that boot doing lying around in the foreground? Two, is that another soldier coming through the trees at the top of the picture? And finally, what's that white box shaped object through the trees?"

He handed the photo back to Des. Des turned the photograph this way and that for a few minutes.

"The boot could simply have been discarded. It's an old building and it looks like some other rubbish is lying about where the tear is, and anyway what's ominous about another soldier coming towards him?"

"It not that it's ominous," said Liam. "It just seems to suggest that some sort of concerted action is going on here and that it's not just Pat posing idly in front of a local building to get his photo taken. The boot is a strange one, it doesn't look that old. Remember, this was taken in nineteen twenties Ireland, not the throw-away society of today. Boots would be repaired and used until they fell off your feet."

He paused and drew a circle around the boot.

"Talking of which," he continued, with a slight cough. "I made a good close up of that boot."

He tapped the circled boot.

"It's lying as if it still had a foot in it."

Des snatched the photo from him.

"Oh come on, Liam! You would hardly notice the thing!" he said pointing to the boot. "Let's not get carried away here. God, I think you talk more sense when you're drinking!"

Liam took another photo from his inside pocket and put it down. "Here's a larger blow-up of the boot by itself."

Des picked it up and stared at it for a few moments. He put it down carefully.

oooOooo

CHAPTER TWELVE

Mallow Station

Pat and Charlie had finished the excellent breakfast provided by Mrs. O'Sullivan and were standing in the hotel lobby when they heard the loud blast of the taxi horn. Mrs O'Sullivan came bustling through to the hall wiping her hands in her apron.

"I'm sorry, Mr McKenna, I hope I'm not keeping you back. I prepared your bill earlier on."

"Don't worry , Mrs O'Sullivan, We've got plenty of time, the taxi's, a bit early. I'll settle up with you now."

"Can you carry out the luggage while I pay the bill?" said Charlie.

Pat gave a nod.

"Sure," he said as he started to gather the luggage together.

She pulled out a small leather bill holder from under the reception desk and handed it over with a smile.

"I think you'll find that the bill is up to date, Mr McKenna."

He opened the folder and looked at the bill. Seventeen shillings a day and two shillings for lunch. A total of one pound and eighteen shillings or about five American dollars for the two of them. Very reasonable considering, thought Charlie. He paid with two pound notes, insisted that she keep the change and explained that a receipt was not required.

Charlie trotted down the short stairway and reached the street. Mrs. O'Sullivan, avoiding the light rain, stood in the doorway, shouted her goodbyes and waved enthusiastically as the taxi reversed, turned noisily, and then raced down Georges Street towards the railway station.

They rattled along Patrick Street and over the River Lee on to Glenmire Station, and were in good time to catch the train. Charlie paid off the driver and moved inside to join the short queue at the ticket office to buy two single tickets for Tralee, changing at Mallow. The rain was beginning to get a bit heavier as they walked along to the covered platform where they found some bench seats. Pat walked back to the stationers and bought a couple of newspapers to read on the journey.

"You might find that of interest," said Pat on his return.

He handed Charlie a special edition of the Cork Examiner, its headline read:

"Enemy Troops in Seaborne Invasion!"

Irish troops the enemy? Charlie wryly reflected how the editorial line of The Examiner had changed somewhat since the local anti-treaty militia had taken over the paper and appointed Mrs McCurtain and that upper class Englishman turned revolutionary, Erskine Childers, as the editorial team. He was half way through the story when he stopped.

"I knew that man," he said to Pat, tapping the column. "Ian Kennedy, I met him a couple of times here, in Cork. He was a Scottish chap from the Highlands, came over with his mother to improve his Gaelic at the college in Ballingeary and got caught up in things. He was called 'Scottie' of course. Got himself killed just outside Douglas last night according to this."

"My God," sighed Charlie. "What a bloody waste!"

"This paper I've got doesn't even mention the landings. Give me a look at yours when you've finished," said Pat.

The platform was beginning to fill up with a variety of passengers, some carrying a large amount of luggage.

"Looks like some people are getting a bit jittery," remarked Charlie. "I hope you remembered to stash the revolvers away."

"I put one in the bag and one in the case with twenty rounds each. I hope you're not expecting to use them?"

"The way things are going, you never know. I know that they've started to blow up some bridges recently, let's hope they've not resorted to robbing the passengers – yet," replied Charlie as he stood up and started to pace up and down.

The train was ten minutes late arriving and was, thankfully, almost empty. Charlie hoisted his case up on the rack, while a slightly nervy Pat elected to keep his kit bag between his knees. They were joined by a couple of businessmen and a young girl, who looked like a house servant. Although it took a bit of time to get the passengers loaded up, everyone managed to find a seat and with a flurry of flag waving and loud whistling, the train steamed noisily from the station - now fifteen minutes behind schedule. The other passengers talked politely and formally to each other but the brothers spoke little on the 45 minute journey, except to exchange newspapers occasionally. The train seemed to stop at every station and sometimes in the middle of nowhere. They were beginning to think that they would miss their connection to Tralee at this rate when after half an hour they suddenly took off at a tremendous rate and raced through the Cork countryside and arrived almost on time.

At Mallow all passengers were asked to disembark by the station guards. The platform teemed with people who seemed oddly quiet, the railwaymen gathered there were sullen and wary. Little wonder, as the anti-treaty forces had recently declared that they were traitors and liable to be shot for their 'cooperation with the National Government'. Charlie needn't have worried about their connection as the Tralee train was running at least an hour late and the journey to Dublin cancelled until further notice. Transport was being arranged for the Dublin passengers to bypass a blown up bridge which, Charlie gathered, could take a bit of time. All of this information was gleaned by a combination of crackled platform announcements, a guard with a megaphone and variety of railroad employees at the pay windows and information desks.

"This is bedlam," said Charlie. "Let's get out of here, go for a walk and get a cup of tea or a pint or something."

"We need to watch our time, we wouldn't want to miss the train or we could be stuck here for long enough."

"I've got a pocket watch on me, somewhere," said Charlie, searching his inside pockets. He pulled out a small chrome plated hunter and opened it up and checked the time.

"Dead on time with the station clock, or near as damn it. We'll be back before half past twelve. Let's go."

The town was busy. Technically it was within Liam Lynch's so called Munster Republic, but everything - the post office, the rail system, the bus service and the rest were run by the Provisional Government. It was a strange mixture of ordinary citizens going about their daily routine and stranded and frustrated travellers looking for somewhere to eat or drink. There were also knots of tired looking armed irregulars hanging around: a mixed crew, some wearing bits of uniform and most looking dirty and unshaven. Many of them looked uncomfortable, as if they were strangers to the area. Pat spotted a hotel nearby that had a reception area and fairly crowded and noisy bar where they eventually found a small table with a couple of straight backed chairs. They parked their luggage and Charlie went to the bar and ordered a couple of large bottles of beer and some glasses.

"Quite honestly, with all the excitement of yesterday, I never gave it much thought, but you never quite told me why we're going to Tralee," said Pat, pouring his stout into a beer glass.

"Do you remember Riley, the quarter master chap we met in Douglas yesterday?" said Charlie, talking just loud enough to be heard by Pat.

"Joe Riley, was that his name? I know who you mean. That older man who walked very upright and marched about, the man that you gave the ammunition van over too."

"That's the man. Well he told me that when he was captured up in Tralee by the Free Staters he was interrogated by an officer by the name of Peebles. Did you ever meet any of the Peebles family? They came from Dromore. Not far from us."

"I remember a Jack Peebles. I think he joined the navy a while ago. Is that the family?"

"Yes, that family. In fact I met Jack on the boat to New York. It was

Jack who told me to get in touch with his brother George, a contractor in Philadelphia. I ended up working for George Peebles for over two years."

"How do you know it's the same fella?" asked Pat.

"George went to America very young and ended up with an American accent. He was also an ex-soldier himself, joined the US army for a while and was discharged as a Captain. As far as I can make out, the National Army has been trying to recruit experienced ex-officers from anywhere they can find them, including America. General Prout who took Waterford was in the US Army. So was General O'Connell, the man they took hostage during the battle of the four courts in Dublin. So I'm assuming that George must have been persuaded to join up with the Free Staters. How he fetched up in Tralee is anybody's guess. Officer with a Yankee accent who came from Letterkenny with a name like Peebles? Who else could it be?"

"Sounds like you're right, but why do we want to see him?"

Before Charlie had time to answer he caught sight of a vaguely familiar face coming through the crowd to greet him.

"I think I know you," said the stranger, stretching out his hand. "You're Charlie, aren't you, been a while since I've seen you."

Charlie stood up to take the man's hand, at the same time desperately trying to remember his name. It simply never crossed Charlie's mind to try to deny his own identity.

"How the devil are you?" said Charlie, enthusiastically shaking away, hoping that the man would speak next and reveal all.

Charlie paused for a moment.

"This is my brother Pat," he said nodding over to Pat. Pat stood up and put out his hand.

"Eddie Kelly. Pleased to meet you, Pat."

Charlie remembered immediately, it was an organised ambush on a patrol of auxiliaries in Tipperary just over a year ago in a place called Glen of Aherlow, where Eddie Kelly was the local company commander. Charlie was sent to provide, and detonate, the land mines that would halt the patrol half way through a narrow country road that would allow the local brigade to engage the enemy. He had only stayed a couple of nights. The first night was spent with Eddie and his wife and young family.

"Well Eddie, old boy, how is it going?" said a relieved Charlie. "Come and join us, I'll get you a drink"

"You're fine Charlie. I've got enough here to last me," said Eddie lifting up a half full glass. "I'll need to be going soon anyway."

"Where are you heading?" asked Pat.

"I was supposed to go to Cork but I'm getting the next train back to Formoy and try to get back to Tipperary Town from there. There's supposed to be one due in ten minutes so I need to watch my time."

"Did you hear about the landings?" asked Charlie.

"Yes I did, and I also hear that we…they might be planning to pull out of the city altogether"

We…they? In that instant Charlie knew Eddie had either changed sides or abandoned the thought of fighting on. He also knew that he had seen the future, from now on every conversation was going be loaded with guarded comments, double meanings, hints, clues and lies, in an effort to gauge the position of anyone you talked to. Charlie thought for a second.

"How are the wife and family? Give them my regards," he said.

Eddie had realised that, under the circumstances, it might have sounded odd that he had decided to return home. He seized on Charlie's comments as a way out.

"I will indeed!" said Eddie quickly. "I just heard my wife's mother has taken ill," he continued, "and my wife wants to go back to her mother's for a few weeks, so I'll need to watch the wee ones. How about yourself?"

"I've got some business in Tralee, just waiting for the next train. It should be here shortly."

Eddie was aware that Charlie was a well connected and high ranking engineering officer who was not always attached to any particular brigade and was given free rein to move around, often on special missions. He was getting nervous, and also knew better than to ask any further questions.

"Tralee? Never been there myself. They say it's nice up there."

"It's alright, I suppose," replied Charlie. "The trouble is that it's now in the hands of the Free Staters."

"Yes. I heard that as well," said Eddie, finishing off his beer in one gulp.

"Well, I best be going," he continued, as he put down his glass and turned towards the door. As he began to shoulder his way through the crowded bar he turned and shouted, "Good luck to both of you."

Pat and Charlie sat down again and picked up their glasses.

"Your man didn't seem too keen to hang around now, did he?" said Pat.

"Sign of the times, Pat. He's given up and wants to go home like many others. He was worried in case we would notice and cause problems. On the other hand he may have changed sides and is keeping an eye on things for the Government, although I doubt it - he always struck me as being a man of principle, although I'm sorry I even mentioned Tralee to him now."

"You were going to tell me about George Peebles."

"Let's leave it until later," replied Charlie, lifting an eyebrow and looking around the bar. "You don't know who's in here."

They talked about the Peebles family for a while as they finished their drinks. After a few minutes they finished up and went back out to the street. It looked as if a couple of trains had departed as the town seemed noticeably quieter even after the short time they were in the bar. After wandering up to Main Street, they separated and looked around the shops to pass the time, then joined up and headed back to the station concourse. Just as well, as the train sitting at platform two was announced to be the train for Killarney and Tralee and was leaving in ten minutes. It took them a few frantic minutes to find the right platform. They finally boarded the train and found to their surprise that it was almost empty. Pat threw the kitbag into a carriage half way down the train. He jumped in and sat beside the window with his back to the engine pulling the bag between his knees: Charlie lifted his suitcase onto the rack and sat opposite, drumming his fingers on the armrest. After five minutes the train gave a shudder and lurched forward, again another cacophony of whistles and flag fluttering before the train finally took off. As soon as it left the station and began chugging through the North Cork countryside, Charlie took off his jacket and loosened his tie.

"Better get comfortable, the journey could be long enough," said Charlie stretching out on the seat. Pat lay back letting his head rest against the window. Perhaps it was the steady rhythm of the train wheels, the excitement of the events of the last twenty four hours, the effects of the stout or more likely a combination of all three that made them nod off for a while. Charlie woke up for a few confused minutes as the train shunted back and forth along the sidings of Killarney and fell back into a fitful slumber for short while. The next time he opened his eyes he gave himself a shake and wakened his brother...

"Wake up Pat. It might not be that long before we have to get off." Pat stood up and gave a long wide yawn and stretched his legs. He sat down again and started to rummage through the kit bag and eventually pulled out a package.

"Here take this, I bought something in that baker's shop on the main street."

Charlie opened the brown bag and pulled out a couple of meat pies and a bottle of lemonade.

"Good thinking Pat! I'm just about ready for this."

They took a pie each and shared the bottle.

"Now then," said Charlie, as he started to bite into the pie. "I was about to tell you about George Peebles."

Charlie started at the beginning, telling Pat of his journey to America and Philadelphia, about Rosie's wedding and then his move up to New York.

"New York was difficult because of the Italians, well not so much the ordinary Italians as their Black Hand gangs. Most of the time they terrorised their own people but generally they wanted a piece of anything that made them money. The Irish however were not an easy target. We had our own gangs who spent most of their time fighting and drinking which made the Black Hand a bit wary of us, although to be honest, most of the fighting and drinking was

122

done amongst ourselves."

He paused for a second and looked out the window.

"When you come to think about it, it's probably the reason the country's in the state it is now."

"Anyway," continued Charlie. "George was a member of the IRB, the Irish Revolutionary Brotherhood, but I think like most of those who join secret societies it was more to increase his business contacts than any heartfelt political ideals. He often tried to get me to join up but I could never be bothered with all that swearing of oaths and rituals, to me it was not much different from the Masons and Orangemen back home."

"I know a few Orangemen but I don't think I've met any Masons or IRB men," said Pat.

"Hardly surprising, considering they're supposed to be secret societies," said Charlie dryly.

"I started to get interested in Irish politics after I got discharged from the army," he continued. "I went to a few political meetings in New York, they were always good crack, free beer and food, dancing and the like. When the war ended things got a bit tighter with work and we all ended up back in Philadelphia, I think it was around March of 1919, which suited me as I was courting Madge McGhee at the time, you know the McGhees from over the hill in Rader."

"Well now you tell me!" said Pat, sitting up. "Of course I know the McGhees and well remember Madge before she left home; she's not much older than me. She was a real beaut, you lucky devil!"

"Several of us went back up to New York one weekend," said Charlie slightly embarrassed by Pat's enthusiasm for Madge. "It was a big rally for De Valera when he came over. There was thousands there. George and I hung on for a few days, making a bit of a holiday of it, and that's when I was introduced to Harry Boland. Does that name ring a bell?"

"I think I've heard of him, didn't he throw his lot in with De Valera after the Treaty?"

"The very man - Boland was interested in recruiting experienced men for 'the war of freedom' as he put it. He knew George well and he was quite impressed when he heard I was an ex-sergeant in the British army. There was a fair bit of drinking going on and he became quite keen on George and me to start organising the smuggling of munitions to Ireland particularly to Cork and the West Country. He reckoned the main action would be there - outsides of Dublin of course."

"But why you and George?" said Pat.

"Well, not so much me, but, as I said, George was in the IRB and Boland knew George had used his contacts in Cork to import French and Belgian mining equipment when we were working on the New York subway. Boland thought that this would provide a first class cover to import all sorts of equipment. The trouble was George couldn't leave the US as business was thin on the ground and it needed him and his spider web of politicians, local fixers and union connections to keep it running. He suggested to Boland that I do it."

"I see. I take it that that's why you knew about bonded warehouses, banks and things."

"I learned that as I went along. Boland and Mick Collins came down to see me. Collins had good banking experience and it was him who showed me the ropes as far as banking and the methods of payments for imports were concerned. I enjoyed it. It was a bit of an adventure and a chance to travel around."

"What about Madge, didn't she get worried?"

"Madge was okay about the whole thing. The first time I came over I stayed for six weeks, got things organised and returned to Philadelphia and started shipping stuff out from the States. All was going well until the end of 1920 when we lost a large consignment up in New York. Everyone thought it was some informer on the Ireland end of the operation. So I had to come back to Cork in December 1920, right in the middle of the Tan Wars, to organise a large shipment of ammunition and rifle spares from France. I managed to get caught up in a fire fight right in the middle of Cork town centre. I got lifted by the police and spent a week in the slammer with twenty others before the local brigade broke in and freed the lot of us. Damn thing was the police had my passport and I couldn't risk trying to get back to the states without one. Not only that but they assumed I was high up in the local IRA and put a price on my head. When I got out I was assigned to the engineering brigade. Later on the men voted for me for the rank of captain and I've spent the best part of the last eighteen months on the run and going from one part of the county to the other to help out. I intended to go back after the Truce but got caught up in this mess. That's why I intend to leave for Dublin as soon as I can. If I can get in touch with Boland or Collins I'm sure I can get my passport renewed and get out of here. As far as I'm concerned - I've done my bit."

Charlie sat back in his seat and finished off his lemonade.

"I can see that, but you still haven't explained why we need to see Peebles?" said Pat.

"We really don't have to see him I suppose. I think I could organise getting the gold out of Ireland myself, but George is smart and has loads of contacts. It just seemed providential that I heard his name and whereabouts yesterday."

"Providential?" said Pat.

"Maybe 'lucky' is a better way of putting it."

"Anyway, we'll soon find out if it's lucky or not," Charlie continued. "That's Tralee railway station I can see up the track, if I'm not mistaken."

oooOooo

CHAPTER THIRTEEN

Julie at the Scotia

Julie looked terrific. It was a bright sunny day and she wore a dark neat tailored suit with a dazzling white blouse. The sun glinted off her blonde highlights and her face was framed by expensive designer sunglasses. One of the few perks, as she pointed out, of working in a retail pharmacy. The effect was marred however when she stumbled over the threadbare carpet and into the gloomy interior of the Scotia Bar.

She felt as if someone had suddenly switched off the lights.

"Hi Julie," shouted Liam unperturbed, "can I get you a drink?"

Julie removed the glasses and rubbed her eyes.

"My God, I thought I had been struck blind for a minute."

Des turned around, grinned, stood up and grabbed her by the waist and gave her a welcoming kiss.

"Hi there! I wasn't expecting to see you!"

"We weren't too busy and they owe me a few hours. I knew you were meeting Liam so I thought I'd join you for a drink," she replied, regaining her composure.

She looked at the table.

"Coffee? Are we going tee-total today?" she asked.

"Want one?" asked Liam from the bar.

"Not likely. Not after the morning I've had. I'll have a gin and tonic, if you don't mind."

"In fact," she said as she sat down. "Make it a double."

She sat in the bench seat opposite Des and looked at the scattered photos.

"I see Liam's been busy," she said.

"Yes he has and he has come up with some rather interesting ideas."

"I'll bet he has, why am I not surprised?"

"He has some interesting thoughts on your Uncle Pat's photo."

"Here's your drink," said Liam putting down a glass of gin and ice with a small bottle of tonic. "I'll let you pour your own tonic."

"By the way, guys, before I forget, I had lunch at Alice's Restaurant with Mick Hasting and his colleague earlier," said Des. He hesitated, deciding to leave out some details. He would explain the suspect's arrest later. "The funeral is on Friday in Holy Cross at 10 o'clock."

"Alice's eh? What did you h…" said Liam. "Never mind, silly question."

"It's my day off this Friday, should be okay for me," he continued as he manoeuvred his bulky body into the booth.

"I might have to arrange some cover but that should be no problem," added Julie.

Liam picked up a photo and handed it to Julie.

"Now then, look at this one closely and answer a few questions if you can."

"Fire away, Sherlock!" said Julie amused at Liam's serious appearance.

"You've been in Donegal umpteen times as a child. Does this look like a typical scene from Donegal?"

Julie peered at the image, and then looked up.

"Mmm …No. I don't suppose it does."

"What makes you say that?" said Des.

"The background, the trees, they look a bit too … well lush, for want of a better word. And the building to the right is a least two stories high and it looks quite wide too, not many farmhouses of that size in Donegal, I would think."

"Have another look at the trees, can you see anything else?" asked Liam.

"That looks like an archway or maybe part of a wall in the

127

middle. Is that someone standing there? In fact it looks like someone coming forward through the arch carrying something, is it another soldier maybe with a gun or rifle?"

"Anything else?"

"There's an object behind the soldier, like a long box or something, something very white."

"Or very glossy or shiny," said Liam. "The box, if it is a box, is the same tone as the buttons on the uniform, so it could be something polished, something that shines in the sunlight."

"I'm not sure where all this is going," said Julie.

"Let's look at the foreground. Can you see that boot to the left?"

"Yes, but what of it?"

"Here's an enlargement of the boot," said Liam pushing one of the other photos over.

Julie looked at it closely.

"I give in, Liam. What am I looking at here?"

"The boot doesn't look empty to me. It looks like it's full of something."

"I suppose it does, so what? There's rubbish lying around all over the place."

There was a brief silence.

"Liam thinks it's a severed boot, you know, with the foot still in it," said Des.

"Oh come on! Guys get a grip!" said Julie laughing. "You're letting your imagination run riot now."

"There's something else that I pointed out to Des. Why was the photograph torn down the edge?"

"It was made to fit a postcard, for God's sake, Liam!"

"So you think the card maker simply ripped off one edge to fit a 6x3 postcard? He or she wouldn't have a paper guillotine or a least a pair of scissors in the shop?"

There was an obvious logic in what he said.

"Maybe Pat ripped off the edge himself."

"Why would he do that?"

"Oh, I don't know," sighed Julie.

She put down the two photos and looked at Des and then at Liam.

"You guys are serious, aren't you? What do you think this is all about?"

"Perhaps something and maybe nothing at all," said Liam, "and anyway it happened a long time ago. It's a bit of a mystery that's all. It's just that I don't think that it's simply a photo of your uncle Pat hanging around some farmyard to get his picture taken. I get the feeling that something happened here."

Julie sat back, poured some tonic into the gin and took a drink.

"So what's your theory?" she said.

"If your uncle saw any active service it would have probably been down in Cork or more likely Kerry. I've been down there. You used the word lush which is quite a good way of describing the countryside in the western parts of Munster. In the glens and valleys it's covered in elm trees, little copses and apple orchards. Pretty much like these," said Liam pointing to the photos.

"Why is that important," said Julie.

"Kerry became the cockpit of the civil war and all sorts of madness and atrocities were committed down there. The majority of the Free State soldiers stationed there were either from Dublin or from the North, and after Michael Collins was assassinated things got a bit out of hand. The Dublin guys idolised Collins and were often not in the mood to take prisoners, especially when the war began to move away from the towns and into the Cork and Kerry mountains. Things were particularly rough round about Tralee."

"I never knew any of this," said Julie. "I always thought the fighting in Ireland was all about the Easter rebellion and the Black and Tans. That's all they seem to sing about as far as I can see."

Liam was silent for a few moments.

"You know, I could have made a fortune composing some of those songs," said Liam shaking his head.

"I call them 'Twis on' songs."

"First of all you start the song with 'T'wis on...' Then you put in the date, for example, 'T'wis on the Twenty First of May...' Next you mention the prevailing weather conditions and where possible, the time of day. Such as 'T'wis on a bright September's morn' or 'T'wis on a cold and wet winter's evening' … although they don't necessarily have to be in that order."

"Now here's a good example"

He burst into song but kept his voice low.

"'T'was on a dreary New Year's Eve, as the shades of night came down"

"See, easy peasy!" he said dramatically.

Both Des and Julie were in fits of giggles by the time he had finished.

"Don't try your theory out in Ireland, Liam," said Julie wiping her eyes.

"No I don't think I would, not unless I was feeling particularly suicidal," he replied smiling. "By the way, don't think I'm picking on my fellow countrymen. I've seen the translations of Polish and Balkan revolution laments. I think there must be some international agreement on these songs - they are all pretty well standard and equally woeful."

Julie sat back for a moment to reflect.

"So you think this photo is connected to an incident of some kind?" she said finally.

"Just a guess. Do you know anything about Pat? Like where he was based during the war, or are there any papers, you know, like army discharge papers that we could find?"

"Not really. Pat was never married and stayed in the old house with his sister Nora. She was the youngest of the McKennas and was married and had a few kids. Nora was Hughie Toner's grandmother."

"Oh I see, I didn't know that was the connection."

"Pat was a bit odd, some people thought he was not right in the head but I always found him kind and pleasant. The man Nora married, Sean Toner, was an absolute rogue. Permanently on the Dole. I don't think he ever did an honest day's work in his life. Always getting involved in whatever skulduggery was going on in that neck of the woods. Selling Poteen and conning old ladies out of bits of old furniture, old grandfather clocks and the like and flogging them to dealers up in Derry. He bullied Pat at every opportunity and used to make fun of our Scottish accents when we were over. My mother hated him with a passion."

She stopped for a moment and turned to Des.

"Come to think of it, I'm surprised that Pat managed to hold on to that store of sovereigns that my mum was on about."

"The way you describe the family, who's to say that he did hold on to them?"

"What sovereigns? What are you talking about?" said Liam.

"Didn't Des mention the gold sovereign that was found on Hughie Toner?"

"Sorry Julie, I hadn't got round to that yet," said Des rummaging around his jacket pocket that he had draped behind him on the chair.

"Mick Hastings said he found a gold sovereign close to Hughie's body," continued Julie, glaring at Des as he continued his search. "It was the same type of sovereign, well, the same year I mean, as the ones my grandfather used to give our family on special occasions. My mother says my grandfather had some sort of roll of them and reckons Uncle Pat had one too."

"Ah! Here it is," said Des.

"I'll take charge of that!" said a relieved Julie snatching the package from Des and handing it over to Liam "I don't trust you, you're always mislaying things. If my mum doesn't get this back, there will be blood on the floor."

"I thought she was quite cool about it," replied Des.

"Don't let that fool you," Julie hissed.

"Anyway, Liam," she continued on a lighter note. "This is what was left of the roll when my grandfather died. Apparently it was found in an old trunk or something."

Liam looked at the wrapper.

"Soarstat Eireann," he said "Irish Free State, must be quite old."

"How's that? Some people still call it the Free State, don't they?" said Julie.

"That's because some people are daft. It hasn't been called the Free State since 1937, when Eamon De Valera decided to rename the country Eire because he thought Ireland was an English word."

"Well, isn't it?"

"No it's not," said Liam patiently. "Ireland is a Viking word like Greenland, Scotland, Poland, Finland, Iceland or even…" he said, "…England. In 1947 the country was renamed as the Republic of Ireland.

"Not," he added with a wave of his finger, "as you'll note, The Irish Republic."

"Since the Good Friday agreement it is known simply as 'Ireland' although if you want to be picky, the football team can still refer to itself as the 'Republic of Ireland' football team to distinguish it from the 'Northern Ireland' football team."

"Seems a lot of carry on just to name a country," said Des.

"I couldn't agree more, however many men and women have died for this 'carry on' as you put it. You could reasonably argue that it was one of the causes of the Civil War."

Liam turned his attention back to the wrapper, opening it out a bit more.

"There's some writing on the inside of the paper. Let's see, I'll try to write it down, wait no need to bother, I can see it now - looks like 'An Roinn Airgeadas'"

"What do you think that means?" said Julie

"Afraid my Gaelic is a bit ropey, but I've heard of "roinn" I think it means cash or money, it also looks kind of official paper, so at a guess it probably means some thing straightforward like the Government Mint or the Treasury - something like that."

"Is that important, or are the coins a red herring? I mean with your story of the photograph and all that," said Julie.

"I don't know. You said that the coin found on Toner was the same year as these, so unless we have a stunning coincidence here, we can assume they both came from the same source. The fact that your uncle Pat appears to also have had a roll of these - and I think we can assume that he had - is quite remarkable."

"Just a minute Liam," said Des "I'm a journalist and I've written about all sorts of strange goings-on and believe me there is always a tendency to try and link things together which are not even connected. To see patterns where none exist. For one thing, the

Toner murderer has been caught. He was a local junkie, absolutely nothing to do with this."

"I know what you mean but I'm not trying to connect them, not in the way you think. Let's go over what we know about these two brothers..."

"Hold on a minute, let me try," said Julie sitting up.

"We know that my grandfather, Charlie, was in the British army during the Great War," she said, "and you reckon he may have made the rank of sergeant, although we have no definite proof of that. My father says that he knows that my grandfather - let's just start calling him Charlie from now on - went to America in 1917 or thereabouts he then seems to have appeared in Cork or County Cork during the war of independence - or so we think. He then seems to have returned to America about 1923. And. according to you, his younger brother Pat must have been in the Free State Army at this time too."

As Julie paused for a moment, Liam leaned forward.

"Can I just stop you there for a moment, Julie?"

He thought for a second, then continued,

"Would you say that Pat and Charlie got on well, I mean, did you ever see any animosity?"

"I would say they seemed to get on fine together," replied Julie, "even if Pat did seem a bit crazy at times. If anything they were almost conspiratorial, you know, they would suddenly stop talking if you walked in to a room unexpectedly and things like that."

"I'll use a bit of guess work here and try to sum up Pat's probable movements as far as the war was concerned," Liam said. "And I'll try to keep it brief. The peace truce was called in June of 1921 and the Free State Army was formed about six months later, at the beginning of 1922, just after the treaty was signed. Fortunately for the Provisional Government, one of the first groups to join up was the Dublin Brigade, mainly, it must be said, due to loyalty to Michael Collins. The Dublin Brigade was battle hardened and one of the best organised units in the country."

He stopped to take a sip of coffee. Des, for a horrible moment, thought that Liam was about to embarrass them again by launching into some obscure song about the adventures of the Dublin Brigade. But thankfully he continued talking.

"By this time the 'old' IRA was swollen enormously in numbers by a sudden influx of 'volunteers' who joined after the war against the forces of the Crown was over. Some people suspect it was a ploy to revel in the glory of being one of 'the boys' without taking much of a risk. Others think it was for simple economic reasons, with the mistaken belief they would automatically be taken into the new Free State Army or get 'called to the barracks' as it was referred to at the time. These Johnnie-come-latelys were sneeringly referred to as the 'Trucelleers' by the old hands. In any event, the Army council of the IRA voted seven to four to support the Provisional Government of the Free State which everyone thought would avoid a conflict. But in a way it was irrelevant, for, from what I can make of it, civil war, seemed to be in the air and almost inevitable. The four opposing staff members walked out and formed the basis of the anti-treaty forces. Even the fact that the Provisional Government and their pro-treaty allies received something like seventy percent of the vote in what was basically a referendum on the treaty, the civil war still broke out. Mind you, the atmosphere wasn't helped by De Valera announcing after the election, the bizarre notion that 'The people don't have the right to be wrong!' How's that for a democratic principle!"

"I didn't know any of this and it all seems terribly complicated," said Julie.

"Yes, I know and I'm sorry if I'm boring you by ranting away. If I sat here all day you would only be hearing half of it and if any other Irishman came in he would probably give you an entirely different version of the same events."

"Anyway," he continued, "I'm just telling you this to give us some sort of time frame for the movements of these guys."

"So what's your conclusion? If you have one," said Julie.

"No conclusions, but a few guesses. I think Charlie played some part at some stage in the war of independence, got involved in the periphery of the civil war on the anti-treaty side and left for the

USA, for some reason, early in 1923 which was several months before the civil war officially ended."

He stopped for a second and stroked his beard, thinking deeply.

"The tie in with Pat on the other hand seems a bit more difficult to fathom. Pat could have joined the army sometime in May or June when the provisional government was recruiting heavily. But would he have joined the 'other side', if I can put it that way, if he knew his brother's position? Possible, of course, and certainly not unique but given their cordial relationship in subsequent years, a bit unlikely. If he was in the National Army and ended up in Cork, he may have taken part in the sea landings around Cork in that August."

"Sea invasions! I thought you gave the impression that the civil war was a minor event on the world stage." said Des.

"It was hardly on a par with the D-day landings but, yes, there were quite a number of seaborne attacks by the National Army where they landed men, field guns and armoured vehicles, quickly, often following up the assault by rapid movements inland. Some historians say the Blitzkrieg tactics were based on military knowledge gained from this period."

He hesitated, "I think that's rather fanciful thinking myself," he added derisively.

"But you're right, as I mentioned on Saturday, the military part of the civil war only lasted about six weeks. It was in the months that followed where the real horror lies."

"My goodness, you make it sound quite terrifying!" said Julie.

"I'm sorry if I seemed to be drifting away from Pat and Charlie but I'm trying to let you see the difficulties involved in them being on opposing sides."

Julie hesitated.

"I know it sounds silly," said Julie, "but to be honest I'm not all that clear who the opposing sides were"

"I'm afraid you're not alone there. Believe it or not some people I know think it was some sort of war between Northern Ireland and the South instead of a vicious fraternal conflict between the Nationalists themselves. Basically the Government side, I mean

135

the Free State Government side, were Pro-Treaty and those against the Anglo-Irish Treaty were obviously Anti-Treaty, the Government referred to the Anti-Treaty forces dismissively as 'the mutineers' or 'the irregulars'. But let's not get bogged down in detail here ..."

He paused for a second.

"I supposed 'bogged down' is a rather unfortunate choice of words considering the subject matter."

"Yes, I suppose it is," Julie laughed.

"You know, maybe Pat didn't even think Charlie was in Cork and assumed he was still in America," she continued.

"Yes, I was coming round to that kind of view myself, it seems the only logical explanation. And yet..."

"You're not convinced," said Julie, finishing her drink.

"I'll need to go," she continued. "I'm going to take a run up to my mother's later on to tell her about the funeral and I want to have a shower first. You can stay on if you like, Des"

"No need," said Liam. "I'm about to go myself."

The three of them walked out together.

"I'll cross the road and catch a bus," said Liam. "Listen, this is all becoming quite intriguing," he added. "I think I'll do a bit of digging in the library and on the Net - find out a bit more. Julie, you could quiz your mum - see if she can remember anything. We could meet up later in the week and have a bit of an update."

"Sounds fine to us," said Julie. "When and where?"

"Come up to the flat on Thursday. We can have a bite to eat."

"It's a date then!" said Des slapping Liam on the shoulder, "...as long as it's not ribs and cabbage!"

CHAPTER FOURTEEN

All Quiet in Tralee

"First thing is finding somewhere to stay," said Charlie, as they stepped from the train. "I don't think there's much in the way of decent hotels in Tralee. Someone told me there are quite a few cheap ones for sailors and the like that pass through the port."

"Why don't we ask the porter or the station master?" said Pat.

"I suppose we'll have to, but I would like to keep our visit as discreet as possible"

Charlie kept walking and continued.

"Don't look now, but see that chap standing over there, beside the newspaper shop, just outside the gate. The one with the grey coat and the soft hat."

Pat gave a guarded glance.

"He looks like a military agent on the look out for visitors. In Dublin we used to call them 'G men' after the G division of the Dublin Metropolitan. He's almost certainly looking out for any strangers coming to town so don't get too excited if he takes an interest in us, or if he follows us for a while."

"He's not exactly hiding the fact, is he?" said Pat, glancing over again.

"No point. Almost everyone would know who he was, so why disguise the fact? Anyway that kind of thing is more about power - to show everyone they are watching you. It's their way of telling everybody that they're in charge."

There couldn't have been more than a dozen passengers getting off at Tralee and they could see that the platforms and general concourse of the station were fairly quiet. Charlie handed the station guard their tickets and walked over to the two porters he spotted standing outside the staff rest room.

"Hi lads!" said Charlie "We're going to be staying up here for a few days. You wouldn't know of a decent hotel around here, would you?"

The G man near the shop lowered his paper and glanced over. The porters looked at Charlie and Pat cautiously.

"The best hotels have been taken over by the army top brass," said the older man, giving the intelligence man a defiant look. "But there are a few lodgings that might take you in for a few nights."

"We'll probably only stay three nights at most. Could we hire your services to take us to one of these places? We've just came up from Cork and been on the go all day - and these bags are getting heavier by the minute."

"Sure, throw your luggage on the barrow. I'll take you down to Kitty Conklin's place. I'm sure she'll have room for you," the porter said. "It'll cost you two shillings for the hire though," he added almost apologetically.

"Sounds okay to me," said Pat, happy to get rid of his heavy kit bag.

As they trundled out of the station and on down to the town square, Charlie knew instinctively that they were being followed. They passed Denny Street on their left - passed the bare plinth where the statue of the Pikeman used to stand before the Tans pulled it down. They walked on for another fifty yards. Charlie was about to ask how much further when the porter turned sharp left.

"Just down here," he shouted as he spun the barrow round.

Charlie took the chance to glance back; the G man was following them about twenty paces behind and not even bothering to disguise the fact. A minute later the porter stopped at a well maintained, fairly large house and rapped the door. A young girl that Charlie assumed to be the housekeeper opened the door almost immediately.

"Ah Sarah! Good afternoon to you, these two gentlemen are looking for a few nights lodgings. I thought Mrs Conklin might oblige."

The housekeeper looked them up and down closely and decided that they were respectable, and more importantly, affluent enough.

"That should be fine. There are a couple of spare rooms available. Please come in, I'm sure you want to speak to Mrs. Conklin about terms."

Charlie handed over two shillings and a sixpence to the porter.

"Have a drink on me and thanks for your help."

The porter took the hire money and the tip gladly, things had been hard going the past few weeks. He gave his thanks, touched his cap and turned back up the road pushing his rattling wheelbarrow in front of him.

They were ushered into a pleasant front room where they were greeted by Mrs Conklin. She was a tall, confident looking woman, with a slight hint of grief around her eyes. Her thick dark hair was tied up with a couple of plain coloured ribbons. The rate, she informed them, was ten shillings a day including dinner. Charlie agreed the terms and asked her if they could extend their stay, if the need arose.

"That should be all right. I have no advance bookings for the rooms you'll be occupying at the moment - what with things being as they are. But let me know your intentions as soon as you can," said Mrs Conklin. "Sarah will show you up to the rooms now and if there is anything you need please, let me know."

The housekeeper led them up the stairs. Charlie was impressed by the size of the house and the rather expensive looking furniture. The rooms they were given were large and airy, and both rooms faced the front and onto the street below. From his window Charlie could see the G man standing on the corner of the street leaning against the wall casually smoking a cigarette. After storing his suitcase in the wardrobe he went next door to see Pat. Pat was standing two or three feet inside the darkened room looking through a space in the curtain.

"Your man looks as if he might stay awhile. I don't think he's seen me, he's hardly even glanced up at these windows so far."

Charlie fiddled with his tie.

"You stay where you are. I'm going out to talk to him."

Pat jumped back from the window.

"Have you gone mad? I thought the idea was to lie low and not be noticed."

"I know, but if he's military intelligence, he probably knows who George Peebles is. If I tell him I know George and would like to get a word to him he'll assume I'm more likely to be friend rather than foe."

"That's a big assumption," said Pat.

"It's a bit of a risk, but we've already been spotted and he might take a closer interest if we are seen to be hanging about Tralee for no apparent reason. If he decides that we have no obvious business here we could be in big trouble. In other words, if we do nothing we might be taking an even bigger risk."

"Yes, you're right, I see what you mean," said Pat. "So what do you want me to do?"

"Not much you can do, just watch from here. If I have to go anywhere with him, try to follow us, but don't try to intervene if anything goes wrong."

"Do you think I should take the revolver?"

"No, that's too dangerous. If you're caught with a concealed weapon they would throw you into the cells without a second thought, anyway what could you do? No, forget carrying a gun. Frankly I'm a bit more worried about the sovereigns. The way things are going around here, if we got turned over I think we could bluff our way through the reason why we are carrying the guns, after all, the country's in chaos at the moment. Explaining the presence of over a thousand pounds in gold sovereigns would be a different proposition altogether."

He paused for a second. The sovereigns would immediately be traced back to the incident at Passage West and the amount of money involved was quite enormous. It also occurred to him that men had been hanged for less recently. He decided not to mention this train of thought to Pat.

"We'll think about that later," he said.

Charlie walked over to the mirror on the wardrobe, straightened his hair and adjusted his tie.

"I'd better go before he decides to go back to the station now that he knows where we're staying."

"Good luck," said a worried looking Pat.

Charlie pulled open the door and made for the stair landing. He walked down the stairs in a leisurely manner, rehearsing his approach to the intelligence agent. As he stepped out onto the street the door locked with a loud click before he suddenly realised he hadn't asked for a key. He continued to walk up the street towards the agent with a polite smile on his face.

"Good afternoon to you, sir!" said Charlie charmingly.

The G man came off the wall, stubbing out his half smoked cigarette on the pavement. He was totally taken aback. It was the first time anyone he had followed or tailed had openly greeted him. Normally they were far too frightened or alarmed to do anything but avoid him at all cost. Charlie knew the chap would be briefly confused so he talked clearly and quickly.

"Since you took the trouble to follow us from the station I must assume you are connected, in some way, to the military command up here." As he spoke Charlie shook his head slightly from side to side and held up his hand palm outward, to indicate that he had no problem with the idea of being followed, and that he understood the agent was only doing his job.

"Don't worry. We've come up from Cork to contact an officer by the name of Peebles, George Peebles. Perhaps you know of him, a large fellow with an American accent."

He stopped briefly to allow the man time to digest this information. He carried on smoothly.

"I know you're too much of a professional to answer me directly but if you could make a discreet inquiry or two I would be grateful. If you could mention to Mr. Peebles that Charlie McKenna would like to meet him and that I'll be staying for two or three days over here." He indicated the house behind him with a casual wave.

"It was a pleasure talking to you," Charlie said half turning. "I was intending to take a walk through the town but I forgot to ask for a damned house key so I'll need to go back. Perhaps we can meet again? Bye for now." With that, he turned and walked back to the house and rapped the door loudly.

Pat was pacing the floor when Charlie walked into the room a couple of minutes later.

"Well, is he still there?"

"No, he's not. He left in a hurry before you even reached the front door. Are we in trouble?"

"Who knows? It depends on how convinced he was by my story but I think he bought it. I asked him to pass on a message to George. I suppose we'll find out soon enough. Anyway I need to go down stairs and organise a key and find out what time they eat around here."

Charlie went downstairs and looked around the ground floor. He had been let in by the housekeeper only a couple of minutes ago and now she was no where to be seen. He was about to put his foot on the stair to go back up, when the front room door opened and Mrs Conklin stepped into the hall.

"Oh, Mr McKenna! Is everything all right?"

"Sorry to disturb you. I was looking for Sarah, the housekeeper. I was wondering if we could have a house key and was about to inquire about mealtimes."

"Perhaps you should come in to the front room and join me for tea. I'll ring down for Sarah from here."

Charlie hesitated. He really should go back upstairs and put his mind to getting the sovereigns located somewhere safe, but to refuse Mrs Conklin's request would seem unmannerly.

"I'd be delighted, of course," said Charlie holding the door open, "after you."

They sat on two large fireside armchairs on either side of a low table with a silver tray full of tea things, including some cakes and biscuits.

"Help yourself to some cake. You'd be doing me a favour. Sarah insists on bringing some up every day. She bakes them herself and they are delicious, but after two years I'm beginning to find them rather a trial."

She pulled out her bag from under the table and poked around inside.

"Here take this key, there are several more downstairs. As for dinner, guests are served next door at seven. Sarah usually rings a bell to let the guests know that it's about to be served, so don't get too worried."

"Thank you," said Charlie pocketing the key. "We may be popping in and out over the next few days."

Mrs Conklin pulled a chord at the side of the fireplace.

"I'll get Sarah to fetch another one for your brother."

She lifted a cup elegantly to her lips and took a sip of tea.

"Have you been in Tralee before?" she inquired.

"Yes, a couple of times on ...er business, but I haven't had much time to look around, perhaps I can see a bit more this time."

"I hope so. Times are..." she hesitated, "...a bit difficult just now."

Again the guarded words, the prying hints and subtle clues, thought Charlie. The verbal dance which you hope can give you some sort of clue about which side the other person is on.

Charlie decided just to play the game and see how things went.

"We've just come up from Cork today. It seems the National Army landed there yesterday morning," he said casually.

"Oh really! You don't sound as if you come from Cork."

"No. My brother and I come from up North - Donegal to be exact. We were down here to collect some equipment for an engineering company I represent. I didn't realise that things were as 'difficult' as you put it, down here."

Mrs Conklin put down her cup.

"The National Army landed in Fenit just over a week ago and took the town in a matter of hours. It appears that the irregulars fled town after trying to burn down the barracks, even so I still wouldn't recommend going into town after dark. There seems to be gun battles every other night."

"I'll bear your advice in mind, Mrs Conklin."

Charlie thought for a moment, trying think of a way of

establishing the whereabouts of Mr. Conklin.

"Is Mr. Conklin's business affected by the…the uncertainty?" he said finally.

She gave Charlie a sharp, pained look.

"There is no Mr. Conklin, he was killed eighteen months ago," she said, "by mistake, or so they told me…"

She hesitated for a second, looked at Charlie trying to gauge his reaction, and then continued.

"He was a senior railway engineer. Got shot in the crossfire when they tried to repair a blown-up piece of track just outside Killarney," she explained.

"I'm sorry to hear that."

"It seems to me IRA and Royal Irish Constabulary became more and more adept at shooting railway workers than they did each other," she added bitterly.

"Yes it's often the bystanders that suffer most," said Charlie tactfully. "However hopefully things might improve from now on."

"Yes," she said, looking into his face for clues, "perhaps."

They were disturbed by a knock on the door. It was Sarah.

"You wanted something, M'am."

"Yes. Would you fetch a spare key for Mr. McKenna? There's a couple in the drawing room table if you have none downstairs."

"Yes, M'am."

Just as Sarah turned there was a rap on the front door. She left the front room door ajar as she went to answer the knock. There was a short, muted exchange before she returned.

"Excuse me. There's a message delivered for Mr. McKenna."

She walked into the room and handed over a folded piece of paper to Charlie, which he opened and read in a few seconds.

"A message from a friend who knows I'm in Tralee," said Charlie smoothly. "I'm afraid I must take leave of you for a while, I must tell my brother."

"Well, it was nice talking to you Mr. McKenna," said Mrs Conklin rising and extending her hand. Charlie shook her hand lightly.

"Thank you for the tea," he said, walking to the door. "I'll see you again."

Sarah pulled the door closed as she left with Charlie.

"I'll bring the other key up to you shortly," she said.

"Thank you. By the way I didn't get a chance to see who brought the note. I was partly expecting a soldier. Did he identify himself by any chance?"

"No, it wasn't a soldier. It was a man wearing a suit and a hat. I think he had a Dublin accent," she said blushing slightly. "A young man, but he didn't leave his name."

"Thank you Sarah. Take your time, there's no rush for the key, I can collect it at dinner and I'll see you then."

He turned and walked up the stairs.

When he entered the room Pat was lying on the bed staring at the ceiling in a reverie.

"I'll read this out to you first then you can have a look," said Charlie.

"Good God! That was a quick reply!" said Pat straightening up.

Charlie smoothed out the note and read it out:

"Charlie McKenna, where the heck have you been?" it says. "What brings you to this part of the world? Unfortunately I may be busy tonight and tomorrow. Come to my office in 27 Denny Street on Friday morning about 10. It's in the old solicitor's office. Bring this letter with you and give it to my secretary.

Regards,

George"

"Here, have a look," Charlie said, throwing the letter on the bed. Pat read it quickly.

"It's on official army paper," said Pat, "that should give us safe conduct."

"You don't know George," said Charlie, sitting down beside the window. "I wouldn't bet on it."

He looked out the widow glancing from side to side to see if anyone was hanging around - no one looked particularly suspicious.

"Dinner's not for a couple of hours yet. Let's get cleaned up and go out for an hour."

***

Charlie returned to his room to get washed, shaved and changed. He rapped on Pat's door fifteen minutes later.

"Let's go," he said.

They walked back to Denny Street to establish George's office; it was at the start of the street surrounded by several similar buildings.

"No wonder the message came so quickly, he's only a minute or two away from our lodgings," said Pat.

They walked the length of a very busy Denny Street, crossed over and walked all the way back.

"Let's walk down to the court house and see if we can find a pub. A drink before dinner would do us no harm... Just mind what you say in there."

They discovered an establishment called Musgrave Brothers, close to the courthouse. They quickly found the public bar and ordered a small jar of stout and two glasses. The bar was almost empty so they could talk quietly and freely.

"I think my nerves are getting bad," said Pat. "I'm not used to all this."

"It'll soon be over. I just want to see George for a while and then we can take the train back to Cork and you can head back north from there if you like. Best bet is to get a steamer to Dublin or even Derry if you can. It's easy enough to get home from Derry."

"Yes, that might be the best bet, although ..." Pat hesitated, "... I'm not sure if I want to go home yet. After all, what's there?"

Charlie looked around and lowered his voice, even although he was unlikely to be overheard.

"Have you lost all your senses? Surely you're not thinking of joining up with the anti-treaty side again."

"Oh no, I'm starting to agree with you. It's rapidly becoming a lost cause. I've read more papers this past day or so than I have for a while. I'm now beginning to think Collins and the rest have a point, maybe it's better to establish an Irish State first and see what happens instead of immediately taking up arms against it because it didn't deliver every dot and comma."

"What about the gold?"

Pat shrugged.

"I'm not really interested in that. It just confuses things."

"Don't be too hasty," said Charlie. "At least keep what you've got in the bank."

"Okay. You've gave me what you've gave me and that's an end of it. The government can take back the rest for all I care."

Charlie leaned back in his chair to think for a minute. Before he joined him down south, only three weeks ago, he had hardly known Pat as an adult; he was, after all, only about nine or ten when he first left for Glasgow. There had been a brief meeting before leaving for America when Pat struck Charlie as a shy and bashful fourteen year old. He had misjudged him, mistaking his quietness for a lack of confidence or a lack of education. He had come to realise over the past few days that Pat was much smarter, better educated and more articulate than he had ever given him credit for.

"Well, if you've made your mind up about the sovereigns, then that's fair enough, but what are you going to do if you don't go back home?"

Pat put his glass on the table and turned to face Charlie.

"I'm going to join the Free State Army," he said.

oooOooo

CHAPTER FIFTEEN

Liam's Mean Abode on Victoria Road

Liam lived in a large handsome sandstone tenement flat overlooking Queen's Park on the South Side. The building had a rather early American look to it. It had a short staircase leading up to the front door - what New Yorkers call a stoop. It even had a miniature statue of libertè perched on the east end of the building. Des and Julie got off the bus at nearby Victoria Road, just at the park gates, and walked round to the tenement entrance and rang up for Liam. Both were slightly out of breath as they climbed the three flights of stairs to the apartment.

Julie was dying to see the flat - her mother had demanded a full report. She had the peculiar prejudice shared by many women including her mother that men are basically hopeless at any kind of housekeeping task, and half hoped her irrational instinct was correct. It was.

"Come into the living room for a few minutes while I get my jacket," announced Liam at the door. He directed them through the large hall and into a room which had a spectacular view over the park. At this time of year the park was overflowing with flowering bushes and shrubs. The late evening sunlight made the towering trees positively glow in a medley of green, brown and bronze. Neat flower beds in every possible geometric shape and colour were dotted around the green open spaces. Not that Julie noticed, her eyes were too busy skimming over the undusted furniture and bizarre bric-a-brac that covered most of the flat surfaces in the apartment. The large coffee table was littered with a mound of newspapers, magazines and badly matched cups, saucers and mugs. An ancient television set sat in the corner. On the mantelpiece above the fireplace stood a gaudy and gilded eighteen inch statue of the 'Child of Prague'. One of the light bulbs on the wall lights on either side of the fireplace was obviously burnt out. Why they were switched on in the first place on such a beautiful sunlight evening was anybody's guess. The only thing that looked well kept and well stocked was a rather magnificent dark oak Victorian bookcase.

"Right, that's me ready," Liam announced as he tottered into the room struggling into a crushed, cream coloured linen jacket.

"I thought you were making us something to eat?" said Des.

"Me, make something to eat?" he said, astounded, as he finally managed to get his arms into the jacket.

"I couldn't cook to save myself, in fact come to think of it," he said, tugging at his beard thoughtfully. "I don't think I've even got an oven."

"Oh come on! Surely you must cook something now and again," said Julie.

"Oh yes! I've got a microwave and a couple of gas rings and I grill the odd steak or hamburger on the whatchamacallit grill, the George Formby thing."

"A George Foreman grill, I think you'll find it's called," said Julie. "When I said we'll have a bite to eat I meant go out for something, not me making it! I've booked a table for us at eight o'clock at the Tapas bar round beside the Vicky Hospital, its only ten minutes from here. My treat, by the way."

Julie was hoping for the grand tour. The kitchen, she decided, would have been of particular interest, but it was not to be as Liam ushered them out the door. Not that he was remotely embarrassed about the flat. It simply never occurred to him that anyone would take the slightest interest in his living arrangements.

They strolled leisurely through the warm sunlit park with the joggers and dog walkers while Julie was busy telling them that she had managed to get a job in the nearby Victoria hospital.

149

"I'm not starting right away. They've still got a bit of work to do in the apothecary but I'm really looking forward to it. I'm getting fed up making up prescriptions for old women and dishing out doses of methadone to half cracked junkies" she said as they came out of the park gate nearest the tapas bar. They crossed the road and entered the restaurant dead on time.

"Good evening Mr. Liam, something to drink perhaps?" said Garcia helping Liam to remove his jacket.

"A bottle of El Muro," gasped Liam, finally flinging the jacket to the floor. "Tinto - and three glasses."

Garcia said nothing as he picked up the jacket and draped it over Liam's chair, a task he was apparently familiar with.

The bottle of wine with three neatly polished glasses appeared instantly and smoothly.

"Now then," Liam said as they all settled down. "What news?"

"Well, my mother almost laughed her head off when I told her of your interpretation of the photo. Said you were always making up stories and you always sound like a plausible rogue - said it was part of your Irish charm."

"I always thought your mother had a rather cynical edge to her," replied Liam haughtily.

"Although my father had an interesting little bit to add to your speculation about the County Kerry thing," she continued. "You know, about it being the main place for activity. Seems old Charlie took my father there once, to the town of Tralee, round about the early fifties or so."

"I remember you telling me he used to go down to the south of Ireland, now and again," said Des.

"It appears that he took my dad and his older brother to Cork for a week's holiday, my dad reckons he was about ten at the time. They stayed in some old fashioned hotel in Cork and then got the train to Tralee. Dad said it seemed to take a long time to get there. They stayed in a guest house somewhere in the centre of the town but the best thing was that they went to a big beach every day. That's why my dad remembers it so well, said they had a great time."

"What would you like to order, Mr. Liam," said Garcia quietly appearing at their table with a menu.

"There are three of us, just make up a dozen tapas, Garcia."

"And don't..." he said quickly, dropping his head and holding up his hand, palm out. "...start reading them all out to us," as Garcia lifted a finger to the top of the menu list. "Just...surprise us."

Des turned up the glasses and poured a large measure for each of them.

Julie took a sip and continued.

"Apparently the guest house they stayed in was enormous and there was an old woman who lived in the upstairs rooms that his dad, Charlie, seemed to know quite well. Anyway, they spent the rest of their holiday there and didn't return to Cork but they got a train to Dublin direct and then a boat back to the Broomielaw in Glasgow. From there they walked back to their old tenement flat in the Gorbals. It seems it wasn't that long a walk. He reckons the whole thing must have made a great impression on him as he remembers it so well."

"Does that add anything to your conspiracy theory, Sherlock?" said Des.

"I'm not finished yet, there is another thing," said Julie.

"What was that?" said Liam

"Dad said that Charlie bought the house in Mount Florida shortly after they returned."

"Nothing odd in that is there?" said Des.

"Don't know about that," said Liam.

He hesitated for a second.

"How much do you think your parent's house is worth?"

"God knows, prices go up and down don't they."

"I'm thinking of relative terms. I've only been in it a couple of times but at a guess it would be at least half a million."

"Probably about that, I don't like to think about it too much, my parents are getting on a bit and it seems a bit ghoulish talking about the value of their property," said Julie beginning to look uncomfortable.

"I agree and I apologise, but my point is that all of a sudden

Charlie buys a big house after returning from Ireland, probably for around £5000 in the early fifties at a guess. And he would have been quite middle aged by then as well."

"You're right, I never thought of it that way. He must have been in his early sixties then. He died when he turned ninety four and that was 1988. I was only..." she glanced at Des and hesitated, "... a very young girl at the time."

Liam drummed his fingers.

"Yes. He would have hardly been in a position to organise a mortgage," he mused.

"Odd place, Tralee," he continued. "I went there once. We were touring round the west coast and a friend of ours wanted to see Dingle bay. Apparently it was where they shot the movie 'Ryan's Daughter' in the late sixties."

"A long and rather tedious film, if I remember it right," said Des.

"I thought it was quite romantic!" countered Julie.

"Anyway," Liam said irritated by their interruptions, "that's hardly the point. We spent a day and a night there, in Tralee I mean, very quiet, about 20,000 of a population. About the same size as Newquay in Cornwall. With the same sort of a seaside atmosphere about the place."

"What's odd about that?" said Julie as the first of the tapas arrived.

"It became a kind of Gaza Strip of its day. An incident happened a few days after a young Irish boy, Kevin Barry, was hanged by the authorities in Mountjoy prison."

He started to sing.

"Just a lad of eighteen summers that...

"Please Liam, for God sake! Not in here ..." hissed Des, looking around.

"Ha, got you there!" said Liam wagging his finger at Des. "You don't think I'm that mad do you! You thought I was going to sing the whole song."

"You are mad!" said Des. "Carry on anyway."

"There's an interesting little story about Mr. Barry, which I'll tell you later, if can remember it," Liam said, scratching his beard and cocking his head in reflection.

"Try one of those," he said suddenly, pointing to a ramekin of cooked potatoes with a thick sauce dip in a smaller dish at the side that had just arrived.

"Spanish patatas bravas, it goes to show you that it's not just the Irish that can create something with the humble spud."

"Where was I? Oh yes! The hanging. Needless to say there was widespread international condemnation at the hanging of such a young boy, and of course, his case was helped by the fact he was not just any old riff raff, but a middle class medical student. Anyway a couple of days of riot and mayhem followed all over Ireland. In the middle of the confusion some of the local Tralee brigade captured a couple of RIC men in the late afternoon, intending to hold them hostage for a few hours. There was a gas works in Tralee at the time. Town gas is created by burning coal at a high temperature in a large oven, giving off gas and making the coal into coke. Sometime in the early hours of the morning the two RIC men were bound up and thrown into the oven - alive." There was a stunned silence.

"Oh my God!" whispered Julie holding her hand to her mouth. "That's unbelievable, how could anyone do that to a fellow human being."

"Thereby lies the problem of any war. Did they do it? Was it true? Or was it simply an atrocity story put about by the authorities to cover up the subsequent rampaging and destruction in Tralee by the local RIC reserve force, or the Black and Tans as they were better known as? According to foreign press reports they laid siege to the town for two weeks and almost starved the entire population to death. Tralee was on the front page of the New York Times for three days."

"Isn't it odd?" said Des "You can go through the archives of any paper reporting a guerrilla war and the same kind of horror stories always appear and they are always committed by the other side. What do you think?"

"The problem was the two men were obviously killed, but their bodies were never found. The local brigade originally claimed the two men were Black and Tans, but they weren't, they were regular RIC policemen who surrendered immediately when confronted by the gunmen. One of them was an Irishman from Galway. Even to this day the whole Tralee episode is shrouded in silence and speculation. Anyway, regardless who did what and why, the point I'm trying to make is this. If you go there now you simply see a sleepy and rather attractive tourist town but in the early twenties it must have been like downtown Beirut. That's why it's interesting that Charlie may have been there and even more interesting that Pat, apparently in the Free State Army, may have also have been there."

He paused to catch his breath, and looked at the table covered in dishes

"Just a minute!" he roared "Garcia, another bottle of wine. Let's get eatin' and a drinkin' here!"

***

"Well done Liam," said Des, dabbing at his mouth. "That was excellent. Couldn't find better in the centre of town."

"Yes sir, and thirsty work too. Garcia, bring us a few of your best Spanish beers."

"Now then, I was talking about Kerry during the Civil War," said Liam as Garcia appeared almost instantly with beers and glasses. "Ah for Gods sake!" he shouted, slapping his head. "Torta de Manzanas! How could I've forgotten about them? Garcia, bring us three portions please, and bring us some carajillos when you serve them, there's a good chap"

Liam pushed aside the last empty ramekins of salted cod and leek. "As I mentioned earlier Kerry was the Beirut of its day and I've yet to hear a plausible explanation for it."

"I'm not sure I follow you when you compare it to Beirut," said Julie.

"Well to be honest, I don't know if that's the right analogy either. It was certainly the place where the bitterest and bloodiest fighting took place during the civil war. Some would argue that the National Army, which in Kerry consisted mostly of Dubliners

154

or Northerners, acted more like an army of occupation than a unifying force of fellow countrymen. They, the army that is, were also used as a kind of police force," he paused and shook his head. "Always a bad idea if you ask me, particularly when you had a period of virtual anarchy in the county."

"What do you mean 'virtual anarchy'," said Julie.

"Well if you think about it, common civil law and order simply ceased to exist. There was no policing and courts of law had become almost unworkable. The local militia dealt out rough and ready justice when required. Summary executions for suspected spying, alleged consorting or working with the enemy took on almost epidemic proportions. They reckoned the IRA killed three times as many Irishmen as they did British around the Kerry and Cork area, and that's not including policemen, many of whom were Irish themselves."

"Strange things happen in wars, you know that," said Des.

"You're right, of course, and I'm not trying to place blame or excuse anyone. I'm just pointing out that at that time, this was an extremely dangerous place to be."

"So back to Charlie and Pat," said Julie.

"It's more Pat than Charlie I'm thinking about," said Liam.

"For six months after the National army took over Kerry," he continued, "attacks and ambushes against them took place on almost a daily basis. Scores of soldiers were killed. They in turn took revenge and it became almost a tit-for-tat war. As it escalated, the atrocities became more commonplace. Round about March of 1923 several terrible events take place which more or less brought about the culmination of the war."

"This would have been after Charlie had left for America," Julie pointed out.

"If your dad's research is correct, and I've no doubt that it is. Then you're right, Charlie would not have been there. But Pat probably was."

"Sorry Liam, carry on," said Julie.

"Throughout the conflict the anti-treaty men had always used road blocks as a tactic," continued Liam, "either to hold up pursuing patrols or as part of a direct ambush ploy. It became almost a ritualised form of warfare. The army would be pelting down some rural lane when they would spot the barricade, they would leap from their vehicles, take up position and start firing. The opposition side would then return fire with the same intensity and so the battle would start. These engagements often lasted for hours, often without a single injury, and very often finishing only when it started to get too dark to see one another."

"Good man, Garcia!" he shouted as Garcia tried to quietly slip three portions of apple pie on to the table.

"Julie, try this with coffee and brandy, fantastic," he said taking a cartoon sized bite of pie with a gulp of carajillo. He munched for few moments, sighed contently, brushed away the crumbs from his beard and continued.

"Trouble with the anti-treaty forces was that they were rapidly losing sympathy among the populace. For many years the ordinary people recognised that the main cause for injustice in Western Ireland was absentee landlords and a worthless crew of landed gentry propped up by a corrupt court system and a partisan police force, the IRC or the 'Peelers' as they used to call them down there."

"...and the British Army," added Julie

"Not to the extent that some would have us believe, in fact the first British soldier to die in Dublin after the Easter rising, nearly five years earlier, was at the hands of our old friend, Kevin Barry. No, the main enemy of the rebels was not the British army but the RIC, although really it's a bit of a mistake to regard them as a police constabulary, they were a bit more like a gendarmerie. But with the RIC disbanded and the British army sent back to dear old Blighty, the locals thought they had won."

Des butted in.

"I'm being a bit of a devil's advocate here, but I suppose the anti-treaty side would say there was no Republic created so they had still to fight on," he said.

"Yes, but against whom? And you're making a mistake when you think republicanism is synonymous with nationalism - perhaps it is now to some extent, but what many nationalists back then wanted was an independent state first of all. How it was governed was largely irrelevant. Arthur Griffith, the founder of Sinn Fein, no less, was a fervent monarchist. His idea was to have a dual monarchy. Rory O'Connor the most ardent anti-treaty of them all seemed to think, amongst many others I may add, that an army takeover would be just the very dab. Why he should have thought a military dictatorship had the same principles as a democratic republic certainly beats me. Anyway we're drifting away from Charlie and Uncle Pat again."

"No surprises there, then!" said Julie lifting up her glass. "By the way, these carajillos are excellent…"

Outside the bar, the light had faded and darkness was settling in. Garcia started to light small candles around the tables, casting dark shadows on the walls.

"Garcia," roared Liam "Another three carajillos for the road."

"Talking about roads," he continued. "Do you remember I mentioned the road blocks?"

"Yes, you mentioned them before you started ranting and raving about nationalism and republicanism and how the anti-treaty side were losing sympathy," said Julie

"Ah!" said Liam, forming his hands into ball. "It's all connected, as we shall see!"

"By the end of the winter of 1922-23, between one thing and another, the anti-treaty guys seemed to be getting more desperate. In early March they started to put hidden mines inside the barricades and arms dumps."

"You mean, like booby traps?" said Des

"Yes, that sort of thing. Around the beginning of March, I'm not too sure of the dates, I haven't completed the research yet, an arms dump was mined and several officers and men of the Free State Army were killed. In revenge, men from the Ballymullen barracks took nine prisoners from the cells, took them to a place called Ballyseedy Crossroads, tied them to a mine and blew them up."

"My God that's awful! Were they all killed?" said Des.

"Not all, one survived to tell the tale. The rest were blown to bits."

"Just a minute, Liam! You're not suggesting that Uncle Pat had something to do with this, are you?" said Julie.

"Just a thought," said Liam waving his hands airily. "Just speculating that's all."

"You are mad, Liam," said Des with a chuckle. "All this from one old photo! Good story though, I like it."

"It's all right for you, Pat's not your uncle," replied Julie.

"Oh for God's sake! He's not your uncle, he's your great uncle. And anyway, it all happened almost a hundred years ago. So don't get too upset about it all."

"That's true, I suppose," she sighed.

"I don't know why I listen to you, Liam Tracey," she continued half angry, half amused. "You're always telling daft Irish stories. I should know better by now."

"Remember Kevin Barry?" asked Liam

"Please, not another song!" wailed Julie.

"Oh no, a true account. Honest!"

He lent back in his chair and took a sip of his drink.

"Young Kevin Barry was due to be hung on the first of November, which…" he said, raising an eyebrow, and looking from Des to Julie, "…we all know is All Saints Day."

"He was held in Mountjoy Prison in Dublin. It was an old prison, in fact, it was an old ex-military prison. Michael Collins and the Dublin Brigade had spent weeks planning a break out and to have the maximum propaganda impact it was planned for the night before Barry's execution. Just as the attack was about to take place, hundreds and hundreds of Dublin women suddenly turned up for a night time vigil and started to walk round the perimeter walls praying loudly and carrying candles. The attack was compromised and had to be called off. Needless to say, the good women of Dublin were hoping the 'power of prayer' would bring about the release of Kevin Barry, when it was, in fact, the 'power of prayer' that done him in! So the next time some clergy talks about the mysterious 'power of prayer', tell him to explain the irony of that story."

Julie groaned good-heartedly "Let's call it a day at that, shall we?"

Liam insisted on paying the entire bill, despite protestations from both Des and Julie, figuring that he owed them a small fortune from the frequent doss downs and overnight stays he had at their flat over the years.

They stopped outside the tapas bar for a few minutes as Liam started his perennial battle with the linen jacket.

Julie looked around casually.

"Here! I just noticed, Des. We could get the bus from that stop up there," said Julie

"Come on, I'll walk you down to the stop outside my door it's only five minutes," replied Liam turning away. " I've just remembered a song about Rory O'Connor, it's got a great line in it. He started singing "You murdered our dear Rory. Your hands are all gory..."

"There's a bus, Julie!" shouted Des over his shoulder. "Start running!"

oooOooo

CHAPTER SIXTEEN

George Peebles

They spent most of the next day resting up and wandering around the town. Later they bought papers and some news magazines and took them back to their rooms where they relaxed, read and occasionally nodded off. As the evening mealtime approached, Charlie heard a quiet knock on the door. He opened it, expecting Pat and was surprised to see Sarah standing there.

"Mrs Conklin was wondering if you could see her for a few minutes if you have time to spare."

"Of course, I'll come down now, give me a moment," he replied. Leaving the door ajar, he went to the mirror, ran his fingers through his hair and adjusted his tie. He looked a bit embarrassed when he returned.

"Oh don't worry, you look fine," said Sarah with a smile.

Charlie followed her down stairs and into the front room.

"Thanks Sarah," said Mrs Conklin. "Could you close the door on your way out?"

Turning to Charlie she waved at the armchairs.

"Have a seat Mr. McKenna. I was going to ask you down earlier but I thought I'd save you the penance of Sarah's baking."

"I thought her cake was first class," said Charlie gallantly, taking a seat.

Mrs. Conklin smiled.

"I'll convey your appreciation."

She hesitated for a few moments.

"I know we agreed terms when you arrived, Mr. McKenna, and please don't take this the wrong way, but I was wondering, that is, if you intended staying for several days, if you could perhaps pay something in advance?"

"Yes of course...." started Charlie.

She held up her hand to stop him rushing on.

"It just that my local bank was apparently 'liberated' by some of the irregulars some days ago, and cash is in somewhat short supply. Don't worry. I'm quite willing to let you stay even if you don't have immediate funds. I just thought you might be in the position to pay an advance having just come up from Cork."

Charlie was both amused and taken by her confident approach to a subject that most people in her situation would have found difficult and perhaps embarrassing.

"You're right, and if I may say so, very perceptive, Mrs Conklin," he said, sitting back in the armchair. "I do have some funds available. How much do you need?"

"Just a few pounds, the bank manager assures me that cash will be sent over from Limerick for Monday morning."

Charlie put his hand into his pocket and pulled out some sovereigns and notes.

"Five pounds enough? I can give you it in coins if you like - sovereigns."

"That's more than enough. To be honest, it's Sarah I was thinking of more than anything else. The way things are, I always like to pay her weekly if I can. You're being very obliging," she said as Charlie handed over the money.

Mrs Conklin held the five coins in the palm of her hand.

"Isn't it odd how sovereigns seem to be much more common these days? When I was young they were a rarity, now they seem to be everywhere. Sign of the times, I suppose."

She held one up to the light.

"These look rather new, Mr McKenna."

"Not so much new as unused, I only er... acquired them a couple of days ago. And you're right they are quite common these days."

Charlie sat thinking for a moment while Mrs. Conklin turned the coins over to look at the dates before she poured out some tea.

"All the same date as well, I see."

"All part of the same bank consignment you'll find," said Charlie with a smile.

"I was wondering…." he continued.

He leaned forward and started again.

"I think I told you," he said, "that I represent an engineering company from up North. My brother Pat and I came down to collect cash for equipment we had supplied to a company in Cork. On the way down through Tipperary and County Cork we were stopped several times by the irregulars, they didn't threaten us or take anything, presumably because we had nothing of value, but it did not look too good for a return journey."

He stopped to take a sip of tea.

"After completing our business in Cork we found ourselves carrying a fair amount of cash and some other items of value. Frankly I was a bit worried about the money being 'liberated', as you so finely put it, on the journey back. So we decided to get the car garaged with one of our associates in Cork for a while, and decided on an alternative method of getting back up North."

Charlie paused for a moment.

"It was suggested that we travel by train up here to Tralee and hopefully obtain passage on a ship from around here to get us up North, but that may take some time. Ideally I would like to put the money somewhere secure, perhaps you could help me out. Do you have a strongbox or a safe in the house?"

"My word! Isn't that's the oddest thing," she replied, standing up. She walked over to the corner of the room to a large sideboard.

"My husband often had to keep money in the house to pay subcontractors and wages for the men. The railway company supplied him with this."

She opened the right hand side door of the sideboard to reveal a small but substantial combination safe.

"The other side is a just a normal cupboard space. Would this be of any use?"

***

On Friday morning Charlie and Pat had a leisurely breakfast around nine o'clock. They had wisely decided on an early night last night and had slept well and, despite Mrs. Conklin's warnings of late night disturbances, all had passed quietly.

"Do you want me to see George Peebles as well?" asked Pat as they turned into Denny Street.

"I've been thinking about that," said Charlie. "It might be better if we left that to tomorrow, I think we'll need to weigh things up after I speak to George."

Charlie slowed down and took out his pocket watch and snapped it open.

"It's quarter to ten now, plenty of time."

He was about to put it away when he impulsively handed over the watch to Pat.

"Here, take this. You have no means of telling the time."

"Don't worry." he continued as Pat protested. "I'll buy a small wrist watch in town for myself later on. I'll meet you in Musgrave's for lunch about one o'clock."

They were almost outside the office by now.

"You should take a walk down to the sea. It's quite a sight at this time of day. You can easily walk there in less than an half an hour, just head down this street and you'll come to the Dingle Road, and from there you should see a sign for a town called Lohercannon. The beach is not far from there. See you later."

Pat said goodbye and good luck and walked on. Charlie continued into George's office.

There was a handwritten notice on the office door in remarkably intricate Gaelic writing, almost a work of art, which he could just about translate as:

'Office of the National Free State Army – Kerry Command'

He turned the handle and walked in.

A smartly dressed subaltern stood up from behind a desk and addressed him.

"Who art thou?" he said in Gaelic.

Charlie almost laughed until he saw the stern look on the young man's face.

"Hast thou an appointment?"

Charlie realised that the officer was not a native Gaelic speaker but had learned the language from some old book or other - it was the language and diction used by medieval scholars.

"I'm afraid," he said carefully and in English. "My Gaelic is not up to your high standard. Er...could we use English for a few moments?"

"If thou must," he replied with a final flourish.

"I'm quite capable of speaking the language of the foreign oppressor," he announced pompously and with a broad Belfast accent.

Charlie handed over the note.

"I've a meeting with George Peebles at Ten."

"Lieutenant Colonel Peebles you mean," he snapped.

"Sorry, Lieutenant Colonel Peebles."

"I'll see if he is available, and your name is..." He looked at the paper again, "...Mr. McKenna."

He turned into a corridor and went upstairs, apparently to another office, returning in a few moments.

"He'll see you in five minutes," he said formally, and sat down behind his desk. He picked up a pen and started flicking through a pile of folders making the occasional note.

There were a couple of minutes of uncomfortable silence, with the loud ticking of the clock on the wall making the silence even more oppressive.

Charlie coughed.

"Sounds as if you come from Belfast," he said eventually.

The officer glanced up.

"I've been to Belfast a few times, nice place," said Charlie.

The clock ticked on.

"I went to see a football match there once," he continued gamely. "Glentoran I think the team was called."

The subaltern looked at Charlie with a raised eyebrow.

"I'm afraid," he said with distain. "I do not watch barrack room games."

Just at that, George Peebles burst through the door.

"Charlie McKenna!" he cried, grabbing him round the shoulders. "How the hell are you!"

He spun him round and looked at him affectionately.

"You've changed, by God, That's what, a year and a half? Come on upstairs, we have plenty to talk about!"

The officer had stood up stiffly by this time.

"No visitors for an hour Mr. Devlin," George said as he walked to the door leading to the corridor.

"What if…"

"Please, Mr. Devlin, emergencies only, feel free to deal with anything else yourself."

They tramped along a wide corridor to an open staircase; George bounded up the stairs two at a time and opened the door to a large well appointed office over looking Denny Street.

"Have a seat, Charlie," said George, indicating a well upholstered Chesterfield.

He went round the desk, pulled out a bottle of Bushmills from a drawer, then moved over to the sideboard and selected two cut glasses. George poured two generous measures, gave one to Charlie and returned to the other side of the desk. He poured a measure of water into his own glass from a water jug and slid the jug over the table to Charlie. Charlie poured in a splash of water.

"Slainte!" said Charlie, taking a sip.

He rubbed his hands along the smooth leather armrest of the chair. "Big improvement from the Mill Street office, George."

"Yes indeed! But not better times I'm afraid. Now tell me what happened. We were all worried sick about you. The last we heard you had been lifted by the 'Peelers' as the guys round here insist on calling them, and got locked up in Cork City Gaol."

Charlie looked at his glass.

"That seems a long time ago," he said. "A lot has happened since then."

"Like what?" said George sardonically. "That bad you can't write or send a cable?"

"I got sprung from the Gaol by the local brigade. Not that they were trying to specifically rescue me. They attacked the prison with mortars and machine guns, there were dozens of them involved. I managed to get out in the general mêlée and found myself hiding out in South Tipperary with a price on my head for the next four months."

"Reward money for you! You weren't exactly a flying column leader, how come?"

"Usual confusion, I had a British passport with US, French and Belgian visas, I also had over two hundred dollars in cash. Their first assumption was that I was high up in the organisation. However, they half believed my story about being a dealer in mining equipment but when I escaped, they naturally assumed I was guilty."

"Why did you take part in the escape?"

"I was rushed out along with the rest. What the hell was I supposed to do? These guys were armed to the teeth. I could hardly say 'Sorry chaps! Big mistake! I'm not really part of the gang, you know. I think I'll just head back to the prison'. I just had to go along with them."

"Okay, I take your point," muttered George.

"In the meantime the local brigade also thought I was some sort of undercover big noise and put me in charge of their so called Engineering Battalion."

"Engineering Battalion? What the heck did they do?" asked George.

"Blew things up. Which is the exact opposite of engineering, I'd have thought. But..." he shrugged his shoulders. "...who's to argue about titles?"

He stopped for another sip.

"I managed to get in touch with Harry Boland eventually and we got your last consignment of gun parts and ammo from that warehouse in Cork. That was about this time last year."

"Yes I know, and I haven't been paid for that yet. I laid out a fortune for that deal!" said George.

"Oh yes, I forgot that the world spins around your financial arrangements, George," said Charlie with a smile. "I think this time you might find difficulty in getting paid."

"I've thought about that, it's one of the reasons I joined up. A couple of months ago the word was put about that the National Army was desperate for officers with some combat experience." He waved his hand vaguely.

"Of course, they took up my offer at once."

He hesitated.

"As for poor Harry ...." he let the words drift away with a shake of his head.

"This sounds like bad news, George. What about Harry?"

"Didn't you hear? He was gunned down up in Skerries, got involved in a gun fight with a National Army patrol sent to arrest him. He survived the shot but then died a few days later. It was only about two weeks ago, about the same time we landed at Fenit."

Charlie drummed his fingers on the leather and looked up to the ceiling, almost but not quite, visibly upset.

"One of the reasons I originally threw my lot in with the anti-treaty side was because of Harry," he said eventually. "That and loyalty to the guys I commanded and worked with - this whole business is insane!"

"Of course it is! Almost all of the Irish American organisations have came out in favour of the Free State. Most see the civil war as an embarrassment. Give the Irish a bit of freedom, the next minute they're at each others throats. That's the way some papers back home have put it. Some of the anti-treaty factions are demanding a thirty two county republic which will be 'Catholic, Gaelic and Celtic'. Not exactly the words that some people up North in our neck of the woods would be happy with. Including a few relatives of mine I might add."

"Don't you think that partition was a too high price to pay?"

"It's possibly a high enough price but not exactly one to create the mayhem and murder that's happening down here," said George beginning to raise his voice.

He leaned over the desk.

"Listen Charlie, I had to interrogate some of the prisoners we caught here about a week ago. They are not all as clued up or as politically aware as you think they are. They talk about a Republic and partition of the North, but if you pressed them, most of them couldn't even point in the direction of North. In fact, some would have been even hard pressed to count to thirty two. Their aim was to get what they regarded as forces of the crown out of Ireland. After that, how Ireland was governed was largely irrelevant. They weren't even all that enthused by a Republic. They could have been governed by a king for all they cared - although we must assume they mean someone Irish, someone of the stamp of Brian Boru, if he could be brought back to life. A lot of these guys are being led up the garden path by some politicians who should know better."

"I'm not convinced that they are all that gullible," said Charlie.

"I'm not saying they are gullible!" said George, now irritated. "I've been involved in a few barneys in my day, they are not always what they seem. The Spanish American War was deliberately started by the Americans as a blatant land grab and was somehow made out to have been started by those undependable, treacherous, warmongering Spaniards by the Hearst controlled newspapers in the States. A blatant lie that the great American public swallowed hook, line and sinker. I could give you more examples, but it'll get us nowhere."

Charlie stood up and walked over to the window. George's surprising conversion to the Free State cause took him a bit by surprise, mainly because he thought George was incapable of that depth of feeling about anything - anything, that is, that he didn't have a financial interest in.

He made up his mind to hold fire on any mention of the sovereigns to George for the time being.

"How are things back in the US," he said finally.

"Nothing great," said George calming down a bit. "Since prohibition those crazy Eye-talians are virtually running New York these days. Those politicians must be clean out of their minds to ban liquor stateside. If you think it's dangerous here you ought to try walking around Manhattan after dark... Manny O'Donnell is doing well on the West Side but it's like Dodge City up there these days, I try to keep out of it if I can. Anyway, my construction business is running a lot smoother now that I've managed to get some city contracts in Philly."

He lit a cheroot.

"My commission here is short. I only signed up for four months so I hope to get back in a couple of weeks time. That's if I can get this payment business squared up, damn nuisance, that it is."

"How are you going to get paid? The stuff went to Harry Boland's anti-treaty men, they're hardly likely to pay you now, the way things are."

"I still have the bill of exchange and it's signed on behalf of the Provisional Irish Government. Now, if I could get a copy of the receipt from the warehouse…"

He hesitated and looked at Charlie slyly.

"With the bill of exchange and a receipt I'm pretty sure I could hire a Dublin lawyer and get paid by the present government."

"Surely you don't expect me …."

George jumped up.

"I'll give you a straight 10 percent," he said quickly. "Anyway it should be money for old rope to you. You must have loads of contacts in Cork."

"I'm just up from there. The place must be a battlefield by now."

"Are you kidding?" George said "I've just heard that, apart from a skirmish near a place called Douglas, Dalton took Cork with hardly a shot being fired. The irregulars seemed to have perfected their war tactics, which seems to be capture the barracks, come out of the barracks and fire a few shots, retreat to the barracks, set fire to the barracks and then bugger off."

"So what do you think?" he continued.

"I suppose… let me think about it," said Charlie.

He returned to his whiskey and his seat.

"There's something that you could do for me."

"What's that?" said George cagily, expecting something that would cost him money.

"My younger brother Pat came down here a while back, mainly for the excitement I suppose. I've worked with him for a few weeks now. He's a dependable lad. He now reckons he would like to throw his lot in with your guys. What do you think?"

"That's not a problem," said George. "The recruiting sergeant's desperate for volunteers. I'll take care of it when you're down in Cork."

"Hold on I only said I'd think about it. I've no intention of rushing back to Cork. Let's leave it a few days. Let's say I go down there this time next week. I need a rest, George."

"I wasn't expecting you to dash off right away! Give me some credit. Next week should be fine. It might give me a bit of time to clear up a few things here anyway. I'll get the paperwork sorted out for Pat as well."

"I'll need to leave you shortly," said Charlie finishing his drink. "Which bank are you using these days? I didn't see a Provincial around here."

"Walk round to the parade, there's one about half way down. You can't miss it. The manager's a young chap called Eamonn Aherne, tell him you know me."

"By God, George, you can get around! You've hardly been here more than a week and you know the local bank manager."

"You know me Charlie, you never know when a financial investment is going to come a knockin'. How's about I'll organise some dinner and a few drinks next week sometime. I can't give an exact day right now as things can get a little crazy around here at times."

"Sounds okay," said Charlie.

"I'll get somebody to bring a message to you after the weekend. There's a market day in town tomorrow. The first since we arrived, I'm just hoping that it doesn't turn into a gunfight before the day is over."

"My landlady mentioned a few nights of gunfire recently, what's the problem? I thought all the irregulars had left."

"It seems there are still a few hot heads around - and plenty of guns. These guys are pretty accustomed to no Law being around, so firing off a few volleys at the local barracks is what passes for entertainment in these parts. Part of the problem is that our men are almost all outsiders, mainly from the Dublin Brigade. But even the battalion that came over to our side from County Clare are considered foreigners by the locals - and they come from just across the water. Hopefully things should get a bit quieter now that Cork has gone, that was their last big town."

"Don't know if I would take a bet on that George. In my opinion, when you've been fighting as long as these guys it gets a bit hard to put the guns away."

"We'll see," said George draining his glass.

Charlie thanked him, walked to the door and turned.

"By the way, who's that stuck up pompous ass you've managed to get as a secretary?"

"Oh him! Stephen Devlin. Or 'Stiofan Ó Doibhilin', as he likes to call himself these days. One of a rake of guys who were invited down from Belfast to join the National Army in the Curragh a few months ago."

He continued to talk as they walked to the top of the stairs.

"He one of your 'Gaelic, Celtic and Catholic' brigade. Thinks the locals are a bunch of unsophisticated yahoos. Probably end up with a bullet in the back of his head if he's not careful."

"Yes, I've met a few like that in my time. The ideal Irishman. "Plus royaliste que la roi'" replied Charlie "...more Royal than the King."

George looked at Charlie curiously for a second.

"Charlie!" he said suddenly enlightened. He slapped Charlie on the back and laughed.

"Now don't you start trying to bamboozle me with your Gaelic. You know that I can speak more Crow Injin than Gaelic."

"It's not Gaelic it's ....Ah! Never mind. See you next week sometime," said Charlie trotting down the stairs.

***

He was bit early for his meeting with Pat. With nearly an hour to kill, he wandered round to the Provincial Bank and made an appointment to see the manager on the Monday morning. That done, he walked up to the courthouse and stood around admiring

171

the statues and the cannons until he noticed Pat entering the nearby Musgrave's Bar.

"A pint for me as well," he said to him as Pat was ordering at the bar.

"And did you enjoy the walk?"

"Grand! As you said, Tralee Bay is a fine sight at this time of day." He took the drinks over to an empty table.

"So, how was George Peebles? Was he glad to see you?"

"Yes, well at least, I think he was. Sometimes George thinks so far ahead where money is concerned, that it's hard to tell what he's thinking."

"Did you tell him about the gold?" said Pat quietly, looking round the bar.

"No. Not yet. I'll need to think that over. It's a bit odd, but George seems to have found a sudden enthusiasm for the Free State."

"Maybe he's seen the sense of it."

"Perhaps, Pat. But George..."

He hesitated.

"It doesn't matter. It's unlikely, but he just might take exception to the source of the gold. I can't take the chance."

Charlie rubbed the back of his neck.

"Anyway, he said there will be no problem if you're still keen on enlisting. I'm going to meet him next week. He wants me to go down to Cork to do a bit of business for him."

"My God, he wasn't long getting you back into the harness, was he?" said Pat.

Charlie laughed.

"That's a good way of putting it, Pat. I never thought of it that way. But I've been thinking it over this past hour. It might be that going back to Cork might suit me."

"I've said that I'm not bothered about the money. You can keep the rest of the gold, it'll only bring bad luck in the end," said Pat without rancour.

"I don't believe in that old rubbish," said Charlie. "Funny, when millionaires and landlords come into money, they don't start on about it bringing bad luck."

"Anyway," he continued, "I'm not going to argue about it. You've made up your mind and that's fine with me. But I'd like to put some more money in your account, not just for yourself, but for the family when you get back there. I'll make arrangements later."

"Okay," said Pat. "That sounds fair enough, let's leave it at that."

oooOooo

CHAPTER SEVENTEEN

A Quick Return to Cork

After the weekend Charlie decided to go to Cork alone. It was a safe bet that Officer Simon Barrett would now be turning every stone to find him and he considered that things could go badly wrong if he was somehow recognised.

The newspapers were in turmoil on Monday morning after the death of President Arthur Griffith who died of a stroke at the weekend. According to George Peebles, whose flair for the dramatic came to the fore, Griffith loudly cursed De Valera with his dying breath.

Pat persisted and, against Charlie's wiser council, had joined up as a volunteer in the Free State Army and was due at Balleymullen barracks at the end of August. In the meantime he was quite content to stay at Mrs. Conklin's till Charlie came back from Cork. Round at the Kerry Command office, George was in an excitable mood.

"This here is the Bill of Exchange," he said, holding up and pointing to an elaborate document. "For God's sake don't lose it!"

"I won't," replied Charlie dryly, slipping it into his brief case. "The trouble is tracking down the receipt - unless they're willing to give me a copy."

"A copy will do fine. I've talked to that young officer - name of Connelly - who has a Law Degree. Says his father has a practice in Temple Bar and will set it up if I can get to Dublin as soon as possible. So don't be hanging around Cork for too long."

"Hanging around Cork? Nice choice of words, George."

"What?"

"Never mind. I'm going to leave early on Friday. I want to make arrangements to see Isaac Cohen first thing Monday morning."

"Good man, expect you back on Tuesday then."

"About this ten percent …"

"Five percent when you come back with the copy of the receipt. And the other five percent when we hit pay dirt in Dublin."

"In dollars - cash?"

"Of course, what else?" said George.

That Friday Charlie prepared himself for the journey, first to Mallow and then on to Cork. He decided not to take the Webley, even although the carrying of a gun was almost 'de rigueur' in this part of the country. There was no point in bringing attention to himself at this stage. According to George, Lynch had abandoned Fermoy and had ordered his remaining men to start operating from the hills. He informed him that National Army soldiers were now trying to watch all trains around Cork, Tipperary and Kerry. Charlie travelled light. He took a small valise and his brief case. Sarah insisted in supplying him with a parcel of sandwiches and sliced cake for the journey.

He reached Mallow at about two o'clock, slightly late, but without any incident or without any signs of activity in the surrounding countryside. The station was fairly busy with plenty of National Army soldiers and some pretty obvious state intelligence agents hanging around. The soldiers greeted the passengers with courtesy and helped some of the elderly off with their bags and luggage - but it all had the look of an extensive public relations operation.

Charlie knew the time of the next train to Cork was scheduled for half past two; all he had to do was find out the platform number. The main information board was outside on the wall of the front of the booking office. This gave him an opportunity to get around at least part of the town. It was different from last week. No bands of ragged men toting ancient rifles and handguns, no frantic passengers looking for information about trains to Dublin. He noted the platform number and returned into the station proper.

As he approached the main concourse he spotted a group of four or five young officers coming towards him, talking loudly, laughing and joking. He recognised one of them immediately - it was the other officer he came across in Passage West, Captain John Kelly. Charlie never broke his stride and looked casually at the group as they passed by; Kelly looked straight at him, smiled and nodded in a friendly manner. Charlie half expected a shout or a yell as he walked by but there was nothing; he kept walking, not daring to turn around. He stopped at a small notice board giving directions to the town centre, feigned some interest and looked back. The officers had stopped walking and began to shout and banter with some colleagues on the other platform. Kelly had stood to the side talking earnestly to a young lady, it was obvious that they had a few lunchtime beers; not drunk, but in high spirits. Charlie gave a short sigh of relief, Kelly hadn't recognised him - but it gave Charlie a jolt.

He kept out of the road of the officers, just in case anything suddenly clicked in Kelly's head, and was again relieved when he boarded the train and it took off almost dead on time. He rolled the recent events over in his mind. He had given up on getting help from George, he was becoming more and more of a loose cannon - it was just too risky. The plan he developed was a bit elaborate and would take time. What he needed was a professional printer to produce a counterfeit import tax certificate for the cases of 'machine parts' in the warehouse. He had good contacts for this and knew exactly who to get in touch with, but it would take at least a week of sitting around Cork and after the scare he got with Kelly he was not sure if it was worth it. He decided to cut his losses with a simpler plan.

He reached Cork by three-thirty and immediately hired a cab to take him the short distance to Cohen's warehouse; he made an arrangement for the taxi to wait for ten minutes.

The familiar chilly receptionist eyed him as he came in the door. "I would like to see Mr. Isaac for a few moments if he's available, if not, can I make an appointment for Monday?" said Charlie, using the semi-formal title that the Cohen Brothers preferred.

"I'll speak to Mr. Isaac," she said briefly, rising and disappearing down a corridor.

The bustling round figure of Isaac Cohen appeared at the front desk seconds later and grabbed Charlie's hand.

"Mr McKenna! Nice to see you, how are things in New York these days?"

"Couldn't say Mr. Isaac, I haven't been back since the last time we met."

"That's odd I thought you were going back right away, that must be well over a year now."

"It's a long story, I'm afraid I got rather overtaken by events in Cork. But not to worry I'm back in business now."

"Good, good. So what can I do for you? Come on into my office." Cohen took a seat behind the desk as Charlie opened up his briefcase and pulled out the bill of exchange.

"I would like you to have a look at this, if you have time. I realise you might have to look out some paper work to match it up or even consult your lawyer. Do you think I could leave it with you over the weekend and make an appointment for Monday morning?"

Cohen scanned the document with a professional eye.

"Mm. I recognise this piece of business, you'll be aware, of course, that the goods have been released?" he said.

"I realise that. Really what I'm looking for is a signed receipt for the goods, if not the original, then a copy of it. We can then approach the Provisional Government for payment."

"We've already been paid for the storage. So it makes little difference to me," said Cohen with a shrug. "But yes, I can see that a receipt would help you out. I think we may even have the original receipt, I am not sure if the gentlemen who came to collect the materials were in a particular hurry to demand a receipt. I'll get a copy made for ourselves and hopefully you can have the original. I'll see what the legal guys upstairs think."

"That would be excellent. Mr Peebles, the director, will be delighted if we can get this business done as quickly as possible."

There was a moment's silence as Cohen placed the document on the desk and continued to look over it.

"There was some thing else," said Charlie.

Cohen looked up, curious.

"Yes."

"I've been doing some business with a Belfast company. They ordered some rods of a very high specification - phosphorous bronze for bearings for steam valves. I eventually sourced them in France and ordered a few cases which I deposited here a week or so ago, the business was conducted by your Mr. O'Donnell."

"Is there a problem?"

"Just a slight one. Unfortunately because of the circumstances in the country, I haven't received the import tax certificate yet. I'm thinking of going up to Belfast this week and would like to take a few samples so they can be tested to meet the specification, say two or three from each case. I'll give you a receipt, of course."

"Yes I understand," replied Cohen, "things are not easy around here at the moment, although they are gradually getting better. I'll get that arranged for Monday as well if I can."

Charlie stood up, leaned over and shook his hand.

"A pleasure, as always," said Charlie

Mr. Isaac walked Charlie to the gate where the taxi driver sat reading a paper. They said their goodbyes and Charlie leaped into the back seat.

"See you Monday," shouted Cohen.

Charlie waved back.

"Conway's Hotel, driver," he said with a grin and slapped the door panel.

"Let's go."

***

Mrs. Sullivan fussed around Charlie as he entered the hotel foyer.

"Ah! Mrs Sullivan, I was thinking of staying a couple of nights. Although I suppose you're far too busy with staff officers to have any rooms."

"There's none of them staying here," she said slightly aggrieved, "most of them are billeted up in the Metropole or the Imperial."

"Oh I see," said Charlie quietly relieved, "room for me then?"

"There's always room for a gentleman like yourself, Mr. McKenna. I'll give you the same room as last time, shall I?"

"That'll be fine."

Charlie spent the weekend reading and going for long walks down by the river, popping into the occasional pub, when the notion took him. The Sunday papers were again full of depressing news of the current conflict and the political changes in the government. Charlie bought three papers and read them in a quiet pub close to the hotel. The North seemed to be particularly active, with fierce fire fights in Dundalk and Monaghan between the National army and the anti-treaty forces. In Monaghan the irregular locals robbed the local post office of £900, shooting and killing the postman in the process. Only yesterday, and nearer hand, two Free State medical officers were shot dead up in Kerry, near Killarney. On the political front Bill Cosgrave was named as the new President of the Free State. As usual, there were one or two local worthies in the pubs who seemed to have inside knowledge of a visit of Michael Collins, the National Army Commander-in-Chief, who they reckoned was due to arrive on Monday or Tuesday. Charlie was inclined to dismiss this as one of the rumours that seemed to fly around Cork on virtually an hourly basis, but it was now the third or fourth time he had heard this same story on his wanderings around town. If true, this would mean a big presence of soldiers on the streets of Cork. He decided he would leave as soon as possible on Monday.

His visit to Cohen's could not have gone better. He arrived just after ten and was ushered into the office by Mr. O'Donnell; Isaac Cohen had the paperwork ready and waiting.

"Our legal man says you can take the original receipt as long as you sign the bottom of this copy of it. We will be expecting our usual fee for the service and will bill your company for it, do you agree to all this?"

"Yes, of course. Where do I sign?"

Cohen turned the document around and slid it over the desk,

pointing to a pencilled cross.

"Regarding the other bit of business, Mr O'Donnell here…" said Cohen waving O'Donnell over to the table "…will take you over to the secured cages where we have agreed you can remove some of the material for sampling. I have drawn up a document for you to sign for this service and there is a small £20 fee involved, retrievable from your final bill of course… You can remove a few items from each case."

Isaac Cohen sat back and gave Charlie a friendly smile. Twenty pounds was not a 'small fee', it was a couple of month's salary for most people – a year's income for a domestic servant - and he knew it, but he had decided to cash in. He had long suspected that Charlie and his associates had been up to something for some time.

"Twenty pounds," said Charlie, raising an eyebrow and looking at the document carefully. He was trying to give himself time to think.

"Twenty pounds is close to the intrinsic value of five or six items from each case, Mr Isaac," he said eventually.

"However I will take five randomly from the cases to provide spares. That will be twenty samples - a nice round figure, I think you'll agree," he added smoothly.

Isaac Cohen looked closely at Charlie.

"Very well Mr. McKenna, I'll get Hannah to fill in the correct amounts. It will be ready when you return to the office."

Opening the boxes, selecting and removing the tubes of sovereigns in an apparently random manner and then placing them in the brief case took nearly twenty minutes under the watchful eye of O'Donnell who had been mesmerised by the verbal exchange between McKenna and Cohen; it was almost, he thought, like watching an elaborate game of cards between two experts where only they knew the rules. When O'Donnell turned to open the gate, Charlie tentatively tested the weight of the brief case, it was heavy but manageable.

All the relevant paperwork was completed when Charlie returned to Cohen's office. Hannah, whom Charlie took to be the harridan in the front office, had made a good job of adjusting the documents and bundling up the work into files. Charlie wrote out a company cheque for the 'fee' and added the receipt to the file. Charlie had a quick look at the file containing George's treasured Bill of Exchange and the original receipt - all in order. He placed everything neatly into his briefcase. They shook hands and walked out to the reception area.

"Don't suppose you could arrange a cab for me? I wasn't expecting to conclude our business so quickly; if I could return to my hotel and get my luggage, I could catch an earlier train."

"I'll try to arrange that Mr. McKenna," said Hannah with what passed as a smile.

By eleven thirty Charlie was speeding his way back north to Tralee with £500 in gold and a receipt worth at least another $1000.

***

"Right!" said George, before Charlie had settled in his seat. "Let's get ourselves off to Dublin."

"For Gods sake George, take it easy! I'm just off the train."

George jumped up and started to pace around the office.

He slapped the file with the bill of exchange and the receipt.

"This is worth ten grand! Ten thousand dollars I thought I had lost and you're telling me to take it easy!"

"Just relax for a minute will you."

George looked fiercely at Charlie but didn't reply.

"Talking of money" continued Charlie "Let's have my share first. You owe me $500 up to now, and I want it before I hear any more talk of Dublin."

George waved his hands airily.

"I'll make you out a cheque, how much is that in limey money?"

"About £125, but I don't see why that should be any concern since you said you'd pay me in dollars and in cash."

George stopped pacing.

"Did I?" he said, genuinely surprised.

"Yes you did, and tomorrow morning we go to your bank and get the money, George."

George threw himself back in the chair with a groan.

"Okay Charlie. A deal is a deal," he said disgruntled. "But I'm still anxious to get over to Dublin as quick as we can."

"How are you going to get away from the army for a week or so for a start?"

"That should be no problem; I'm quite thick with the division commander, Brigadier Paddy Daly. Daly is a lunatic. He has this fanatical loyalty to Mick Collins but he's also an ambitious git. He was quite impressed when he saw me talking to an old US army buddy of mine Johnny Prout, at a gathering in Dublin a couple of months ago. Prout is now a Major General and is winning hand over fist down in Waterford and Tipperary. Daly is jealous, I'll talk to him tomorrow. I'll think of something, don't worry"

"You go to the bank tomorrow and organise the cash," said Charlie. "It may take longer than you think for a local bank to rustle up five hundred bucks, let's face it we're hardly in downtown Manhattan. Send me a message when that's done. In the meantime, I'll try to organise a trip to Dublin that doesn't require an armed guard."

Charlie stood up and walked to the door.

"Let's hope things quieten down for the next few days."

***

Charlie had a busy Tuesday. He had arranged to meet Mrs Conklin after breakfast to discuss some matters of business which as, he put it, might be to their mutual interest. Mrs Conklin was intrigued.

He had thought long and hard about his next move. He had almost two thousand pounds in gold sovereigns, over a hundred pounds in notes plus the added bonus of a thousand dollars in cash from George. If he included the money he already had in the Provincial, he was well on his way to being a rich man. His main and immediate concern was the gold. It was secure enough where it was – if only he could persuade Mrs Conklin to keep it in the safe for him for a good length of time, say a year or two, then he could get back to America and return at a later date when things had calmed down a bit.

After breakfast Pat had decided to take his usual walk down to the beach and would probably not return until around one o'clock when they would meet up, as Pat suggested, in Musgrave's for a lunch and a beer. Charlie retired to his room to tidy up. At eleven prompt, Sarah came to the door and ushered him downstairs and into the front living room.

"Good morning, Mrs. Conklin. Thank you for giving me some of your time," he said, as he took a seat beside the unlit fire. The table was covered with the usual spread of tea cups, biscuits and sliced cake.

"Good morning, Mr. McKenna," she said pleasantly and fell silent. She had decided to let Charlie do the talking for the time being.

"As you know I went back to Cork for a few days and I've largely concluded my business down there. As I told you it was my intention to sail up North from here if it was possible, but something else has turned up. I really need to get to Dublin within the week and I'm not sure if I'll be coming back to Tralee for a fair bit of time. Maybe years perhaps."

Mrs Conklin sat up.

"Years?" she said, surprised.

"Maybe, I'm not sure. I have interests in America that may need attending too as well. The problem is, and I don't need to tell you, things are a bit unstable in Ireland at moment. I'm not sure it would be wise to travel with large amounts of money with me."

"Why don't you deposit it in the bank? I know I had a problem but my money was returned by the bank. The way things are going it would be safe enough there I would have thought."

"Possibly, but there are several reasons I would prefer not to. What I have is not currency or bank notes but things of great value. A bank would need something like a strong room or personal deposit boxes to hold them safely. I've already made inquires around Tralee and no such facilities are available. In any event, with the amount of robberies undertaken by the anti-treaty forces,

I'm not even sure that they could guarantee security."

"By things of value, I take it you mean the items that you're keeping in the safe?" she said looking over to the cupboard.

"Exactly, and your safe is ideal and probably as secure as anything else. It's hard to believe that the irregulars, for all their faults, would stoop to the barefaced robbery of ordinary citizens. I would pay you for the use of course, and I'm sure I could count on your discretion."

Charlie paused for a moment.

"Without being too presumptuous, I believe you could use some funds - perhaps to tide you over?"

Mrs Conklin was quiet for a moment then poured out some tea.

"I must admit that in the short term I could do with some more cash," she said finally.

"However I was considering a bank loan. The railway company awarded me half my husband's pension, paid quarterly and I have some money of my own. I also have some shares which I'm reluctant to cash in at the moment given the present situation."

She paused, handing over a cup to Charlie.

"What exactly did you have in mind?"

"You've started taking in guests recently. Do you intend to continue?"

"Yes I have, and until the recent fighting I was quite busy. You would be surprised how many people come here to enjoy the local scenery and the fishing. Some American golfers have booked in for next month, apparently the local course is well known over there. Why do you ask?"

"I was considering some investment in your business – a small interest free loan, say, for several years. In return I could keep my property in your safe without the bother of a complicated rental arrangement."

Mrs. Conklin stood up and walked to the window to mull this over. She had been giving a bit of thought to her future recently. She had been happily married for nearly twenty years and was now in her early forties and had no intention of remarrying and, although she had no children of her own, she was quite happy to indulge her sisters' children. One of her nieces had a child recently making her a great aunt, a role she was happy to play. Sarah, the housemother, was her niece, the daughter of her late husband's brother who had been killed in the Great War. Her mother had died in childbirth shortly after, losing the child and making Sarah an orphan at a very young age. Kitty Conklin had come to regard her almost as her own daughter and was beginning to think of her future.

She turned round.

"What sort of investment did you have in mind, Mr. McKenna?"

"I was thinking of about two hundred pounds. With that amount you could convert some more of the rooms for paying guests. Your house is large but not big enough for a hotel - a good class guest house perhaps?"

Two hundred pounds was a substantial amount of money, she thought, probably as much as her husband had paid for the house twenty years ago, probably a third of its present value. Oddly enough the idea of running a more superior guest house was something she had been considering.

"What securities are you thinking of to invest such an amount?"

"To be honest I hadn't given that aspect much consideration. I thought I would get your reaction first before I went any further."

She sat down slowly and reached over for the tea pot. The corners of her mouth were beginning to turn up in an almost conspiratorial smile.

"Have some more tea, Mr. McKenna. I think you and I could do business."

***

The next morning Charlie was almost fully dressed and was dabbing at his chin after shaving when there was a rapid chapping at his door. A flustered Sarah handed him a note.

"Someone came to the door with this for you. He said he'd wait for a reply."

Presumably the same chap who brought the first note, thought Charlie wryly as he started to read.

'Bad News. Come at once. George'

"Tell him I'll finish dressing and I'll be round at the office in ten minutes," he said unconcerned. Bad news for George could mean anything from having a bad haircut to losing money on a horse.

"I'll go back down and tell him. Don't worry about breakfast I'll make something for you when you come back." said Sarah as she dashed down the stairs. Charlie smiled and shook his head as he finished off fixing his tie and collar.

It had just gone nine when he entered the office. Stiofan Ó Doibhilin looked anxious and agitated.

"Go straight on up," he said.

It was the first time he had spoken to Charlie in English without the usual charade of lambasting him in mangled medieval Gaelic for five minutes. It made Charlie worried.

The door was hardly open when George threw a newspaper fly sheet on to the table.

"Look at this!" he cried, pointing to the paper.

Charlie read the headline hardly believing his eyes.

Collins shot in ambush!

"I just got a call half an hour ago. He's dead."

Charlie sat down.

"That poster came up on the train from Cork for the local newsagents. They're printing a special edition right now; it should be up here by lunch time."

"I can't believe it. There was a rumour that he was coming to Cork on Monday. What the hell happened?"

"Not a lot of news. Apparently his armed convoy was visiting Skibereen, and was ambushed on the way back, some god forsaken place called Beal na blah or blag or something. Collins was the only casualty, killed outright. It seems it took ages to get back to Cork city, I think that's why the news was slow to get out. I can hardly believe it myself!"

Charlie could hardly take it all in.

"The world has gone mad," he said as he stood up. "Harry Boland, Arthur Griffith and now Mick Collins – all within a couple of weeks. Who's left?"

186

"Dick Mulcahy, or Cosgrave, I suppose. That's if you don't count that conniving snake in the grass, De Valera"

"De Valera?" Charlie said with a sneer. "He usually disappears when the going gets tough, can't see him getting very far. In fact the more you think of it, the more you'd come to believe the British government were paying him as an agent, the mess he's made of things."

There was a short silence as Charlie tried to gather his thoughts together.

George looked up at the ceiling.

"Still," he said, with a slight cough, "things could be worse."

Charlie looked at him in disbelief.

"Things could be worse! Just how the hell could things be worse George?"

"I've seen Daly just half an hour ago. He is going crazy, by the way - wanted to take out all the anti-treaty prisoners and shoot them on the spot – and I recommended that I accompany the body back to Dublin, it seems they're taking him back to Dublin by sea from Cork."

Charlie's jaw dropped.

"You…"

"I suggested that I could represent the Brigadier himself and the Kerry Command," added George quickly. He stood up and pulled at his jacket nervously.

"You could come as well."

"In fact," he added brightly, as if the thought had just suddenly occurred to him. "We could get this business of the bill of exchange finished."

Charlie stood speechless.

"Er ..We would be killing two birds with the one stone, so to speak," he added, his voice dropping.

Charlie turned round and looked out the window. He was exasperated. There was little point in ranting and shouting at George – he was beyond redemption. His reaction to any event was never seen from any other perspective other than his own – how does this affect me? Can I gain anything by this? It wasn't a malicious reaction, it was almost guileless more than anything else. In a way it was part of his charm. George Peebles was probably one of the few people in Ireland this morning that could see something positive in the assassination of Michael Collins. In fact, thought Charlie bitterly, he probably regarded it as a bit of luck.

George started babbling about armoured cars and convoys.

Charlie turned from the window in anger.

"Shut up George!" he shouted.

George stood stunned.

"Is there something wrong? No need to shout, old man," he said, genuinely alarmed and hurt.

Charlie took a deep breath and held up his hand.

"Sorry for shouting. Just be quiet for a minute George. I need to think."

He began to pace the room.

"I'll go out for a walk. I'll be back shortly"

"Ok, ok, take it easy," said George guardedly, as Charlie closed the door behind him.

As he walked through the bottom floor office he was taken aback to see Devlin kneeling with his head bowed. He was about to say something as he opened the front door when he noticed that Devlin had beads between his clasped hands - he was saying the Rosary. Charlie said nothing and walked out to the street.

He stood on the pavement outside for a minute with his back to the door trying to gather his thoughts. Grey and black clouds scuttled above him, and he could feel a slightly chilled breeze and a slight smattering of rain on his face: first signs of the end of summer.

He turned up his collar and started to walk down Denny Street.

Charlie looked around him and became aware that the streets were almost empty and deathly quiet. There was an occasional twitch of a curtain in the larger town houses and the odd pale, ghostly face appearing fleetingly across a window pane. It was almost unnerving. The rumour of Collins' death, he figured, must have run quickly through the town.

What was their mood, these people, thought Charlie - delight or distress?

Boland, Griffith and now Mick Collins all dead in a matter of weeks, where would it all end? Charlie was becoming morose: the atmosphere was becoming more and more oppressive; he had to get out of here, out of Tralee, out of the West, out of Ireland. He was at a point where he felt he no longer cared: the French were right, revolutions devour their children.

He crossed over the road and started to walk back.

The hell with it, he thought angrily. Get things organised here and get back to America. That was his best bet. He considered George's jaunt back to Cork. Disregarding his distaste at George's typical crass and opportunistic offer to Daly, in many ways it was ideal. If he could manage to keep out of the clutches of Barrett in Cork, he could be in Dublin in a few days from now, get George's business sorted and get the first boat to New York. If he could get his passport organised at the same time, so much the better. He had already seen Mrs Conklin's solicitor, a typical provincial hand-wringing Jeremiah who had drawn up a contract in the form of a thirty year mortgage at two percent per year for twenty five percent equity of the house. Charlie was indifferent, thirty years was so long away it might have been in the next millennium - he would be nearly sixty years old by then, an age that was impossible for him to imagine. Pat, he decided, was catered for. He had deposited a hundred pounds in Pat's account as prearranged and was intending to give him a couple of rolls of sovereigns which Pat could keep or dispose of as he felt fit.

Charlie's step got a bit lighter as he crossed the road to return to the office. Several things were now beginning to resolve and consolidate themselves in his mind. Sure, he thought, there were a few loose ends to tie up but perhaps the trip to Cork and then on to Dublin would give him the opportunity to get out of this sorry mess.

Now that he had made up his mind he returned to the office in a less sombre mood. As he walked through the front office he could see the prematurely balding head of the still kneeling Devlin nodding rhythmically – he was still busy saying his rosary.

Charlie ignored him and bounded up the stairs and threw open the door.

"Right then George, what's all this about an armed convoy?"

oooOooo

CHAPTER EIGHTEEN

The Funeral

Holy Cross church, with its Italianate façade, was built in the early part of the twentieth century for the parishioners that teemed into the surrounding overcrowded Govanhill tenements. In those days it could easily hold, and expect, a thousand worshippers for a mass. The area itself, despite its congestion, was a bit more up market than the inner city slums that clung to the banks of the Clyde and its shipbuilding. In its heyday the congregation, most of whom were of the decent aspiring working and middle classes, commissioned several additions over the years, such as marble side chapels, marble alter rails and several marble floors. All things considered a rather impressive venue for a religious service.

However these days it is now unusual to have more than a hundred hardy souls in for the daily mass and maybe a few hundred more or so for a Sunday mass - depending on the weather. It was, however, a remarkably popular venue for funerals for the great and good of Glasgow's South Side.

Julie took the car and had left early to pick up her parents. She always gave herself plenty time to cajole her mother, a notorious late comer, into leaving at least on time for any social event that they attended together. Des jumped on a bus to meet up with Liam on Victoria Road, where they could take the short walk down to Holy Cross.

"We're far too early," complained Liam. This time dressed in a dark blue suit which looked as if he had at least tried it on before buying it, although the overall effect was spoiled by a badly knotted black tie.

"The walk will do you good," said Des.

Des told Liam that he had a bit of luck. An English based Sunday newspaper had commissioned a five hundred word article about Toner and his tenuous Irish connections. He had started to read through the books Liam had given him for a bit of research.

"Good man! Even if you only get as far as the first chapter you'll be as wise as the nitwits I've got to contend with."

"The stuff on Collins is interesting. I remember seeing that movie - with what's his name - Liam Neeson - in it. What was it called again?"

Liam stopped and turned to Des in exasperation.

"It was called 'Michael Collins' - believe it or not."

"Damn, of course it was!" replied Des.

Liam continued walking.

"Mind you, I can understand your memory lapse. They might as well have called it 'Shootout at Bigorra Gulch" for all the light it shone on the subject. Oddly enough this Sunday is the anniversary of his assassination. You might want to tie all that in."

"That's an idea. Any thoughts on it yourself?" said Des.

"On Collins? Not really. He was young, good looking and dead. Dead politicians are always projected into the future as a great loss to whatever nation they come from. Collins was no different. Although I've little doubt he would have changed the course of Irish history..." he paused for a second, "...one way or another."

They could now see the front of the church. Liam continued.

"There's an interesting photograph of Collins. One that was taken at Arthur Griffith's funeral, it's the one where he's looking to the side as he adjusts his leather gloves..."

"Yes. I've seen that. It's in both books, looks a very classical pose."

"In both books? It's in every damn book that ever mentions Collins," replied Liam.

"You know," he continued, pulling at his shirt collar. "I've thought about that photograph a lot and why it is used so often. It somehow reminds me of an image of Fascism. In fact he strikes a pose that looks more like your Italian chum, Mussolini, than anything else."

Des stopped briefly.

"Fascism! Mussolini! Now isn't that odd. 'Morte Fascista' - death to the Fascists - my only words in Italian and I've used them twice this week'" said Des.

"What?"

"Nothing. Just spooky - a daft coincidence."

"Look there's Mick Hastings on the corner!" said Des "Sorry, Liam, I interrupted you. What were you saying?"

"We'll leave it just now…. Hi Mick, how's it going?"

***

All three walked the short distance to the front of the church where various groups were beginning to form. Des, Liam and Mick were joined by others, most were mutual friends or old school chums.

"I didn't know you were pally with Hughie Toner, Mick." someone said.

"I'm not really, but my mum knows his mum well, I think they went to school together."

This was regarded as good a reason as any to attend a funeral in Holy Cross.

The crowd were not exactly in a jolly mood but neither were they particularly solemn – after all it wasn't a tragedy. It wasn't as if Toner was a child or a teenager. He was always regarded as a bit of a tearaway, moved in dangerous circles where getting knifed was regarded with the same indifference as an industrial accident. He was almost fifty; he wasn't married so there were no offspring involved. No need to get too upset then.

Julie and Grace appeared, early for a change.

"Good morning, ladies," said Liam. "By God, Grace, I swear you look younger every time I see you!"

"Oh don't give me any of your old blarney, Liam!" she snapped, turning slightly pink. "I'm far too used to it. And what have you

193

been up to? I haven't seen you for ages and now Julie tells me you've turned poor old Uncle Pat into a mass murderer on the evidence of that silly postcard."

"I did not! I merely speculated on the anomalies and coincidences that the photo threw up," Liam announced, straightening up his shoulders. "That's a long way from accusations of mass murder."

"Still got the gift of the gab I see. Was that young Mick Hastings I spotted standing over here when I got out of the car? Is his mother here I wonder?"

"Yes," said Des, "he's standing over there with her now."

"I'll away over and see her. I've not seen her for ages either. I'll see you two later at the purvey, and you as well Liam. You can give me some of your latest ridiculous theories."

Grace pushed her way through the gathering crowd to the door of the church where Mrs. Hastings was standing with a few others.

"Oh well! You know Mum - sees someone more important than you, and she's off," said Julie apologetically to Liam.

"No harm, I'll enjoy having a chat with her later."

The crowd moved around talking loudly. Hastily forming one company before blending mysteriously and forming another. Clouds of cigarette smoke drifted and wafted around the horde of mourners like a weird morning mist. Everyone seemed almost conditioned by tradition to mingle, linger and chatter outside until the last possible minute. Suddenly everyone started to move into the church at the same time, as if given a mystical signal and, by the same strange potent protocol, all were seated and coughing discreetly just seconds before the opening hymn struck up.

As usual, the funeral service was simply shoehorned into the normal daily mass. The main mourners occupied the front seats on the left, on the right were the regular daily communicants, some of whom were slightly miffed at this change to their routine.

At least, Liam noted as the mass progressed, the elderly priest seemed to have some passing acquaintance with Hughie Toner. He had been to many funeral services where the celebrant seemed to have little or no idea who was in the coffin. Liam passed the time studying the Stations of the Cross that lined the outer nave.

They were large and rather splendid illustrations created in an interesting post-renaissance style. He wondered idly if they were simply prints or elaborately painted copies. Julie and Grace on the other hand spent their time whispering to each other, pointing out this one and that one. The congregation numbered a good four or five hundred, most of whom were not regular attendees at any kind of religious service. When they were required to stand, kneel or sit they took their cue from those regular parishioners at the front. The result was often a giant human Mexican wave that flowed from the alter rail to the front door and back again. Hymns were enthusiastically sung out of tune and responses were shouted out from the front of the church then picked up at the back giving a bizarre echoing Doppler effect. The mass finally ended in a whirl of enthusiastic handshakes and loud shouts of 'Peace be with you'. Some interesting variations were heard towards the back of the church.

The elderly priest trotted nimbly down the altar steps followed by a young altar boy who staggered under the weight of a smouldering chancel, a pail of holy water containing what appeared to be a whitewashing brush and numerous other bits and bobs of religious paraphernalia. There was momentary confusion as the coffin bearers jostled and vied with each other for the more prominent positions - the front two spots apparently being the most prestigious. They had no sooner arranged themselves in formation when the priest elbowed them aside to commence his last duties to the dead. The brush was dipped into the pail and lashed at the coffin with the enthusiasm of a fire-fighter tackling a blaze, while the altar boy followed waving the opened chancel back and forth. A few of the regulars started coughing and rubbing their streaming eyes as a powerful waft of burning incense caught in the back of their throats, while others pulled out handkerchiefs in an attempt to dry their hair and clothes. Eventually, after many incantations and more liberal lashings of holy water and incense, the coffin was raised by the pall bearers and led down the aisle at a surprisingly fast lick by the priest. Everyone stood up quietly with downcast eyes as the coffin passed back out along the main aisle, followed by the main mourners. As the coffin passed the congregation they left their seats giving discreet nods, waves and smiles to suddenly recognised old friends and followed the procession outside.

When Liam squeezed out of the main doors and into the small courtyard, he looked around for Des or Julie. People were again gathering in knots and beginning to banter and laugh as the tension of the service gave way to relief. Plumes of smoke appeared everywhere as smokers puffed away as if the last forty five minutes had been a prison sentence. He found them talking to Grace and Eddie on the pavement just outside the low wall of the Church.

"Are you going up to the cemetery, Liam? I should be able to squeeze you in," asked Julie.

"I might as well, the pubs are not opened yet," replied Liam. "Only joking!" he added hastily as Grace glared at him.

"Where's the purvey? I could be doing with a bite to eat," said Eddie.

This produced an even more malevolent scowl from Grace.

"Don't you ever listen! The priest said everyone is invited back to the 'Marie Steward' after the burial."

"The Marie Steward eh! Good! They do a decent spread in there," replied Eddie, who had become totally immune to Grace's bad tempered outbursts over the years.

"Let's get into the car, the funeral party looks as if it's ready to get going," said Julie.

***

Eddie sat in the passenger's seat while Liam sat in the middle of the back with Grace and Des on either side.

"Goodness me, Liam!" said Grace "You've put on the beef. I can hardly breathe back here!"

"A few extra pounds, nothing more. I'll soon burn them off come winter," he replied.

"We'll see. Anyway, what's your latest theory on poor old Pat?" said Grace.

"Well," began Liam, "as Julie probably told you, I think Pat might have been stationed around Cork or Kerry, more likely Kerry. The Kerry brigade was by far the most active during the Civil War."

"Why was that?" asked Grace.

"Several reasons, but mainly because they were simply the best armed. They captured and took over a town called Kenmare in the early stage of the war and executed two of the officers. One was Tom "Scarteen" O'Connor and the other was his brother. They took 120 first class rifles and, more importantly, 20,000 rounds of ammunition. This made them a pretty well armed and a very dangerous guerrilla group. Throughout the winter of 1922/23 most of the rest of the country became quieter as the Free State Government starting taking an extremely hard line. They were executing prisoners on an almost daily basis. County Kerry became almost the last stand of the diehards. Anyway, early in March the irregulars planted a mine in a field under an arms dump in a place called Knocknagoshel."

"For Gods sake, Liam! We're not getting a written exam on the Irish Civil War after this are we?" said Julie from the driver's seat.

"Just a bit of background, that's all!" said Liam, rather irked.

"The arms dump was then reported to the local barracks," he continued. "The officers sent out to investigate were blown to pieces. Two of them were highly regarded soldiers, the members of 'The Squad', veterans who had taken part in the War of Independence. The Kerry Command was led by a fanatical follower of Collins called Paddy Daly. He decided to take retribution by ordering anti-partition prisoners to clear anything that was suspected of being mined - road blocks and the like. Some of the Dublin guard decided this was a good way to get rid of a few troublesome prisoners. So they mined the road blocks themselves. Nine prisoners were taken out of Ballymullen barracks near Tralee and tied to a barricade. Eight were either blown up or machine gunned. Believe it or not, one prisoner survived to tell the tale."

"My God, that's awful," said Grace. "I can't believe that the Irish would do that to each other! They seem so easy going and good natured."

"I believe it!" said Des gruffly. "Every war has atrocity stories, believe me, I'm a journalist, and I've been there. I can't see why the Irish would be any different. I'm sure it wasn't all laughing leprechauns during the Civil War."

"Are you saying that Pat took part in one of these ...these executions? I thought you said they were committed by the Dublin Guard," said Grace.

"The Dublin guard formed the shock troops, if you like, of the Free State Army. But I suppose any soldier in the army could have been drawn into it, including Pat."

Julie pulled the car into the cemetery, followed the funeral cortège up the winding road to the top terrace and stopped.

Before leaving the car, Grace turned to Liam.

"You," she said slowly, with a shake of her head, "are out of your mind!"

***

The view from the graveside was spectacular. It was a clear cloudless day and the top tier of the cemetery overlooked the Clyde valley. The hills of the Campsie Fells could be seen the other side of Glasgow, to the North - opposite the graveside. On the left, to the West, was the impressive grey blue outline of the Argyll Mountains. The top of Ben Lomond could be seen peeking over the foothills. Those who were closest took an interest in the proceedings, the rest, on the periphery stood around quietly, admiring the view. When the last bit of earth clunked against the coffin the main mourners moved towards the official cars. Some of the family, Toner's mother and sister, were weeping. The other members of the family looked more bewildered than anything else.

Liam and the rest had to stand around, while one of the undertakers arranged and directed the traffic out and down through the winding one-way road system. Des was about to join them when he noticed the detective he had met in Alice's Restaurant, standing at the side. He appeared to be watching someone in the crowd. However the movement of the front cars distracted him and he looked around casually and spotted Des. He smiled, waved in recognition and walked over to him.

"Hi there, Des."

"Hi, Alex isn't it, Alex Munro?"

"Yes, that's right, how's it going?"

"Fine. I didn't see you at the church. See anyone interesting?"

"As a matter of fact, yes. Strictly off the record, of course. Someone we've been keeping a weather eye on for a while. Small time. Jimmy Gilmore. Claims to be a member of the Real IRA, although I usually find that anyone claiming to a member of any organisation usually isn't. There he's there, just getting into that white car."

Des looked around and saw a youngish, medium sized, dark haired, agitated man bending down to get into the back of a car just twenty feet away.

"I see him."

Des turned back.

"I take it you're finished up here? You could hardly go to the purvey unnoticed."

Munro laughed.

"Yes, I think that would look a bit odd. I'm still on duty for the rest of the day so I'm just going back down to the station. I wonder if Mick's going to the purvey? I didn't manage to catch him before the service."

"He'll probably take his mother. As it happens, she was quite friendly with Toner's mother."

"That's a bit of a coincidence. Anyway, you can mention Gilmore to Mick, but tell him not to get too involved. Gilmore's got a reputation of being a bit flaky."

"Must admit he looked a bit uptight when I looked over."

The undertaker started to wave at Julie's car.

"Come on Des!" she shouted from the car window "We're next away."

"Nice meeting you again, Alex. Might see you later," said Des

Des hurried over and manoeuvred himself into the crowded back seat.

"Has anyone heard of Jimmy Gilmore?" he asked without

thinking.

"I think I've met him once at a wedding a few years back," said Julie, concentrating on the traffic as it snaked its way down the narrow road. "A young nervy, dark haired man, if I remember. Sounded as if he had a Belfast accent - he and Hughie seemed quite pally."

"Ah, him," replied Grace, "another one of the famous Toner tribe. Some sort of cousin of the late deceased I'm led to believe."

"I'm not sure if he was an actual blood relative," said Eddie defensively from the front.

"Another would-be gangster if you ask me," said Grace coldly. "The Toners were always in and out of the shadows claiming to be part of some large mysterious organisation. Always on the fringes of some sort of skulduggery."

"He looked a bit ...agitated" said Des.

Julie had slowed down as the car approached the exit.

"I wouldn't worry about the likes of Gilmore," said Grace to no one in particular. "They're the type that likes to swagger about, posing and acting tough. It's all incredibly boring and irritating, but they're usually pretty harmless..."

She hesitated for a brief second as the car swerved slightly to turn into the main road.

"...by and large."

oooOooo

CHAPTER NINETEEN

Boat Journeys

"Just tell him I work for the Philadelphia Inquirer," said Charlie, "...and tell him to send over a recent photograph of himself – tell him a head and shoulder shot would be good."

George's jaw dropped slightly, hesitated for a moment before he picked up the phone.

"George Peebles here. Get me General Daly," he barked.

He cupped his hand round the mouthpiece.

"How the hell do you think these things up, Charlie?"

Charlie shrugged.

"As long as he falls for it, who cares? Tell him I'm writing a piece on the military action in the Irish west coast and would like his opinion on how things are turning out, and that I would be grateful for a lift down to Cork to cover the assassination of Collins. Generals like to get their name in the paper. Daly will be no different, get him to write down a few of his thoughts on paper and give them to you to pass on. Anyway I've got things to do. Send over a message to Mrs. Conklin's when you've organised everything and I'll see you in the morning."

"Let's try to make it daybreak, around 6 am. We don't want any trouble from the irregulars," said George.

"Mind you," he added, raising his eyebrows. "Judging by the amount of booze that most of them consume I'm surprised that any of them ever see the light of day."

He shooed Charlie away as he began to speak into the phone. The floor creaked as Charlie got up quickly and opened the door and ambled down the stairs. Devlin was nowhere to be seen, he looked around the room and spotted a note on the table.

"Attending 12.00 mass. Back at one."

The note was scribbled in English - Devlin must have been short of time. Charlie shook his head, and left the office turning down towards the Provincial Bank.

The rest of the day was busy. He had a stultifying meeting with the bank manager, the solicitor and Mrs. Conklin which stretched out to over an hour. He returned with Mrs. Conklin to the house and asked if she would mind opening the safe for a few minutes.

"I'll leave you to it," she said as she twisted the combination lock.

"No it's okay, you can stay."

"I'll leave, if you don't mind. I'm beginning to think the less I know the better," she said. "I'll go and organise the tea – I'll be back in ten minutes."

Charlie opened the safe and sat back, he was beginning to lose track of things now, and had to think for a minute to even have a rough idea of much he had left. In a way it didn't matter, things were moving at such a speed that he was not in a mind to do nitpicking calculations. He counted the rolls. He remembered that there were 96 rolls in the original case plus the ones he taken from the warehouse. He put aside 100 rolls - £2,500, there were only a few left. The business with Mrs. Conklin had cost near enough £250 which he paid by cheque, so he could forget that for the time being. He had also paid in another hundred into Pat's account as arranged and he intended to give him a couple of rolls to keep as an emergency or even as a keepsake. He would give these to Mrs. Conklin until Pat was discharged from the army. He put the remaining few in various pockets, closed the safe door, rubbed his brow with both his hands as if to clear his head, and finally spun the dial.

He had just stood up and was arranging his jacket when he heard a tap at the door.

"It's okay, you can come in," he said lightly. "I'm not up to anything."

"The tea will be along in a minute. Please, take a seat," said Mrs Conklin moving over to one of the fireside chairs.

"Don't mind if I do, I've one or two things I want to talk over with you."

Sarah came in almost immediately and started to arrange the tea things and sensing that they were waiting for her to leave before they started to talk, she didn't hang around.

"I hope there's nothing wrong, Mr. McKenna."

"No, nothing, it's just that I'll need to leave tomorrow. I was going to mention it at the bank but I wasn't too sure about mentioning any of my business in front of that slippery eel of a solicitor. I got the distinct impression that he likes to know a bit too much about his clients for my liking."

"He's really alright, but I take your point. It's difficult to know who to trust these days. Anyway," she continued. "I'm not too surprised that you're leaving, you more or less said so last week."

"I wasn't expecting to leave for another week or so, but I'm leaving tomorrow morning, first thing."

"I take it that it's something to do with yesterday's events. Oh don't worry," she said quickly, waving her hand as he was about to speak. "I'm not going to pry, let's stick to the practicalities. What time are you leaving?"

"I want to be out of here by 5.30 but don't get Sarah up or anything like that. I should get a message to confirm this and if it's any different, I'll let Sarah know right away."

"I'll get her to leave something out for your breakfast and something for your journey."

"That sounds grand. Talking of practicalities I'll leave another ten pounds to cover my bill and it should be enough to cover Pat's bill until he gets called up to the barracks, anything that's left you can give to Sarah as a tip."

"That's more than generous, Mr. McKenna. Sarah will appreciate your good will."

"In fact if she could get a couple of shirts washed and ironed for the morning I would be very grateful. I'll leave this for her," he added, taking out a ten shilling note and putting it on the table.

"I'm sure she'll organise that for you."

They had some tea as Charlie outlined his plan to give Pat some of the rolls of coins which he discreetly described as some 'items of value'. Mrs. Conklin made no comment on the arrangement and had no problem holding onto the rolls until Pat needed them, or was about to go home.

Charlie finished his tea and stood up.

"I'm afraid I'll have to leave you, I've still got one or two things to do."

Mrs Conklin rose.

"I don't suppose you know when you might return?"

"I'm afraid it may be some time."

Charlie stretched out and took her hand.

"I won't see you before I leave. So…" he kissed the back of her hand "I'll say goodbye."

She reddened slightly.

He nodded and turned to leave.

"Goodbye, Mr. McKenna…" she said hesitantly, "…and good luck."

Charlie wandered around the shops and managed to pick up a large second hand leather holdall. He returned to the lodgings and spent the rest of the day packing his bags. He thought long and hard about taking the Webley revolver until he finally decided he would take it to Cork just in case things got rough. It seemed like an age but it was only a couple of weeks since the confrontation outside Passage West. Charlie, after a look in the mirror, convinced himself that he wouldn't be recognised, but a niggling doubt remained. He lifted the bags and left them in the small cupboard in the hallway so he wouldn't make too much noise in the morning. Later he had dinner with Pat and, after a couple of beers at Musgrave's where he filled him in on his plans, he retired for an early night.

***

The streets were quiet and daylight was appearing across the roofs as Charlie quietly turned the key in the lock and posted it through the door. He assumed he would have been first to arrive and was surprised to see a harassed George hanging around the office door as he turned the corner into Denny Street.

"What's up, George?"

"I told that fool Devlin to leave the key in the sergeant's office when he finished up last night! He must have ...

Devlin marched smartly round the corner just as George was about to curse him.

"Don't even attempt to explain yourself - in Gaelic or otherwise. Just hand over the key." "I thought I would come round and give you a hand on your journey, Colonel," replied Devlin brightly.

"Don't bother we'll manage," said George, taking the key. "Away back to your bed."

"But..."

"On you go, back to the barracks. Come back to the office at nine as usual, there's a load of work you'll need to be doing."

Devlin looked crestfallen as he turned and walked back up the street, giving a doglike lingering look as he turned the corner. As soon as he was out of sight George tried turning the key in the lock.

"Bloody pest that man! Been angling all day yesterday to get on the convoy down to Cork."

"Why not? He's your adjutant after all."

"Not of my choice I can tell you! Anyway the seat is occupied by someone that Daly insists we take along."

"Who's that," said Charlie casually.

"Someone from Tipperary called Regan who came over to the National Army last week, apparently he commanded a brigade during the Tan War and he thinks he might be of help to Dalton down in Cork."

George concentrated on getting the lock opened.

"That's odd, I don't remember anyone..." Charlie hesitated. He had met or knew almost all of the officers in Tipperary, none of whom were called Regan but his experience over the last few weeks had taught him that some people can quickly re-invent their past with remarkable imagination. Best say nothing and wait.

"What was that?" said George finally opening the door.

"Nothing. Nothing at all."

They were both distracted as a motor cyclist and side-car roared into the street followed by two other vehicles, one a fairly large Crossley and a smaller Lancia. Drivers included, guessed Charlie, there were no more than half a dozen soldiers in the convoy.

"I'll nip upstairs and get my papers," said George. "Back in a minute."

While he was gone Charlie suddenly noticed a young, curly headed man in civil dress walking up Denny Street looking at the door numbers. He assumed that this was Regan. Charlie did not recognise him as someone he had met. Seeing the motor bike and the cars, the man headed straight towards them.

"You wouldn't be Colonel Peebles, would you?" he asked Charlie as he approached the office.

"I'm not, but he'll be down in a minute," Charlie replied as he heard George clattering down the stairs.

"Ah!" shouted George jovially and held out his hand. "You must be Regan."

"Terence Regan, although some call me 'Rusty'," said Regan.

"And this is Charlie McKenna," said George after shaking Regan's hand and waving in Charlie's direction.

Regan turned and shook Charlie's hand with enthusiasm. Charlie was unimpressed. Only children and small fry hoodlums had nicknames in his experience and, more often than not, the nicknames were created by themselves, for themselves.

"I've been over in America myself," continued Regan, noticing George's accent "...Chicago mostly."

"Nice place, been there once," replied George.

Charlie stood back a bit and let George ramble on about Chicago and who he knew there. Regan matched him in acquaintances and began to talk with a slight accent and using American slang terms like 'swell' and 'so-and-so was on the level'.

Although he had a bit of boyish charm Charlie found him

irritating and tiresome. He was also pretty convinced he was lying about his former activities and did not relish the thought of sharing a three hour journey with him and George babbling on about their mutual pals.

"George," he said finally, "let's be getting going. By the way did you get that photo and letter from Daly?"

George looked at him slightly baffled.

"What? …Oh yes I forgot," said George searching his pockets.

"I'll sit in the Lancia and take some notes and leave you two to carry on reminiscing in the Crossley."

"But why bother…"

George cut him short.

"It'll save me time writing out copy on Daly when I get to Cork," said Charlie quickly and turned to Regan.

"I'm a reporter for the Philadelphia Enquirer - I'm sure George would have got round to telling you sometime."

"Yes, yes, of course I would've," said George suddenly remembering the cover story. He fished out an envelope from his inside pocket.

"Here you are."

"Right. I'll get in the back seat, it'll give me a chance to read these over, and you two get into the car in front. We'll stop at Macroom to stretch our legs."

"Sure thing!" said Regan enthusiastically.

"I'm off," said Charlie through gritted teeth. "See you later."

As they made their way through the streets of Tralee to the main road south, Charlie had a quick look at Daly's notes and then threw them to the side. He had wanted a bit of time to think and Regan's arrival had at least given him an excuse to get out of George's way. The sun was now well up and he glanced at the dark and baleful landscape of Ballyseedy Wood to his right and thought over the events of the past few weeks.

He was now beginning to have some regrets about the gold. He felt he was not in control. He had simply been driven by events, but thinking it through, there was not much more he could have done. What he did was impulsive. The country was in chaos, if

Charlie hadn't taken the shipment someone else, probably less scrupulous, would have. The amount of money involved was immense yet bank and post office robbery was rife over the past two or three months: sums of over £5000 were often "liberated" in a single day and very rarely for the right reasons. Could he have left the sovereigns somewhere to be found? Not really, he thought, found by whom? The consignment would have disappeared: he was becoming aware that he was simply justifying his own actions. Although he was an honest man by nature, he was not a fool. He had no intention of giving any of the money he had taken so far, back to the authorities, it was far too risky for a start. The way things were going and with a bit of ill fortune, he could be easily taken out and shot, with or without a trial. He wondered if he should contact someone about the hoard in the warehouse. Yet again, who was to guarantee that it wouldn't simply disappear in the confusion? No, he concluded, he would just have to live with it for the time being. He was sure he would put all this behind him when he got back to America which in turn made him think of his passport. Technically there was no need for a passport to go to America. There were other methods, but a passport would almost certainly guarantee his entry with little or no baggage check. He could try several of his contacts but this too could be perilous as he was still not sure of his position regarding the authorities. He wondered if there was another way...

***

He was aroused from his sleep by the sound of the partition glass being slid open.

"Macroom coming up. Do you still want to stop?" said the young soldier in the front.

Charlie rubbed his eyes.

"I must have nodded off," he said trying to get his bearings. "Best stop at the barracks or as near as you can."

"That's okay, we'll be there in a couple of minutes," replied the boy. "I'll give the horn a blast so the cycle driver will know when to stop."

"You must have made good time," said Charlie looking at his watch.

"We came through Killarney. There were no hold-ups and hardly any traffic."

Charlie suppressed a yawn and rubbed the back of his neck, he was feeling stiff and he was keen to get out and stretch his legs.

The car had hardly stopped before Charlie had opened the door, jumped out and walked back to the Lancia. He pulled open the car door.

"A short stop, George and then we're off."

"What's the problem, Charlie? The National Army's here, are they not?"

"In theory. But let's not press our luck – let your men take a walk about in turns, but don't leave any of the vehicles unattended and tell them to be on their guard."

He walked back to his own car and gave the same instructions. By this time George and Regan were on the pavement and Regan had lit a cigarette.

"Let's make it half an hour at the most," said Charlie. "If we leave then we should make Cork by ten at the latest."

"Ok. Let's see if we can get a cup of tea over at that hotel beside the castle," said George.

Regan was becoming slightly confused, as it seemed to be Charlie, a mere reporter, who seemed to be giving all the orders around here. George Peebles, he noticed, didn't seem concerned in the slightest about this state of affairs.

***

"I wonder if I could get a uniform made in time for the funeral," mused George, picking up a slice of toasted bread.

"I think I might be able to help you out there, I know a decent tailor who could probably rattle up a uniform if the price was right. I'll get him to come over and see you at lunch time, name's Goldstein."

"Goldstein," said Regan with a slight sneer. "Sounds like a Jew to me."

209

"He sounded like a Cork man to me," replied Charlie curtly. "By the way, where are you from yourself?"

"He's from Clonmel," answered George.

"That's right and I was there until two weeks ago when the National Army besieged the town. I could tell you things that happened there that would make your hair stand on end," said Regan. "I gave myself up to save any more bloodshed."

I'll bet you did, thought Charlie. Then he reflected for a moment, maybe Regan was telling the truth. He was now beginning to remember mention of a Regan in one of the Tipperary Brigades, but this Regan didn't look the part some how. Clonmel, he knew, was a stronghold of the anti-treaty forces - there were hundreds of well armed men milling about the town when he was last there and they weren't exactly running around in panic. He was about to ask him a few questions when he stopped himself. It would be impossible to check up his story. Anyway, he thought, to hell with it - what does it matter?

"I think I'll phone ahead and book a room for you, George," said Charlie rising from the table. "I'll see if I can get you into the Imperial."

"What about you and Rusty?"

"I'll be staying at Conway's. As for Mr. Regan, I think the military might want a say in where he stays. Back in a minute."

A few minutes later Charlie returned.

"That's it arranged, the Imperial will let you book in after twelve," he said without sitting down.

"We're finished here," replied George, putting down his cup. "I think we'll get going now."

They managed to round up the men without too much trouble and headed back down the main Cork road. The motor cyclist said he knew Cork quite well and would stop when they reached George Street just after the Parnell Bridge.

The road got quite busy as they reached the southwest outskirts of the city and the drivers greeted the one or two military vehicles on the road with enthusiastic horn blasts. When they stopped, Charlie jumped out and walked up to the Lancia.

"All over to you now, George. I'll get Goldstein up to the Imperial as quick as he can make it. I'll get my luggage and walk up to Conway's from here - it's just as quick."

He pulled out a small card.

"Phone me at Conway's when you get news of the arrangements."

He looked into the car.

"Good luck, Mr. Regan. See you sometime."

"Sure thing, buddy!" said Regan.

Charlie waved, and turned away with a grimace.

***

At the tailors Goldstein greeted him like a long lost friend and agreed to go to the Imperial to make George a uniform as soon as he could. Charlie trudged his way up to Conway's lugging his bags which now felt as if they contained dumbbells. Mrs. O'Sullivan treated him with the same enthusiasm and insisted that he come down for lunch after he had put away his bags and freshened up. Following a plate of Mrs. O'Sullivan's smoked eel and bacon, and after downing a glass of stout, Charlie walked over to the news stall and bought a Cork Examiner and retired to his room to loaf around. He was lying with the paper over his face when Mrs O'Sullivan tapped the door to tell him there was a telephone call.

"Charlie, are you there?" roared George down the phone.

"Yes I'm here, no need to shout."

"I've got news," he shouted at the same volume. "They're taking Collins back to Dublin by boat tomorrow night and I've got two berths."

"Okay, I'll drop over to see you at lunch time tomorrow to get all the details."

"Your fellow Goldstein came over and took my measurements, by God that man's a fast worker. He's coming back at five o'clock for a first fitting, says it should be ready by twelve tomorrow."

"Can't wait," said Charlie dryly. "See you tomorrow then."

Now awake and refreshed, Charlie got into some more casual clothes and had a walk around Cork organising a few bank appointments, dropping in for the odd beer here and there. He realised that it was likely to be a long time before he would see Cork again – if ever. It was a pity, he liked Cork. It was a more genuinely friendly and cosmopolitan place than anywhere else in Ireland. It had nothing of the tangible bitterness of Belfast or false bonhomie of the professional Dubliners who sniggered behind the backs of the country folk, whom they contemptuously referred to as 'Culchies'. He also managed to pick up an illicit copy of the latest anti-treaty 'Stop Press-War News' which he read in his bed later. It made no mention of Collins's assassination.

Even after an early rise Charlie had a busy morning with one thing and another, and didn't get over to the Imperial until well after one. A bus-boy was dispatched to George's room and came back with the message to go on straight up. He gave a rap on the door and heard George shouting him in.

"Well! What do you think?" he said standing in front of a large mirror.

Charlie was stunned for a moment. Goldstein was standing in the middle of the room and caught Charlie's eye, he shrugged his shoulders spreading his hands out as if to say, 'Not my fault'.

"Mr. Goldstein could you leave us for a moment?" said Charlie.

Goldstein scampered away saying he'd be back in five minutes.

"I hope you're not seriously thinking of wearing this… this outfit to the funeral."

"What's wrong with it?" said George smoothing down the pockets.

"Have you ever seen a Gilbert and Sullivan opera?" said Charlie.

"What?"

"Obviously not," said Charlie softly.

Charlie had to think of another tack; George did not take ridicule too kindly.

Standing back he could see that the uniform was a bizarre confection of gold braid, epaulettes, lanyards, buttons, cuffs and sashes.

All that's missing is a plumed hat, though Charlie wryly.

"Listen George. Your uniform looks great but this is likely to be a state funeral of the highest order, they will be looking for a bit of decorum and solemnity. I think your uniform, might be suited to something like, say, a passing out parade."

"That's funny - that's what Goldstein said." said George, slightly put out.

"He's got experience about these things. Maybe you should take his advice."

Goldstein came back in a few minutes later.

"I've been thinking," said George. "Maybe the uniform's a bit too fussy, a bit too much braid perhaps."

"Don't worry Mr. Peebles I can soon fix that!" said a relieved Goldstein, already ripping off the epaulettes.

Within minutes he had the uniform stripped down and was beginning to add polished leather belts and straps which he had in his bag.

George paraded in front of the mirror.

"Yes, much better," said George, tugging at the lapels in front of the mirror. By now totally convinced that the uniform change was his idea in the first place.

"After all," he said strutting around the room, "this is a State Funeral, Mr. Goldstein!"

"Now George, tell me what's been arranged," said Charlie.

"We'll need to get down to Queenstown later on today. They've commandeered a cross channel liner called 'Classic' and it's leaving tonight on the right tide, whatever the hell that means. I managed to get hold of the Lancia, it's coming here about five."

"If that's the case I'll need to get moving. I need to arrange to get my luggage down here this afternoon," said Charlie.

"By the way, your uniform looks great - good choice," he continued. As he moved to the door he gave Goldstein a surreptitious wink.

"Thanks Charlie, see you later," said George without turning round, being far too busy adjusting straps and tightening belts.

Charlie walked back to Conway's at a brisk pace and called on Mrs O'Sullivan.

"I wonder if you could arrange for my luggage to be taken down to the Imperial within the next hour or so."

Mrs. O'Sullivan gave a short gasp.

"I hope you're not …"

"Oh don't worry I have no complaints. It just that I have to leave for Dublin tonight and I'm being picked up at the Imperial."

"I take it that this has something to do with … recent events," said Mrs. O'Sullivan slightly embarrassed by seeming to pry.

"In a way, yes. Could you also make up my bill?"

"Surely, Mr. McKenna. I'll get young Seamus to get the luggage down to the Imperial on the wheelbarrow. If you could bring your luggage down to the hall in about twenty minutes."

"Here give him this," said Charlie, handing over a half crown. "I'll go up and get the bags."

After changing into a clean shirt and collar he brought down the luggage. He decided to return to his room to finish off his newspaper and allow some time for the luggage to get to the Imperial. Mrs O'Sullivan had his bill ready when he returned to the hotel reception. Charlie did not want to upset her, nor did he like long goodbyes or sentimental departures.

"I may be back in a few weeks."

"You know there will always be a place for you here, Mr McKenna, Good luck to you."

Charlie took a leisurely stroll down to the Imperial. It was a pleasant, calm warm day and it was hard to believe the turmoil that existed here a couple of weeks ago was gone. He turned into the hotel and admired the marble floor of the lobby as he walked through. He was pleased to see his luggage stacked beside the porter's lodge as he approached the desk.

"Could you call Colonel Peebles? Room 312 I think it is."

"No need," replied the receptionist, using his hand to indicate the open area at the side of the foyer. "He's over there in the bar."

Charlie looked over to a group of four or five officers. Although George had his back to him, he recognised his uniform and his outline. Suddenly a clearly excited George moved to his right waving his arms and Charlie could see most of the officers. He turned away immediately; he recognised two of them - and one was Lieutenant Colonel Simon Barrett.

Charlie took a moment to regain his composure.

"Ah yes! I see him. Thank you very much," he said, suddenly patting his pocket.

"Damn, I forget to buy some matches."

"There's a tobacconist just next door, sir," replied the receptionist.

"Good, I'll nip out and buy a box before joining Colonel Peebles. Back in a minute," said Charlie turning away from the desk. He needed a couple of minutes to think.

Could he avoid meeting with Barrett? Possibly, but he would have to leave a message to meet George outside the hotel and give him some story about how he needed to avoid Barrett. He could do this quite easily; George could be quite gullible at times. Trouble was, if Barrett was going to Dublin he could hardly avoid bumping into him at some stage, to act furtively now would only make him look as if he had something to hide. An added complication was the fact that he recognised another of the officers as Emmett Dalton who, even from the hotel lobby, looked absolutely ghastly. He had never actually met Dalton but had seen him on several occasions in the Great War, particularly during the Battle of the Somme where Dalton was a senior officer in the Dublin Fusiliers. Not that there was any chance of Dalton recognising him, but it might be awkward if George started talking about military adventures as he was sure to do. He walked outside and turned left towards the shop and bought a box of matches. By the time he returned to the lobby he had made up his mind. He would have to meet Barrett and take it from there.

He marched up to the bar and slapped George on the back.

"How are you, George?"

"Ah, you made it!" said George, turning round.

"This is ..."

"Charlie McKenna of the Philadelphian Examiner," said Charlie, cutting him short and putting out his hand to the nearest officer whom he had earlier recognised as General Dalton.

"Emmett Dalton. Pleasure to meet you," said Dalton distractedly, looking even paler at closer quarters.

"And you too," said Charlie.

After shaking hands with Dalton, he turned to the other officers.

"Lieutenant Colonel Barrett," said Barrett holding out his hand. He looked at Charlie closely, not with recognition, but simply with the curiosity of an observant man.

Charlie knew he was safe for the time being.

"George," said Charlie quickly, "I've taken the liberty of booking a table at Harvey's for an early dinner. We might have a long night ahead of us. I said we would take an early table at 4 o'clock"

They looked at the clock above the bar, it was three forty-five.

"We'll need to leave shortly."

"Good thinking Charlie, I'll finish this drink and go."

George continued his conversation with the others, one of whom he had discovered had been born in America. He talked to him as if they had been friends for years.

"A reporter you say. From an American paper," said Barrett, turning to Charlie.

"Yes, just back from Tralee, I've been up there a while."

"Ah yes. County Kerry, haven't been there myself, the irregulars seemed to be pretty active there."

"I'm afraid I kept pretty much to the town. It's fairly quiet at the moment but there's the occasional ambush to liven things up," he paused for a moment. "Are you going to Dublin tonight?" he added lightly.

"'fraid not. I'm far too busy down here. Besides, as our American friends here would say, someone's got to hold the fort."

Charlie smiled at the remark.

"Okay George, let's get going."

He turned back to Barrett, holding out his hand.

"See you again sometime."

It took another minute to prise George away and over to Harvey's. At dinner George told Charlie about the Beal na blath ambush and how Dalton had held the dying Collins in his arms. Apparently the 20 mile trip back to Cork, took a horrifying 12 hours in the dark.

"No wonder you thought Dalton looked so bad," said George.

"You're right. Hard to believe it was only a couple of days ago," Charlie replied. "I suppose he's bearing up well, considering."

George continued to chatter away, helped by the couple of Jamesons he had taken earlier, and they finished eating just after five. They were just turning into the South Mall as the Lancia was pulling up at the entrance to the Imperial.

"Right! Let's get our stuff into the car and make our way down," said George. "God knows when this boat is going to sail."

It took a bit of time to get loaded up but it was still light when they finally got on the road. As they approached Queenstown they could see that many of the road signs were replaced with the Gaelic title of Cobh.

"What's this cob place?" said George.

"It's pronounced Cove, the original name before Queenstown. There's no letter v in written Gaelic, so they write bh instead," said Charlie.

George grunted and, as with most things that did not affect him directly, it went in one ear and out the other.

There were a few road blocks with nervous Free State troops inspecting vehicles and paperwork. Even so there was a fair crowd standing around the quay where the 'Classic' was berthed. The quiet crowd was held back a hundred yards or so by a ring of armed soldiers. Charlie could hear a low murmur of the rosary being led off by a priest. They parked the car and approached the officer in charge who waved them through after a quick look at their papers.

It appeared that the coffin had already been loaded up and as they walked up the gang plank they could see an armoured car being lowered into the hold. They were met by the chief officer who allocated them adjoining berths and instructed them to meet in the passenger's lounge in fifteen minutes.

There were nearly thirty people gathered in the bar as George and Charlie entered, mainly officers and dignitaries with a few newspapermen.

"The bar is opened and you can have a drink here until the boat sets sail." said the chief officer briskly. "There is no food available other than light snacks at the bar and the bar will close shortly after sailing. The captain has instructed that you then retire to your cabins and stay there until told otherwise – there will be no wandering about the deck area. I will send a crew member around after the boat has tied up at the North Wall in Dublin and the coffin has been removed."

He gave a sharp salute and walked out of the lounge.

"That's us told then," muttered George. "Fancy a drink?"

"Just a whiskey and then I'm off to my cabin, it's been a long day," said Charlie.

***

Charlie was getting ready for bed as the ship cast off. He looked out of the starboard porthole and watched the well lit quayside rapidly disappear as the ship turned south. The other porthole faced astern and inward, facing the main deck. He could already hear George snoring in the adjoining cabin.

Several hours had passed when Charlie awoke. He was slightly disoriented and it took a few moments to grasp that he was aboard a ship. He realised what had stirred him was the sudden calm as the engines stopped. He threw back the bed covers. From the starboard porthole he could just about see the outline of quays and piers of what he assumed was Dublin. The ship was riding high on the incoming tide of the Liffey and still travelling at a fair speed without the engine running. From the other port hole the silent empty deck was lit up in a bright ethereal white light against the black of the night. Only the ghostly and lonely figure of the captain could be seen standing on the bridge. Charlie returned to his bunk and sat on the edge. He could still hear George gently snoring in the silence surrounding him. He lay back and stared at the ceiling.

A light tapping at the door woke him up again; he must have dropped off.

"Tea is being served in the lounge," said a muffled voice.

There was some activity in the passageway outside as he started to get dressed. He looked out the starboard porthole; they must have berthed and unloaded very quickly and quietly. The dock area was almost deserted with only two or three military personnel hanging around. He could just make out the shape of the armoured car sitting on the quayside under a dull gaslight. George was passing as he opened the cabin door.

"Damn boat! Never slept a wink all night," he muttered as he passed. "Let's get some tea, I'm parched."

They were instructed in the lounge to get their paperwork and luggage organised and that they should be disembarking within the hour. General Collins' remains were already being prepared for a state funeral and public viewing in the City Hall. The funeral, they were told, would be from the Pro Cathedral in three days time - on the 28th August.

"We'll book into the Shelbourne, it will be handy for everything, I'll get us a taxi," said Charlie as they walked down the gangplank.

"I need to get to Temple Bar to see this lawyer fella," said an agitated George.

"For God's sake, George! It's only five in the morning – relax will you."

Two or three taxis formed a shuttle service to the city centre and they managed to reach the Shelbourne as the sun was rising behind the hotel. Charlie arranged a breakfast and a room call for eight o'clock and they retired to their rooms for a lie down.

***

"Right then, that's me off," announced George, draining his breakfast teacup.

"Hold on a minute, what plans do you have?" said Charlie.

"I want to see this Connelly guy, the lawyer, and get this money sorted out."

"Then what?"

"I need to get to Army HQ to organise resigning my commission after the funeral."

"…and then."

"Haven't thought about that yet."

"I'll organise our travel plans for after the funeral," said Charlie

"... and while you're at HQ, see if you can get me some credentials for the funeral, here take this letter from Daly – let's keep up the 'reporter from America' line. Meet me back here at one o'clock for lunch."

"And what are you going to do while I'm racing around Dublin?"

"Don't worry about me. I've got plenty to do," said Charlie, rising from the table.

Actually Charlie didn't have that much to do but he wanted a long early walk around Dublin. Anytime he had been there it was always rushed and fraught with danger with little time to do anything or look at anything. He took the short walk up to the river Liffey, passed Trinity College, and across the O'Connell Bridge to Sackville Street. The half ruined GPO building was on his left; it was a melancholy sight. He remembered his brother Pat telling him, with pride, that a Donegal man was killed there during the Easter Rising. At the time he was about to tell Pat the unfortunate fact that the only Donegal man killed in the uprising was in the British Army. But he didn't have the heart and thought better of it. What difference did it make?

He wondered how many more myths would come out of this conflict; plenty, he surmised.

The road ahead was still littered with rubble from the fighting in July. He turned right trying to find the best route back down towards the Liffey, hoping to find a shipping agent down by the Quays. He found several and managed to get a booking for two days after the funeral. He crossed over Sackville Street again into Bachelors Walk to browse through some of the second hand bookshops there and was delighted to pick up a good copy of 'Riddle of the Sands' by Erskine Childers; it was a book he had spent time trying to track down. There were one or two other books he picked up, including an old fashioned French Reader. He headed back to the Shelbourne with plenty of time to spare.

"So, how did it go?" said Charlie over lunch.

"Couldn't have gone better!" announced George slapping his knee. "Connelly reckons the Government have been given a whole load of money by the English to get the government up and running, including paying compensation. And he reckons with the paperwork we have, we should get paid out right away - if we give him some money to 'oil the wheels', as he put it."

"It makes sense. Get the new government into debt and then they owe you more than just money."

"What?" said George slightly distracted.

"Rebels make poor administrators," said Charlie. "Taking pot shots at the police or army are one thing, administering a civil service that can run an economy and a treasury department is another."

He could see George's eyes beginning to glaze over.

"Anyway, what's this 'oiling the wheels' going to cost you?"

"£250, plus his fee of £250," he hesitated. "You mean what it's costing us, don't you, not me alone."

"Sure," said Charlie, "I'm getting 10 percent so I'll pay fifty of the five hundred pounds. Fifty quid as we call it."

"Only fifty?" said George looking at him closely and drummed his fingers on the table cloth. Charlie was good with figures and George was not quite sure if he was being outsmarted or not.

"Look George, £50 is over two hundred bucks; my total take is $1000. What if I gave you 10 percent of that?"

George reddened slightly.

"That's only one hundred and twenty bucks – thirty pounds," said Charlie.

"No, fifty will do fine," said George, uneasily.

"Good – and you can pick up the bill for lunch. Let's eat, I'm starved."

***

Forking up the last of the ham and sausage of a thick Dublin Coddle, George told him that he could resign his commission any time after the funeral. The bigwigs, he said, thought that the military war was now over.

"I wouldn't bet on that," said Charlie. "Anyway, you're still taking part in the funeral, are you?"

"Of course! They've already drawn up preparations and plans. I'm to be behind the coffin with most of the other officers."

"Good, I'll try to keep an eye out for you then," he paused, "…if I go."

George looked surprised.

"Are you thinking of not going? I managed to get a couple of passes for the cathedral service."

"I've been thinking. I've seen enough funerals these past few years to last me a lifetime. I'll make my mind up on the day and even if I do go, I won't be attending the mass. I'll find somewhere on the route to watch it. Give the pass to someone else. Connolly the lawyer might be impressed, and it could help to oil those damn wheels he seems so keen on."

"By Jove!" said George, "that's not a bad …

"In any event," Charlie continued quickly, "I've organised our return to the States. We're leaving two days after the funeral."

"Are we leaving from here or are we going back to Queenstown?"

"Neither. We're going to Le Havre."

"Where?"

"Le Havre, it's in France," said Charlie. "I need to go to Paris for a week or two then we get the SS France to New York on the 15th of next month. We should be stateside by the 22nd. "

"But…"

"Don't worry you'll enjoy it, I speak the lingo quite well and I'll show you the sights. The Eiffel tower, the Moulin Rouge and all that- I'll even show you where they built the Statue of Liberty."

Charlie was a bit wary of George's reaction but George sat up in his seat, excited.

"You might not believe this, but funny enough, I've all always fancied going to Paris…"

He hesitated and looked at Charlie quizzically.

"…They built the Statue of Liberty in Paris?"

***

The ticket for the memorial service was passed on to a senior civil servant in the Treasury who showed his gratitude by issuing a cheque to George's company the day before the funeral; George was beside himself with joy. Charlie watched the funeral cortège slowly passing down Sackville Street from the top of Clery's Department store, well worth the two shillings demanded by the janitor. It was both moving and unnerving for Charlie. There was a terrible sadness about the whole affair; the crowd that lined the streets was immense and unsettlingly quiet and morose. After a while Charlie began to feel ill at ease with the sound of army boots stamping along cobbled streets. He waited until the coffin and the column of officers behind had passed and then made his way back to the Shelbourne. He sat around the lounge drinking tea and reading his books until George appeared after dinner, half drunk and in good spirits.

"What an occasion! They say half a million lined the streets."

"So they say in the evening papers," said Charlie.

"Did you see me?"

"Yes, you looked very smart."

Of course it was impossible to identify anyone from where he was positioned, but George would never know. He was about to add that as far as he was concerned it seemed to be more a Free State show of strength as a much as anything else.

But he thought better of it.

"I think I'll have an early night, George. Tomorrow's our last day and I still have a few things to do."

The next morning Charlie packed his valise for the journey and arranged for the rest of his luggage to be put aboard the ship after lunch. George spent an age saying his goodbyes to all and sundry in the lounge before Charlie managed to squeeze him into the taxi he had ordered half an hour earlier. As they drove through the city, the atmosphere seemed to be calmer and more relaxed after the exhilaration of the funeral two days earlier. The quayside was busy with travellers and sightseers and they had to push their way towards the gangplank where George fell into company with a couple of giggling and delightful ladies, two American tourists from Boston.

After settling in his cabin, Charlie wandered around the ship observing the sailors preparing to get underway. The engines were already thumping away and within twenty minutes they were on the move. Charlie stood on the stern watching the city slowly disappearing and the bay of Dublin beginning to widen out. A flock of screeching herring gulls followed in the wake of the ship trying to catch the bread thrown by the excited youngsters on the bottom deck.

Charlie became aware of George at his side.

"Saying your last goodbyes, Charlie?" he said, with a surprisingly soft voice.

Charlie said nothing.

"It doesn't bother me," George continued "I've been in America for so long that it doesn't mean that much now."

Charlie looked across the Bay silently. He could just make out the blue outline of the Wicklow Mountains in the distance.

"I've made arrangements to meet those American tourists for tea later."

Charlie turned, tapping his palm on the ship rail for a moment.

"I'll be back," he said, pausing for a moment. "…sometime."

He suddenly grabbed George by the shoulders and turned him away from the rail.

"Let's go!" he said with a laugh. "Let's see if we can use some of our Irish charm on those young American girls."

oooOooo

CHAPTER TWENTY

Ballyseedy Crossroads

Life in Balleymullen barracks was grim for the ordinary soldier, a living reality of the old soldiers' maxim that war consists of long periods of sheer boredom interspersed with moments of utter terror. Barrack activities included endless exercises, square bashing and parades. When not on duty, soldiers polished their kit and assembled and reassembled their rifles or, if they had a pass, went into town to flirt with the local girls, which was an activity fraught with danger for either sex.

Through the cold, wet and dismal weather, the intermittent war staggered on through the rest of the year and into 1923. Many patrols were sent out and homes invaded on the whim of an army of informers and mischief makers, some men were arrested on the flimsiest excuse. Patrols were ambushed for no apparent military gain except for looting of weapons by the anti-treaty irregulars. Local disputes over land rights that would have been settled by diplomacy and courts were resolved by shootouts of Wild West proportions. Some patrols seemed to be arranged with the sole purpose of engaging the enemy in noisy and pointless fire fights. As time moved on, the engagements became more and more vicious as the death toll began to mount. Some engagements simply became revenge attacks with no military pretext whatsoever.

Pat's nerves were becoming increasingly stretched. He started drinking more than he was used to. Unlike his colleagues, money was never a problem. He had more than most and spent freely without being too reckless. Where an ordinary soldier was lucky to draw a couple of pounds a month, an extra two or three pounds a month taken from the bank made the difference between being on the edge of poverty and comparatively rich. His only big expense was a Kodak camera he saw in a Tralee pawnshop for five pounds, which he bought on a drunken impulse. Even with that, by the end of February he still had more than eighty pounds of his own money left.

In the meantime, the anti-treaty forces were becoming increasingly desperate, and more worrying for them, unpopular. They began to bully and harass farmers for food and accommodation. Ill thought-out tactics like high-jacking and robbing grocery delivery vans and blowing up roads, rail tracks and bridges for no apparent tactical reason, merely infuriated and inconvenienced the non-combatants. The execution of prisoners was also beginning to take its toll; during January the state was executing the equivalent of one a day, an act that would have brought wholesale destruction, major civil disobedience and riots if committed under British rule. Yet hardly as much as a single peaceful demonstration was organised or a word raised. The population had simply become war weary.

At the beginning of March, Pat was involved in a long running battle in the Garrane Mountains where they lost three men including a friend of his from Galway. Five anti-treaty men were killed and six were captured and taken to Ballymullen barracks. The battle left Pat exhausted, shattered and drained.

The next day a patrol was called out from Castleisland where the bulk of the Dublin guards were stationed. A letter was passed into headquarters informing them that that the local anti-treaty forces had an arms dump near a town called Knocknagoshel. The letter was a forgery. The arms dump was mined with a massive bomb which was triggered when the guns were lifted out. Two privates and three National army officers were blown to pieces including Michael Dunn and Charlie Stapleton, two veterans of the war of independence and members of 'the squad', Michael Collin's hand picked special operation unit in Dublin.

Paddy Daly was furious, almost fit for tying. These men had been personal friends of his and he demanded retribution. Later that day an order was issued forbidding any national army personnel to take any road blocks apart. Instead anti-treaty prisoners would be forced to dismantle them, if the barricades were mined, then hard lines.

Pat and a couple of friends hung about the barracks most of that afternoon and early evening. They were allocated early morning sentry duties for the following day and decided to rest up after some strenuous early morning training conducted by an overenthusiastic P.E instructor. The time was passed by playing cards and drinking light beer and porter bought in from the local pub in jugs. Around nine o'clock in the evening as it was getting dark, a platoon of Dublin guards, easily recognised by their smart dark green uniforms and dark brown leather holsters and belts, drew up into the gas lit exercise square in two lorries.

Pat and the others heard their arrival and looked out the barrack room window. They recognised some of the guards as the notorious 'visiting committee' or the 'away team'.

"I'm not sure if this looks too good," said someone behind Pat.

There was a commotion over in the prison cells as the guards started to drag out some of the prisoners. Four or five prisoners were thrown against the wall and the guards started firing their revolvers. The men in the barracks leapt back from the window.

"Surely to God they're not going to shoot them in cold blood!" shouted one of them. It was a young eighteen year old boy from Waterford, Brendan, who looked about thirteen.

The shooting continued for another few minutes then suddenly stopped. Pat moved quickly back to the window.

"They haven't shot them. They were just trying to frighten them. Look, the wall is full of bullet holes all around them."

Two of the prisoners were lying on the ground where they were kicked to their feet by the guards. The next hour passed like a horrifying dream as the guards continued to act out mock executions and deliver beatings. Screams from the prisoners echoed across the square from the cells where God knows what atrocities were being committed. Unable to sleep, Pat produced a bottle of whiskey which he shared with his colleagues. Eventually the noise and racket stopped. Brendan, emboldened by the liquor, crept up to the window.

"They're loading them into a lorry now," he whispered.

A minute later they could hear the lorry starting up and rumbling across the cobbled square and out the main entrance. The silence that the lorry left was unsettling.

"Right," said the corporal, sounding more confident than he was. "Let's finish off the drink and get off to bed. We've an early start tomorrow. The sergeant major will be here at seven on the dot so get moving."

***

The door crashed open – it was six o'clock.

"Right you lot," roared an officer with an unmistakable Dublin accent, "get shifted. We've a job for you boys."

Pat and the rest of them staggered out of the bunks, still half asleep and half drunk.

"You've got ten minutes," he shouted and slammed the door.

Someone fumbled with the tilly lamp and managed to get it up and running. The dim yellow light helped the soldiers, with much cursing, to find their gear and get dressed at the same time. They were near enough ready when the officer returned. The corporal was summoned to the door and was taken outside. Parked on the square the corporal could make out an old lorry, he was amazed that he managed to sleep through its arrival.

"Get your men ready to leave in this lorry within the next fifteen minutes. I'm expecting another one to arrive shortly. The second lorry will follow you as you leave," said the officer.

"Where are we headed, sir," asked the corporal.

"Never you mind! Just get going,"

The extra time allowed them to get a bit better organised. Some shoved some food and water in their knapsack, some took cigarettes and matches, Pat stowed away some biscuits and at the last minute, his camera. Brendan, the young Waterford boy, was delegated to stand outside and give them a shout the minute the other vehicle appeared. Around six thirty the lights of the second lorry appeared loaded with wooden crates, or at least that's what Brendan took it to be in the gas lit gloom. He gave a call to the lads inside. The soldiers clattered out noisily and started to clamber aboard the first lorry. There were no seats so they had to stretch out, shifting and pushing each other on the wooden floor. Moments later the engine started up and the ancient vehicle lurched its way across the square and out on to the road, within a mile the paved street gave way to the usual rough stone surface. The journey was incredibly uncomfortable as the lorry lurched from side to side on the uneven road. It was still dark although crimson streaks of dawn could be seen to the east. The engine noise was so loud that they couldn't talk. They were expecting a long journey, perhaps to Castleisland, although no one actually bothered to ask where they were going. After ten minutes on the stone road they were stopped by two or three Dublin guards who looked into the lorry and waved them on. To the men's delight and surprise, they were stopped about five minutes later and told to get out. They could have only travelled five or six miles.

They clambered and jumped off the back of the lorry, stretching their legs and arms, still not quite awake yet. The driver had switched off the engine and had parked about thirty yards from a large derelict house on a crossroad. It looked as if it might have been an old pub or inn at one time, it was hard to tell. The sun was now beginning to appear behind the hillside.

They stood quietly in the silence of dawn, the only sounds being the tick of the engine as it cooled down and the occasional ominous caw of a crow in the trees. The other lorry trundled in behind them two minutes later. Another officer, a staff sergeant, jumped out and stood at the tailgate.

"I want four men to unload the other truck," said the officer finally.

Four men were immediately detailed to remove the boxes, it was not long till everyone became aware, now that the sun was almost up, that they were not just boxes - they were polished pine coffins.

"Put them behind the house for now," instructed the officer. "The rest of you come with me."

As they grabbed their kit and marched, out of habit, in twos down the road, it was beginning to become apparent to them that something disastrous had happened here. There was a large hole blown in the road near the house and heaps of debris seemed to lie close to its edge.

About ten yards before the crater the captain stopped and addressed them.

"Before we go any further I want to tell you something. Yesterday a company of our men were lured to a cowardly trap by the irregulars and blown to pieces," he said. "Five were killed outright, another two had their legs blown off and will never walk again…"

"…our men." he repeated and remained silent for a moment.

"From now on all barricades will be dismantled by the irregulars. Last night this barricade was discovered here, at Ballysheedy Crossroad. As instructed, we gathered up prisoners to dismantle the barricade. Unfortunately it was mined and, it seems, all the prisoners were killed."

He paused again.

"It's our job to give the remains back to their families for a Christian burial. I know this will be an unpleasant task but it's got be done. Remember as you work, that this was laid out, not as a military ambush tactic, but as a murderous trap. Constructed by these spineless, treacherous mutineers for us and that these bodies could be just as easy any one of you – you or any one of your comrades."

He stopped and looked back at the progress of the other lorry and saw the other officer giving the same explanation to the rest of the men.

"You can stand at ease. We will wait until the others are finished unloading before we start."

The men shifted nervously, some took out cigarettes for a smoke, unwilling to go near the blast area until the last possible moment. Pat walked around horrified and tried to take a casual look at his surroundings, not wanting to appear too ghoulish. He had seen the devastating work of land mines before; they normally blasted debris and material over a fairly large area. This one looked to have a curious shape, most of the debris and the bodies seemed to be surrounding the hole in a symmetrical fashion as if placed there. Some of the bodies looked badly burned and surrounded the hole with their feet pointing to the centre. He realised with growing horror that several bloody limbs and extremities like feet and some hands lay a short distance away. Yet a few of the victims of the blast appeared to Pat to be not that badly wounded and looked as if they might have survived had they had been given attention. There was also an odd gap in the circle beside the wall at the other side of the road. Pat went back to the rest of the men and sat down and pulled over his bag. He was looking for some aspirin that he knew he had at the bottom of his bag - he was beginning to get a headache. He started pulling things from his bag as the officer sauntered over.

"That looks a good camera, did you get it in Dublin?" he said.

"No. I bought it in Tralee - in a pawn shop," replied Pat.

"Can I see it? My father has a photography shop up in Dublin. I'm sure I've seen one of these before, a Kodak vest pocket, I think," he said as he picked it up and turned it around in his hand. "Ah yes, this one's called 'the special' it has a leather case rather than the usual enamel finish."

Pat was astonished at the officer's calm reaction to the grisly devastation around him; he was talking to Pat as if he had casually bumped into him in a pub.

The officer held up the camera looking at the lens.

"This is ideal light for a good photograph," muttered the officer looking around. "Early morning sun over your shoulder in front of a whitewashed building ..."

He looked at Pat and waved him over to the old house.

"Stand over there and I'll take a snap. Don't stand too close to the barricade though."

Almost totally bewildered and bemused, Pat put his bag aside and did as he was told.

231

"That's okay, right there."

The officer looked at the scene through the lens.

"Stand up straight, more like a soldier!" he said twisting the lens, "…and try a smile."

The camera clicked as the other officer appeared from the back of the house.

"Will we start now?" he shouted.

The captain silently handed the camera back to Pat and turned to the rest of the platoon.

"Take the coffins down now, one at a time." he said quietly. "After we load the lorry, we need to get the hole filled in. The guards will keep the traffic back until nine o'clock, so let's work as fast as we can."

The work party completed their gruesome task in good time and returned to the barracks: the rest of the day was a nerve-wracking shambles. News of what had happened spread like wildfire through the town of Tralee and relatives and friends of the prisoners started to gather at the barrack gates. Rumour grew that the men had been tied around the barricade and that the mine was detonated by the National Army troops themselves. Pat was convinced that this was exactly what had happened and that the ropes binding them together had been cut off and disposed of shortly after the blast to conceal what had happened. There were also what Pat suspected to be bullet holes in some of the less injured men although sometimes they were working that fast it was difficult to tell. They had brought nine coffins but there were only the remains of eight prisoners. It seemed that one of them had been blown clear which accounted for the space near the wall. They started to search around but could find nothing. The captain thought the body may have been blown into the nearby River Lee somehow and ordered the soldiers to call off the search, finish off and get back to the barracks. When they returned another company of men was despatched immediately to find the missing prisoner; dead or alive was the order. The body wasn't found.

Late in the afternoon the gates opened and a platoon of guards escorted the lorry filled with eight coffins through the streets into the town where they were finally delivered to the relatives, the guards then made a hasty retreat. When the guards left, some of the relatives tore open the coffins to discover the mutilated bodies of their loved ones and a riot ensued. A fire fight developed outside the barracks with dozens of shots being exchanged until darkness fell; one soldier was shot and killed.

In the course of the next week two other 'barricades' were dismantled by anti-treaty prisoners in county Kerry, killing another nine. Another seven irregulars were executed by the state around the rest of the country. Pat went through two bottles of whiskey in two weeks.

***

Towards the end of March, around mid morning, the eight men in the clean up squad were rounded up and taken to a large room in the administration block where they stood around unconcerned, chatting and talking. The large door at the far end opened up and a Colonel Brigadier, who none of them recognised, walked in. He was followed by two lieutenants.

"Line up, men," said one of the lieutenants.

The soldiers, taken aback, shuffled into a reasonable line, not with quite barrack square precision, but good enough for the occasion.

"Okay. Stand at ease."

The brigadier stood in front of them.

"I know you men were asked to carry out a task recently that, given the circumstances, many would have found difficult to cope with. I admire your forbearance."

He stopped talking and started to pace back and forth along the line of men looking at each of them with genuine concern.

"However our political leaders in the Dail, have ordered an inquiry into this unfortunate incident. Perhaps rightly so, some may think. However this will take a few weeks to organise."

He paused again.

"The purpose of the inquiry will be to find out who instigated and perpetrated this act, not to persecute the ordinary rank and file soldiers like yourselves. May I say, to all of you, that you have served well here and under difficult circumstances - you have done your bit. I know you men were only involved when this…this action had already been carried out and I don't want you becoming embroiled in a legal inquiry - it would be grossly unfair. It has been decided to send you to a different posting, probably somewhere less active, like Dublin or the Curragh. You'll be informed by your commanding officer shortly."

He stopped in front of Pat for the second time, seeming to make up his mind about something.

"Okay men that's all. You can be dismissed."

The men visibly relaxed and were beginning to file out the door when one of the lieutenants called out.

"Private McKenna, could you wait behind?"

The rest of the men piled out chattering excitedly about their next possible posting. Pat stood in the middle of the room.

"Brigadier Barrett would like a word, follow me."

The name meant nothing to Pat; he was never good with names.

He was taken through a side door to a large office, Brigadier Barrett sat behind a large polished desk looking through some files. The lieutenant told Pat to be seated.

After a few minutes Barrett told the lieutenant that he wouldn't be needed for now and that he could leave. He then turned his attention to Pat.

"I've been looking through your file here, Private McKenna. I see you volunteered last August with a recommendation from a Colonel Peebles is that right?"

"That's right, sir."

"How did you get to know Colonel Peebles?"

"Oh. He was a friend of my brother Charlie, sir. They knew each from America," said Pat quite innocently.

"Your brother Charlie, was a Captain in the IRA during the Tan War, I believe?"

"Yes, sir."

Barrett picked up a piece of paper.

"Yes, I have a wanted poster of him from the British authorities here, no photo I'm afraid," said Barrett with a thin smile

Pat was uncomfortable now, he wondered where all this was leading.

"Can I ask you, where were you before you came to Tralee?"

"I was in Cork, sir"

"With your brother, Charlie?"

"Yes that's right." said Pat. His throat was getting dry; the past six months had put all the events in Cork out of his mind.

"Ever heard of a place called Passage West?"

All the pieces began to fall into place. Barrett must have been one of the officers they had ambushed on the day of the invasion, he must have been promoted in the time since then... Pat began to turn white, he didn't reply.

The Brigadier stood up and walked to the window.

"I can tell from your demeanour that I'm right."

He turned around.

"You and your brother, with two others, held up and robbed the National Provisional Government of several firearms and a large quantity of ammunition..." he turned around.

"...and of twelve thousand pounds in gold sovereigns."

Pat was squirming in his seat.

"It wasn't ..."

"It wasn't quite like that? Mm... Not the way a jury would see it." He hesitated.

"Not that we seem to bother too much about juries these days," he said with a disapproving grimace. "In any event, a military court would have you hung in a matter of days."

Barrett sat down again.

"I'll ask you this once. Where did Charlie put the money?"

Pat was silent for a moment.

"It's in a warehouse in Cork. I wanted nothing to do with it," Pat said eventually.

Barrett looked a bit surprised at Pat's answer - he expected him to deny all knowledge of the event, blame some one else or simply say nothing.

"A warehouse? What kind of warehouse? You mean it might be still there?" said Barrett leaning forward.

"It might be. Charlie only took one case and put the rest in a bonded warehouse. He booked it in for a year, it might still be there, but I don't really know."

"What was the name of the warehouse?"

"Cohen's, I think."

"Cohen's? A big place, not far from the railway station?"

"Yes. That's it."

Barrett reached for the phone.

"I need a staff car immediately, send it round to the front gate. Get an armed van ready as well."

He put down the phone.

"Well Private McKenna, that bit of information has probably saved your neck. We're going on a trip to Cork shortly."

He looked at his watch.

"The transport might take fifteen minutes or so. Why don't you tell me a bit more about this bonded warehouse."

***

They made the outskirts of Cork in just over two hours. Pat sat in the front with the driver while Barrett and his adjutant sat in the back going over several documents. The lightweight armoured van raced in front of them in case of any attack, but the roads were trouble free and quiet. It took another twenty minutes to manoeuvre through the late lunch time streets of Cork, now much busier than Pat could remember, until they eventually reached King Street. They turned right and then finally turned under the enormous sign for Cohen's warehouse.

Barrett marched into the reception area flanked by his adjutant, Pat trailing behind.

"I would like to speak to the owner or the manager of these premises, if you please." said Barrett while removing his leather travelling gloves. He spoke with remarkable authority.

"Certainly I'll get Mr. Isaac. General... er?"

"Brigadier Barrett, madam."

A minute later the bustling figure of Isaac Cohen appeared,

straightening his tie as he approached.

"How can I help, Brigadier?"

"Some Government business, perhaps it would be better in your office?"

"Of course. Let me lead the way."

Cohen sat in his office chair behind the desk, the officers took the two seats. Pat stood beside the door.

"To business, Mr Cohen, and also to the point," said Barrett.

"A government vehicle was hijacked near Cork around August of last year," he continued. "In that vehicle were five blue boxes, containing some twelve thousand pounds in gold sovereigns, property of the Treasury. I believe these boxes are stored in these premises."

Isaac Cohen was dumbfounded.

"Twelve thousand in gold, that's preposterous!" he gasped.

"I doubt if the person who deposited the boxes would have given you an accurate description of the contents."

"Just a minute, you don't expect me to examine every box that comes in here do you?"

"I suppose that would be unreasonable. Perhaps we could have a look at your letting arrangements for last August?"

"I'll get O'Donnell down here. He deals with that side of things."

O'Donnell duly arrived armed with his neat ledger for August and joined them in the now crowded office. He laid the ledger on the desk so that Barrett could see it.

"Let's have a look at the entries for the eighth of August, shall we?" said Barrett

"Not a lot of business that day," said O'Donnell, "just a small let for a Belfast company. Gorman of Belfast that should be on the ticket. Four boxes of phosphorous bronze in rods. Signed in by a Mr. Charles McKenna."

Barrett sat back a bit to think. He was impressed; all this work was done on the same day. Charlie McKenna was proving to be a considerably resourceful man.

"I'm afraid we're going to have a look at these boxes, Mr O'Donnell."

"Just a minute, you can't come in here demanding to see our customer's goods and opening their boxes, this is a legal government bonded warehouse not a bloody pawnshop!" cried Isaac Cohen.

"I'm a lawyer by profession, Mr Cohen. How long do you think it would take me to get a magistrates order."

"Probably a couple of days."

"Try a couple of hours, if that," replied Barrett, tapping his gloves into his hand.

"You depend on government co-operation in your line of business, Mr Cohen. You use customs officials, tax inspectors and the like. I could make life difficult."

Cohen looked blankly at Barrett, trying to weigh things up.

"O'Donnell, take these men over to the holding shed and show them what they want," he said suddenly. "I'll join you in a moment."

As soon as they left the office, he rushed into the reception area.

"Hannah! Get me the receipt books for the end of August and take them to my room right away."

O'Donnell led the party through the warehouse grounds to a building with a large sign saying Block 3. They were met by a large warehouse man who unlocked the door of the building and let them in. As they walked along O'Donnell produced a key ring.

"Room sixteen," he announced simply, opened the door and walked through.

"Cage Five is what you're looking for," he said curtly. He was annoyed at the idea of anyone, other than a paying customer, being allowed even this far into the building.

Pat looked at the now familiar set-up with the steel bars cemented at floor and ceiling level and stared at the four boxes stacked neatly inside with a certain amount of dread.

"Open the cage, Mr O'Donnell and tell your warehouseman to bring a crowbar."

***

Isaac Cohen found the receipt quickly. What to do next? His first instinct was put a match to it. Letting McKenna take twenty samples was not necessarily unusual but to charge him twenty pounds implied that Cohen knew the boxes contained something more valuable than some goddamn bronze rods. But what if McKenna had been caught and told them exactly what had happened and explained that he managed to remove another twenty rolls of sovereigns by what virtually amounted to a bribe? There was also the problem of supplying McKenna with a receipt for material that had been removed from the warehouse during the period of the truce. What if they started to investigate that bit of business? He shoved the paper into his pocket and headed to Block 3. He would tough this one out. He had friends in the government, some of whom owed him favours.

The boxes were lying opened when Cohen arrived.

"Ah. Mr Cohen! Glad you could join us," said Barrett. "I'm afraid we didn't have a key. We just opened the boxes as best we could."

Barrett picked up one of the rolls and split the paper in the middle with a small penknife. He turned around and snapped the rod in two and pointed the two ends towards Cohen.

"Odd colour for Phosphorous Bronze, wouldn't you say Mr Cohen?"

Isaac Cohen shrugged his shoulders and spread his hands.

"I can only take people on trust, Brigadier."

"There seems to be some rolls missing. I've been assured that none of the other boxes had been opened when they arrived here."

"I can explain that," said Cohen producing the receipt. "Mr McKenna returned towards the end of August and asked if he could take some samples to show some prospective clients and to check that the material was of the right specification."

"Let me see that," said Barrett reaching out.

Barrett started to read through the document.

"You'll notice I charged him a small fee."

"So I see," replied Barrett looking up. "...although I'd hardly call twenty pounds a small fee."

"To be completely repaid when he completed the paperwork and

239

removed the goods," lied Cohen smoothly.

Barrett eyed Cohen suspiciously. His story was plausible and anyway, he decided, to get back as much gold as they did was almost a miracle. So what if Cohen skimmed a bit? He had recovered four out of the five boxes - almost 80% of a consignment that had been given up as lost.

He handed the receipt back to Cohen.

"Consider yourself lucky Mr. Cohen," he said looking him in the eye for a second.

"Right! I'm leaving Lieutenant Jarvis while I go to the magistrate for a warrant to get this stuff out of here - let's keep it all legal shall we?"

"You," he said pointing to Pat. "Follow me."

As they walked through the warehouse back to the staff car, Barrett said,

"I must admit a certain admiration for your brother's way of working. How he manages to manipulate people is quite remarkable. Do you know where he is now?"

"No I don't, sir. I haven't seen him since he left for Dublin with George Peebles."

"Ah yes! The legendary Colonel Peebles. Resigned his commission after his term was up and went to Paris for a while and then back to America - your brother went with him."

"How do you know that?"

"He renewed his passport in Paris and, as Paris is where his passport was originally issued, he got it no problem."

He stopped and looked at Pat.

"I dare say he probably knew that - as I said, very resourceful."

They walked on for a few minutes in silence.

"What will happen to me, sir?"

"Nothing. You will return with me to Ballymullen and you will be transferred tomorrow to Dublin. That should give you the time to get your affairs in order. Anyway with what we've recovered today, and a bit of luck, this war should be over in a few weeks."

He stopped and turned round to Pat.

"I believe you to be an honest man Pat and if you've gained

anything from this affair then keep it. I'm not interested. Although if you manage to get word to your brother, advise him to stay well away from Ireland for a fair bit of time. I also want your word that you will tell no one of this - and I mean no one."

"Yes sir, I'll tell no one."

Barrett stopped for a second.

"Mind you," he said drolly, pulling on his gloves. "It's not that anyone is likely to believe you."

oooOooo

CHAPTER TWENTY ONE

The Purvey

The Marie Steward hotel, although it boasted several bedrooms, was a hotel in name only. Its main purpose was to provide a catering service - a 'purvey' as the people of the South Side called it - for the dozen or so Christian churches of all denominations and the two synagogues that lay within a half mile radius. It handled christenings, bar mitzvahs, holy communions, weddings and funerals - it was always busy. Overnight guests were actively discouraged and anyone foolish enough to book in for an overnight stay was treated as a nuisance, an unwanted interloper and an interference to the main business of the place. However, those organising a purvey, particularly those who were footing the bill, were greeted warmly by the oleaginous owner, who claimed to be a professional ex-football player although no one seemed to quite remember him playing in any of the many teams he claimed to have played for.

The owner said he could 'squeeze' the Toner party in and he said it as if he was doing them a favour. A buffet rather than the full sit down, he pointed out, between 11.00 and 2.00 when he was expecting - he forcefully reminded them - a full house of wedding guests which had been booked up ages ago.

The funeral guests were guided into a large lounge with a bar and French windows that opened onto a well kept lawn where there were five or six garden tables dotted around. On one side of the lounge there were three tables groaning with plates of sandwiches and rolls. Mainly rolls. Rolls filled with every conceivable breakfast item. Rolls and bacon, rolls and fried egg, rolls and black pudding, rolls and potato scones, rolls and sausages of every geometrical shape - square, round or links. Beside the rolls was a collection of sauces, including a vinegary brown sauce, of a type that is only ever seen in lower class chip shops, and a selection of ketchups in a variety of shades and tints of red - some Dijon mustard was supplied for the more discerning. The whole spread was flanked on either side by enormous urns of tea and coffee. The drinkers raced to the bar while the smokers galloped out to the lawn for a quick puff and to allow the food queue to ease down.

By the time Liam joined Grace and Eddie, Eddie had already polished off two bacon rolls and was starting on a third under the menacing eye of Grace.

"Bit early for the stout, Liam," said Grace.

"It's never too early for stout! This is my second pint," he said putting the glass down on the table. "I'm away in to get a couple of rolls."

Des and Julie came over with a plate of food and cups of tea.

"Have you spoken to Noreen or Eileen yet?" Grace asked Julie anxiously.

"No, not yet, but I think we should let everything calm down a bit. It's bit a crazy in there at the moment. There's a flaming rugby scrum around that tea urn," said Julie putting down her plate.

"By the way mum, before I forget, here are those coins we took on Sunday."

"Thanks love," said Grace.

She put the wrapped coins into her bag, took out her purse and removed another sovereign.

"Here, take this one back, that's the one Charlie gave you. I'll replace it with one from the roll. Now that you're getting married you might as well keep it ....keep it as a memento of Ireland."

Julie was raking about her handbag looking for her purse as Liam arrived back with a bacon filled roll.

"Ah," he said, "the famous sovereigns. Let's have another look at this one, Julie"

"Here," she said handing it over, "It's just the same as the rest, same date and everything."

Julie closed her handbag and slung it over her shoulder."

"Odd that," said Liam turning it over in his hand, "1916 – same year as the Easter Rising in Dublin"

"What's the big deal about that?" said Julie.

"Nothing I suppose, I'm just trying to figure out why Charlie seemed to have all these damn gold coins and why they all appear to have the same date. Maybe it was something sentimental or perhaps he bought them as an investment."

"Possibly," said Julie looking around. Her mother had already turned away and was speaking to Des.

"When you think how much he left when he passed away," she added quietly, "but would people invest in sovereigns in those days?"

"I'm not sure. Inflation was fairly low between the First and Second World wars but the value of gold went up considerably in the same period."

He tossed the coin in his hand.

"Then again that's with hindsight of course; the price of gold hardly changed for almost two hundred years before the First World War. I think it's debatable if anyone had a crystal ball or the prescience to invest in gold back then."

"Maybe he bought them as presents as he needed them."

Liam raised an eyebrow.

"Bought them rolled up in a nineteen twenties Free State wrapper? And your uncle Pat also bought some with the same date by coincidence?"

He handed back the coin to Julie with a shrug.

"Probably more to it than that, but I don't think we'll ever find out," he sighed.

Julie popped the coin into her jacket pocket absentmindedly.

"My God, Liam," she said with a smile as Liam bit into his roll, "you see conspiracy and intrigue everywhere."

They were joined by Mick and his mother a few moments later, and after half an hour, the hot sun had induced a soft languor in the well fed crowd. The socialising became less frantic and conducted at an easier pace as people moved from group to group effortlessly. Everything had slowed down so much that Des had begun to notice Jimmy Gilmore wandering around from table to table, eyes looking somewhat glazed, and got a bit concerned. He would have been even more concerned if he had known Gilmore had just done a line of coke in the toilet.

Eventually Noreen Toner came over to the table and was greeted with words of heart felt sympathy and warm hugs. Eddie, her brother, took her aside, hugged her tightly, his eyes glazing as he told her how hard it must be and to be sure to give him a call - for anything, anything at all.

Noreen was younger than Grace but looked ten years her senior. Compared to Grace, who was tall and quite elegant, she was short and slightly portly, her face haggard and careworn before her time. Grace took her aside and talked of better times and happier days when the children were young. Talked of long summer holidays in Ireland where their families often met with mutual friends and relatives. Noreen began to relax and smile. She had turned to talk to Mick's mother when Gilmore, who appeared to be wandering around aimlessly, joined the fringes of the company. Mick's mother was introducing Mick to Noreen.

"You know, Noreen it's the oddest thing. Our Mick's in the police force and he was one of the first on the scene when Hughie was found. Isn't that right, Mick?"

Mick looked utterly embarrassed.

"Just a coincidence Mrs Toner," he said. He coughed slightly and continued. "I know it's not much of a consolation, but we got the man who did it and we're sure to get a conviction."

Des was keeping an eye on Gilmore, who seemed to take a sudden interest when he found out Mick was a cop but he had to look away quickly when he himself was suddenly introduced to Noreen. After chatting for a few minutes she drifted away to another table. Des looked around for Gilmore but he was nowhere to be seen.

Eileen, Toner's younger sister, came over to talk to Julie. Julie introduced her to Liam and Mick.

"I like your accent," said Eileen to Liam. "You must come from the North."

"I'm from Tyrone, but I've been over here for years now."

"Des is doing a piece on Hughie for one of the Sunday papers and Liam is helping Des with some research." said Julie.

"Oh. What kind of research?" Eileen asked Julie.

"Well it started off about a gold sovereign that was found on Hughie, but we got a bit sidetracked when we found an old photograph of Uncle Pat."

"You mean old Uncle Pat from Donegal?"

Julie pulled out a copy of the photo and showed it to Eileen.

"This was in that envelope of photos that you took back from Ireland last year."

"Was it? I only had a quick look at them before I gave them to your mum. Is that Uncle Pat? He looks quite nice in this. I always remember him as wandering about the old house muttering to himself. Talking of Uncle Pat, I've got something of his in here." Eileen started to rummage about in her handbag.

"Uncle Pat gave me this the year before he died," she said, pulling out an old pocket watch. "Said I could keep it, although why he decided to give it to me is bit of a mystery. I thought at the time it was because I was one of his favourites or something - although I must admit he was half-cracked by then. I've always kept it with me. I felt as if I didn't, something bad would happen."

"Can I have a look?" said Liam. "I'm beginning to think of Pat as something of a personal friend these days."

"Sure," said Eileen handing it over.

He opened the front to show the clock face, turned it round and snapped open the back.

"Oh imagine that! I've had it for years and didn't know the back opened up!" cried Eileen.

"Yes, it's what they call a full hunter pocket watch. Look there's an inscription on the inside. I'll let you read it first," said Liam handing it back.

Eileen squinted her eyes and turned the watch away from the

sunlight.

"To Charlie from George Peebles. New Year 1920."

Eileen handed it back to Liam.

"I didn't realise it was that old. It must have belonged to his brother Charlie originally."

Liam looked at the watch closely.

"It says New York, not New Year," said Liam.

"Does it? My eyesight is going to the dogs these days."

"New York? I though you said Charlie stayed in Philadelphia?" said Julie to Eddie.

"That what he always told us," said Eddie.

"...and I wonder who George Peebles was?" she mused.

"I think I can remember there were folk called Peebles around Dunmore when I was a boy, but I think they're all gone now. Either over here or gone to America," said Eddie.

"Ah well, the mystery deepens," said Liam, "by the way, something else crossed my mind when I saw that photo again."

"Pray tell," said Grace.

"I wonder whose camera it was, and who took the photo?"

"What difference does that make?" asked Julie.

"When you see it closely, it's a good exposure and for all the background disturbance, quite well composed - almost professional. And it's pretty clear that it was taken with a relatively expensive camera. I think the army paid around 10 shillings a week then, if that - hardly enough to buy an expensive item like a camera."

Liam frowned as he juggled the watch in his hand before handing it back to Eileen. Grace caught his look.

"You can't half tell them, Liam! I suppose with your fantastic powers of deduction, you'll be telling us next that watch obviously proves that, after Pat massacred half the anti-treaty forces in Tralee, Charlie went off to New York and became a Mafia hit man," Grace said good humouredly.

"Stranger things have happened," said Liam waving his finger at Grace.

"God give us strength!" replied Grace, raising her eyes to heaven.

***

After one o'clock people started to drift away especially after the owner started to deliberately and noisily vacuum the carpet, loudly instructing those who were sitting down to lift their feet so he could get under the table.

Liam announced that he intended to pop down to Heraghty's Bar for a couple of beers and to catch up with some chums.

"You might as well go with him for an hour or so Des. I'll take mum and dad back to the house and I'll pick you up later. Why don't you come into town with us Liam? We'll treat you to a kebab dinner in Zorba's."

"Sounds okay to me," said Liam.

"I'll give you a ring when I leave the house, Des."

Everyone started to move out shouting goodbyes and giving air kisses. Mick fell into step with Des and Liam.

"I'll give you pair a walk down to Vicky Road. I'm meeting someone later on in town so I might as well just catch a train from Queen's Park station."

As they walked through the heart of Govanhill they remarked on how run down the place had become over the past few years. The once tidy streets were now litter strewn and where once the pavements were full of playing children, there now roamed dead-eyed junkies. Many of the windows of the tenements were either smashed or covered in plywood; it was hard to believe that people still lived there. For all that, they were not particularly uneasy or afraid. They were used to this place. The school that Des and Mick attended was just along the road and still going strong. As youngsters they roamed these streets freely and knew the area like the back of their hand. Liam knew the place well too; his first digs were on Allison Street, the main artery of the district. In and around Allison Street were a couple of Irish pubs and some well known Indian and Pakistani restaurants. Almost Liam's idea of heaven.

"Let's have a quick beer in here," said Liam pointing to a corner bar named 'The Coughing Sheep'.

It was a fairly large bar that had its main access on the corner but could also be entered from a side door on the main street.

"Two bottles of beer and a pint of stout, young lady," said Liam to the lithe, hard bodied, blonde barmaid, "and have one yourself".

The pub was about half full with about a dozen or so lunch time customers. As the barmaid put the drinks on the bar, Des caught sight of Jimmy Gilmore coming out of the toilet, where he had just snorted his third line of coke that day. Des was in a bit of a quandary. Should he tell Mick or should he just leave it? On the other hand, he thought, the way Liam drank beer they would probably be out of here in five minutes. He looked over to the corner where Gilmore was standing. There were three of them, talking loudly and laughing at their own jokes. Gilmore and one of the others had distinctive Belfast accents, the other sounded Glaswegian and, as far as Des could make out, Gilmore had not noticed them. Mick and Liam were engaged in a quiet chat about the attributes or otherwise of the various local Indian restaurants. In the meantime, the barmaid clattered and scurried about the bar, frenetically wiping the bar surfaces, and washing and polishing glasses like a woman possessed.

Mick's phone rang.

He answered, putting one finger in his ear to cut out the noise from the bar and stood nodding at the phone.

"I'll get a taxi. I'll be there in ten minutes or so," he said, raising his voice just loud enough to be heard by Gilmore and the others at the end of the bar.

"Sorry guys, something just turned up. I'll need to get a taxi into town."

"That's okay," said Liam. "Listen, I've got the number for a black hack, he'll pick you up right away if he's anywhere near here."

To Des's alarm, Gilmore was now taking an interest in what was going on, and the slow dawn of recognition was beginning to appear in his bloodshot eyes.

Liam used his own phone and told the driver the fare's name was Hastings.

"He'll be here in two minutes. He's on the rank at Victoria

Infirmary."

"Well done, Liam," said Des anxiously. "Let go outside and wait."

"Are you stone mad? I've still got a half a pint here, besides the driver will come in for Mick. Take your time, for God's sake."

Des took a look down the bar. Gilmore was feverishly talking to the two others who took the occasional glance up at Mick, who had casually resumed his conversation with Liam. The seconds crawled by. Des was beginning to sweat.

At last the door opened and a head popped in.

"Taxi for Hastings?"

"That's me," said Mick.

"Hi there," said the driver recognising Liam.

"Listen mate, I've had to park up the street a bit, but don't worry, take your time and finish your drink and I'll see you in a minute."

Liam finished his pint in one draught, Des put his unfinished beer on the bar.

"Come on, let's go," he said.

"What the hell's wrong with you Des? You're jumping about as if you had ants in your pants," said Liam.

"Don't want to keep the driver waiting, do we?"

Liam gave Des an odd look.

"Okay, okay. We're going."

The trio walked out the main corner door led on by a harried looking Des.

"Just a minute Des, for Gods sake," Liam halted and started to pat his pockets to check he had his phone.

"Where did I put...its okay I've got it here," he said, producing the phone from his inside pocket.

They were about to move off when they were stopped by a loud shout.

"Hey you!"

They turned round bemused.

"You!" shouted Gilmore, pointing to Mick. "You're a Peeler. You've been spying on us, haven't you?"

For a second there was silence. Then Liam laughed loudly.

"A Peeler! You mean a policeman. Nobody has called a cop a

peeler since the nineteen twenties. What planet are you from?"

"Who's talking to you, bigmouth?" said Gilmore aggressively.

"Look guys let's forget it. Let's go and get the taxi," said Des.

"Why don't you go back to Belfast and try your hard man act on the Falls Road, you bampot. See how long you'd last there!" shouted Liam. At this point the two other men in the bar came out to see what was going on. Seemingly encouraged by this audience Gilmore suddenly pulled a gun from his waistband and pointed it at Liam. Des almost fainted.

"Who the hell do you think you're talking to bigmouth?" said an increasingly agitated Gilmore.

"Ah get lost! You think you can frighten me with an imitation plastic gun?" said Liam.

"Look's real enough to me. Let's go Liam!" cried Des.

"Only thing is," said Liam calmly, "if we turn around - if it is a real gun he'll probably shoot us in the back."

Liam looked at Gilmore with disdain.

"Isn't that your usual modus operandi, hard man?"

"What?" said Gilmore, bemused by Liam's lack of fear.

Liam turned to the others.

"Let's get out of here, before I really lose my temper with this eejet."

The three of them turned around to walk away.

Gilmore's mood changed almost instantly from bewilderment to fury: he became beside himself with anger and rage. His cocaine habit had already made him a dangerous paranoid. He was a walking time bomb. He lifted the gun, turned it to a parked van that Liam and the others were passing. A loud shot through the windscreen; that would give that bigmouth something to think about, he sniggered to himself, as he pointed the wavering gun in the general direction of the van.

The bullet slammed into a street lamppost just in front of the van, ricocheted off with a whine and cracked into Mick Hastings head at the top of his spine. Des seemed to be taking part in a slow motion movie; he heard the bang, the crack and the thud distinctly and clearly, although they must have only been milliseconds apart.

Mick staggered forward a few paces as if he had been pushed from behind then fell face first on to the pavement with a sickening thump. His peripheral vision caught a glimpse of the taxi driver furiously tapping numbers into his phone and behind him he could hear the screams of the frantic barmaid.

Both Des and Liam immediately fell to their knees beside Mick. He lay with his face slightly twisted to the left, his eyes still open and his head lying in a quickly spreading pool of dark blood. At the back of his head was a hole the size of a golf ball where the bullet, probably mangled after smashing into the lamppost, had entered. Des looked at Liam who looked totally ashen with mixture of shock and anger. They said nothing; it was obvious that Mick was dead. Liam turned round and leapt up. One of Gilmore's mates had already squeezed him into a car and was now running round to the driver's side. With a bellow Liam lunged across the pavement. The third man, the one with the Glasgow accent stood in front of Liam, a skinhead, a big hard looking lump.

"Where do you thi…"

He was cut short as Liam pulled back his right arm and smashed his balled fist into his face. The crack of bone and gristle as the hard man slumped to pavement brought yet another loud scream from the barmaid; but the intervention had worked. By the time Liam had pushed the hysterical barmaid aside, the car was gone.

***

The paramedics covered Mick's head first before they manoeuvred him onto the stretcher. They made little attempt at pretending he was anything other than dead. Two uniformed police were busy taping off the area when another carload of cops arrived.

"Do you think we should go with the ambulance?" asked Des, still dazed.

"Best not, sir. D.S. Munro just called in I think he wants a word," said one of the policemen who had overheard him. He looked at Des.

Des looked dreadful.

"He'll be here in a minute," he added sympathetically.

Des phoned Julie but was almost unable to talk. Liam took the phone from him and tried to explain what had happened. There was a stunned silence from the other end.

"Julie, I know you need time to react to all this. We need to go down to the police station now, so I'll get Des to phone back in an hour or so."

He pressed the cancel call button.

Munro came shortly after and took them down to the station, just five minutes away.

They sat giving statements and descriptions for an hour with Munro and another detective. Both Des and Liam were still in a state of shock. Des was beginning to blame himself for the incident.

"If only I had warned Mick about Gilmore," he repeated several times

"I know it's hard but don't start blaming yourself, you didn't pull the trigger," said Munro.

"I feel as bad, I should have just ignored the lunatic. Should have never risen to the bait," said Liam. "What I can't understand is how the hell he managed to get a goddamn gun in the first place."

"We can thank our broken nosed chum Kevin Campbell for that. He's still in the intensive care unit at the Victoria Infirmary, by the way."

"Who?" said Liam, not quite understanding.

"That halfwit you lamped outside the pub, Kevin Campbell."

"Oh, him" said Liam.

"Inspector McKinney is still interviewing him. Campbell is what you might describe as a failed criminal. Got away with an armed robbery about two years ago. Some Mister Big from the West End organised a bank robbery in Maryhill, the gang got away with £50,000 in cash. The problem was that Mister Big took half, leaving twenty five grand between the five gang members."

"That's only five thousand each" said Des distantly.

"Agreed, not much for a crime that carries a twelve year minimum sentence, but then again, few criminals grasp the theory of the risk-to-reward ratio. To show his magnanimity Mister Big said that they could hold onto the guns that he had generously supplied. Campbell stashed the gun away in his brother's garage and took his family to Las Vegas and blew the lot in a week. He was lifted by the police after a row with the taxi driver who took the family back from Glasgow airport and charged them fifteen quid. He allegedly accused the taxi driver of 'Daylight Robbery'".

Munro stood up.

"Apparently a sense of irony is another of Campbell's weak points," he added dryly.

Munro started to walk around the room.

"Campbell copped a six months sentence last year for robbing a local shop of £150 and four bottles of malt whisky: at least four witnesses recognised him running up Calder Street with a clanking carry-out bag. According to McKinney he had decided to turn over a new leaf after coming out of the slammer last year. Says he knew Gilmore through Hughie Toner and met him last night in some pub on Vicky Road. They got chatting and he arranged to sell the gun and three bullets for a hundred quid in The Coughing Sheep this afternoon. It was a small calibre Browning hand gun. Campbell claims he never even knew how to fire the damn thing. He passed it over in the toilet while Gilmore was snorting a line of coke."

Munro stopped talking; it was becoming obvious that neither Des nor Liam were quite taking it all in.

He told them briefly that Gilmore would be caught quickly, possibly even today. It was obvious that Gilmore was a loose cannon and any allies he may or may not have had would soon distance themselves from someone that would be crazy enough to shoot a police officer in what was basically a pub brawl. Gilmore, he said, had no hiding place.

"Do you mind if I phone Julie now," asked Des after a while.

"Sure go ahead, we're almost finished here. I think it would be better if you came back tomorrow, after you've had a rest and thought things through."

Des talked to Julie briefly; she said the whole thing was now all over the television and radio news, the latest bulletin said a car on the Ayr road had been pulled up and the occupants taken in for questioning.

"I'll come down now and pick you both up in five minutes."

Both men were in a quiet and subdued state as they sat in the back of the car. Julie handed them a pill each, she pulled a small bottle of water from the glove compartment.

"Take one of these. It's a mild sedative, it'll calm you down. Liam, you can stay with us tonight. I'll make up a bed in the spare room."

Liam grunted from a distance.

The centre of town was the usual busy Friday late afternoon. Julie cursed as she took a wrong turn and ended up going over the Stockwell Bridge. She decided to park her car on the North side of the Clyde, not her normal routine but she was in no mood to turn back and plough her way through the one way traffic system or to contend with Glasgow Council's manic obsession for putting traffics lights on every street corner. She would come back later in the evening and move it when things were quieter. They left the car park and walked up Clyde Street in silence, dodging the happy crowds anxious to get the weekend started. Des looked around at the crowds, almost confused; it was hard to believe that it was only this time last week that he got that phone call from Mick. At the suspension bridge they waited for a break in the traffic to cross over. The solitary beggar eyed them as they approached. Like a fairground fortune teller, a good moocher can gauge the mood of his potential customer from a distance, and these guys did not look happy. They had an unsettling aura of grief about them - not the best people to approach for a handout. He decided not to waste his breath giving them the usual routine banter and optimistic weather forecast. He took a sudden interest in his shoes. The dog, lying down using his front paws as a pillow, gave a bored yawn; he was sure he could see some squirrels scampering around the parklands that edged the south bank of the river.

As they passed the beggar Julie suddenly stopped.

"You keep going... I'll catch up in a minute."

Both men muttered and walked on.

Julie stood facing the uneasy beggar.

She put her hand into her jacket pocket and pulled out a coin and held it up between her fingers.

"Do you know what this is?"

The man looked up and leaned forward.

"I may be a homeless jakie, miss…" he replied warily, "…but I'm not a fool." He half suspected some sort of practical joke was being played out at his expense.

He hesitated.

Nothing ventured, nothing gained, he eventually decided.

"That there is a British gold sovereign."

He looked closer.

"Circa 1916, I'd opine."

"Here," said Julie dropping it into his plastic cup. "Take it."

She turned on her heels and continued to walk across the bridge trying to catch up with the two men who had now stopped in the middle.

The beggar tipped out the coin, still half convinced of a prank. He look at it in amazement, it was real. There was a decent pawn shop he knew just up in Argyle Street, it would still be open, if he hurried. He reckoned on a hundred quid, maybe more - no questions asked - easy.

"Right Tyson, you can take the rest of the day off," he said untying the old bit of clothes line that served as lead. "I'll get you a pie from the bakers when I get back."

The dog shot over the bridge like a rocket, his overgrown toenails making a strange scampering, scraping sound.

As he approached Des and Liam, the dog stopped and slunk along the side of the narrow bridge eyeing the men warily before taking off again. Julie approached both of them. They were standing silently, still half confused with shock and the growing numbing effect of the sedative. They had their hands in their pockets gazing at the river, almost hypnotised by the sunlight dancing off the still waters of the Clyde. She put her left arm into Des's arm and the other arm into Liam's and took one step forward.

"Let's go," she said.

Paradise Road by **Stephen O'Donnell** is the story of Kevin McGarry a young man from the West of Scotland, who as a youngster was one of the most talented footballers of his generation in Scotland. Through a combination of injury and disillusionment, Kevin is forced to abandon any thoughts of playing the game he loves, professionally. Instead he settles for following his favourite team, Glasgow Celtic, as a spectator, while at the same time resignedly and with a characteristically wry Scottish sense of humour, trying to eke out a living as a joiner.

It is a story of hopes and dreams, idealism and disillusionment, of growth in the face of adversity and disappointment. Paradise Road examines some of the major themes affecting football today, such as the power and role of the media, standards in the Scottish game and the sectarianism which pervades not only football in Glasgow but also the wider community. More than simply a novel about football or football fandom, the book offers a portrait of the character and experiences of a section of the Irish Catholic community of the West of Scotland, and considers the role of young working-class men in our modern, post-industrial society.

The road Kevin travels towards self discovery, fulfilment and maturity leads him to Prague, enabling a more detached view of the Scotland that formed him and the Europe that beckons him.

"Written in a thoughtful, provocative yet engaging style, Paradise Road is a book that will enthral, challenge and reward in equal measure. It will be a powerful addition to the growing debate on some of the key issues facing contemporary Scotland"

Paradise Road can be purchased on *www.ringwoodpublishing.com* for £9.99 excluding p&p or ordered by post or e-mail for the same price.

The e-book version is be available for £5.99 from the Kindle Book Store or Amazon.co.uk

Good Deed by **Steve Christie** is a fast paced crime novel that captures the reader from beginning to end.

The gripping story of Good Deed rattles along relentlessly, leaving the reader breathless but enthralled. Good Deed introduces a new Scottish detective hero, DI Ronnie Buchanan, who is certain to quickly attract a legion of fans.

The events crammed into Good Deed take Buchanan from his base in Aberdeen on a frantic journey around all the major Scottish cities as his increasingly deadly pursuit of a mysterious criminal master mind known only as Vince comes to a breath-taking climax back in Aberdeen.

"The pace of Good Deed is exceptional and unremitting. It is the kind of book that demands to be read in one sitting, but most readers will be so breathless as the saga unfolds without pause that they will need occasional rests before eagerly returning for more."

Good Deed is Steve Christie's first novel. Based in Edinburgh, the good news is that he is already hard at work on the follow up to Good Deed, which will also feature Ronnie Buchanan.

Ringwood is confident that both Steve Christie and Ronnie Buchanan are names that will become very familiar to all lovers of quality crime fiction.

Good Deed can be purchased on *www.ringwoodpublishing.com* for £9.99 excluding p&p or ordered by post or e-mail for the same price.

The e-book version is be available for £5.99 from the Kindle Book Store or Amazon.co.uk

Whisky From Small Glasses by **DA Meyrick** is a stunningly impressive crime novel. Set in a small Scottish rural town, it reveals the seething cauldron of sex, drugs, violence, corruption and murder that lies beneath the dour surface of Kinloch life. It starts with one body found in the sea. Two more bodies are quickly added as it becomes clear a serial killer is at large. Further ramifications include police and harbour staff corruption and the involvement of a Latvian drugs smuggling ring. The book introduces Chief Detective Inspector Jim Daley who is destined to join the ranks of outstanding Scottish fictional detectives. Daley's complex relationships, with his bosses; his colleagues; and his unfaithful but passionately loved wife, drive the story of **Whisky From Small Glasses** forward to a dramatic and almost unbearable conclusion.

Whisky From Small Glasses is a book that is likely to endure, and will be the first in a series of crime novels set in rural South West Scotland that will transcend their genre and will comment on how such rural communities are coming to terms with 21st Century life and all its complexities.

"Whisky From Small Glasses is well named. It can be savoured and enjoyed just like a fine measure of the hard stuff. It engages and rewards as it thrills and delights. Like all the best crime fiction it transcends its genre as it enlightens the reader about the realities of a community that at first sight is stuck in a mid20th century time warp but underneath the veneer of stability is struggling to cope with the influx of modern values and modern, and not so modern, vices. The relationships around the chief character CDI Jim Daley are wonderfully drawn and are used to drive the story line forward relentlessly to a powerful conclusion, that leaves the reader anxious to follow the main character in his next adventure".

Whisky From Small Glasses can be purchased on *www.ringwoodpublishing.com* for £9.99 excluding p&p or ordered by post or e-mail for the same price.

The e-book version is be available for £5.99 from the Kindle Book Store or Amazon.co.uk

"Celtic Submari" by **Sandy Jamieson** will appeal to all those interested in the power of goodness, decency, integrity and friendship to make a positive difference in a complex world through football.

Rivals for 90 minutes, Friends for Always

The book explains how an invasion of Vila-real by 10,000 Celtic supporters in 2004 created a set of circumstances that has led to a lasting friendship between supporters of Villarreal and Celtic. This friendship is unique in world football and offers the wider football world a model of camaraderie and togetherness that shows how football can be a force for good.

Celtic supporters everywhere can take pride in the story of how their example of camaraderie and good behaviour in 2004 inspired the formation of the Villarreal Celtic Submari. The Submari has proved to be an extraordinary example of the way in which decent people can help others through football and friendship.

Lessons for Scotland

Celtic Submari also explores why the subsequent visit of Glasgow Rangers to Villarreal did not result in a similar outburst of mutual friendship but saw instead Rangers fined for the poor behaviour of some of their supporters. This book investigates the cultural differences between Celtic and Rangers supporters which explain their different behaviours abroad. It offers an enhanced understanding of some of the elements of the sectarian sourness that so scars Scottish football. It puts forward radical solutions drawing on the Villarreal Submari model.

It shows why both Celtic and Rangers supporters need to learn from the model practiced by the Villarreal Submari if Scottish football is to eradicate its sectarian sickness.

Celtic Submari can be purchased on *www.ringwoodpublishing.com* for £9.99 excluding p&p or ordered by post or e-mail for the same price.

The e-book version is be available for £7.20 from the Kindle Book Store or Amazon.co.uk